TALES

of

COLES COUNTY, ILLINOIS

TALES

of

COLES COUNTY, ILLINOIS

FINAL EDITION

By

MICHAEL KLEEN

TALES OF COLES COUNTY, ILLINOIS

Hardcover Edition

This book was printed in the United States by Lightning Source, Inc.

Library of Congress Control Number: 2020915265
ISBN-13: 978-1-61876-025-8

Lake Ridge Press
Woodbridge, Virginia

www.michaelkleen.com

CONTENTS

HIDDEN HISTORY

PRAISE FOR THE AUTHOR

"One Eastern student took several events from the darker side of Charleston's history and creatively blended them into a fictional story in his book entitled, 'Tales of Coles County, Illinois'... The concept of the book is a great one. It makes the history of Coles County a more interesting read, and tricks people into reading history without feeling like they're going through a history book."

- Daily Eastern News
October 28, 2005

"Long before TV stations like SyFy and the Travel Channel took an interest in the area, Michael Kleen was researching and writing about remarkable episodes from the county's past. With a blend of fact and fiction, *Tales of Coles County* is a unique look at the history and places that make Coles County such an interesting place to visit."

- JG-TC
August 12, 2013

"The legend of the ghost of Pemberton Hall is the most well known in the area, but Michael Kleen, author of 'The Tales of Coles County,' has many more to share."

- Daily Eastern News
October 25, 2013

"The wonder of things we do not understand, the things that none of our senses can comprehend or decode: all of this is connected to the idea of what could be; the things we do not know, but that we still believe to be possible. All this and more is what Michael Kleen dedicates his life work to."

- Lake Land College *Navigator News*
Vol. 13 Issue 5 – February 2014

FOREWORD

I met Michael in 2013 when I asked him to speak at an event commemorating the 150th Anniversary of the Charleston Riot. Michael discovered as a history student at Eastern Illinois University how unique Coles County is, with its varied history and connection to President Abraham Lincoln. His passion for history adds a different perspective to known tales and brings to light little-known ones.

The first time I read Tales of Coles County, as a genealogist and someone whose roots go back to Coles County in the 1820s, I wanted to learn more about the stories he told. His perspective on these stories piqued my interest to do my own research using his book as my guide. Why didn't I know about some of these stories? I asked myself. Many of them were intertwined with my family, and I had never heard of them before.

The Charleston Riot was the most northern skirmish of the Civil War where Union soldiers lost their lives. Many do not realize this happened in the home county of Lincoln's parents. My 2nd great grandfather was injured in the Riot, and my grandfather recounted this story to me many times as a child. But Michael's book raises questions for me on other historical events. My great aunt was an early resident of Pemberton Hall and lived there during the time of Mary Hawkins, and my grandmother was a nurse during Mary's time at the Montgomery Sanitarium. Yet there's no mention of Mary in any of their diaries or letters.

My great grandfather's farm was a half a mile from Ashmore Estates, which was surrounded by Galbreath family farms. Yet no one ever uttered a word about it. No one, not even my great aunt, mentioned a three-story building being built on the flat prairie. The biggest mystery is St. Omer Cemetery, where a cousin's wife is buried under a spherical monument with a death date of February 31, 1882. No one ever has mentioned the lore of her being a witch. Thanks to Michael, these stories are being told and documented for future generations.

But you don't have to be from Coles County or Illinois to appreciate these interesting tales. If you love history or a good mystery, you'll love *Tales of Coles County* and *Legends and Lore of Coles County, Illinois.*

Ann Winkler Hinrichs

PREFACE

I always thought Coles County was unique, but even I was surprised when CNN rebroadcast a June 2010 WTHI Channel 10 News in Terre Haute report on Lerna's "world's fastest pop machine." Purchased in the late 1970s by Ivan Thompson for his welding business, the weathered orange, clattering soda machine has become a tourist attraction in this village of 280 in Pleasant Grove Township. As a student at Eastern Illinois University in Charleston, I often brought my friends to it while I showed them sites around Coles County. They never failed to be amazed by how quickly the cans fell into the delivery tray. Like the independently-owned Burger King in Mattoon, the "world's fastest pop machine" adds charm to life in the county, a charm that has made an impression on the outside world.

It was August 17, 2000 when I first entered Room 772 in Carman Hall, the freshman dorm, and I hardly thought I would spend the next eight years at Eastern Illinois University, despite it being my first and only choice. My parents met there. My mom attended Eastern from 1965 to 1966, and my dad attended from 1963 to 1967. My great-uncle John Kleen also attended EIU. You could say the university was a family tradition, but the circumstances that led me to stay for the better part of a decade were unexpected and unplanned.

Caught up in the day-to-day drama of college life, I was plagued with indecision and all the troubles of an uncertain future. I took a semester off, changed majors, and dropped one too many classes, until I found myself an undergrad for six long years. Rather than leave Eastern, I decided to earn my graduate degree there. I knew the professors, and Coleman Hall, where I took endless philosophy, history, and creative writing classes, was like a second home. I finally left in the spring of 2008. Over the years, however, I became familiar with Coles County in ways I never anticipated. Charleston was no longer like a second home—it was home, and by the time I said goodbye, I knew a great deal about the history and the people of Coles County.

I attended EIU during a transition period, when campus was perpetually under construction—whether it was the new food court in the student union, Booth Library, or the fine arts center. I was a freshman when the Electronic Writing Portfolio requirement was introduced. I met three of EIU's presidents:

Carol Surles, Lou Hencken, and Bill Perry; walked in two homecoming parades; wrote a bi-weekly opinion column for the *Daily Eastern News*; and even watched the infamous Blair Hall fire of April 28, 2004. I miss the ivy-covered walls of Old Main, Chubby's Pizza, and the wooded ridges and ravines of Fox Ridge State Park. Most of all, I miss my friends and acquaintances, and regret the overlooked opportunities.

ALBERT AND MARIE KLEEN (MY FATHER AND GRANDMOTHER) IN FRONT OF COLEMAN HALL AT EIU, MARCH 1966.

I still remember when Hardees sat on the corner of 4th Street and Lincoln Avenue where a brand-new Jimmy John's sits today, and when Jimmy John's (the original!) was located in a small shop in the alley behind Positively 4th Street Records. I remember late nights at Lincoln Gardens, lunch at Boxa, Campus Perk in the basement of Thomas Hall, when Panther Paw was called Stix, and Lincoln Avenue's perpetually abandoned restaurant: How Yall Are?

As I tasted my first experience living on my own, I made it my mission to explore every nook and cranny of Charleston and Coles County—my new home. I hoped former students left behind something for me to discover, even if it was only a name carved into a study carrel in the library. I imagined I found my dad's name among the colorful tapestry of signatures imbedded into the cedar, like a time capsule reaching out from one generation to another. In return, I hoped to leave something of myself behind, so that one day my own son or daughter would find something to remind them that I once walked those same halls.

It started with an abandoned building the winter of my sophomore year. My roommate mentioned it—"that abandoned insane asylum out in the country"—but it wasn't until I returned from winter break in January 2001 I learned that place was called Ashmore Estates. Two friends, Monica and Oona (both seniors), took me out there. When Monica and Oona were freshmen, Mike Rice and Matt Fear, the "Men of Adventure," wrote a satirical piece for the Halloween issue of the Verge section of the *Daily Eastern News* on how to make Ashmore Estates into a "highly illegal" Halloween escapade. "No one is really sure what this building once housed," they wrote. "But there are stories. These tales revolve around pagan rituals and dismembered bodies. We aren't sure if any of them are true or not, but they sure do make for three floors... of unadulterated fun."

Like countless others before us, Monica, Oona, and I parked alongside the gravel road a few yards from the building and walked through a thin layer of snow on the fallow corn field. Like the "Men of Adventure," I knew nothing about what this building was or what it had been. As we carefully explored its interior, any story about it seemed possible. It was years before I knew anything about its real history.

In the meantime, I began to search for ghost stories and legends in and around the area. There were a few listed on the Internet, but other than Mary Hawkins and Pemberton Hall, none had appeared in any books on the subject. Slowly, I put together a list: Ashmore Estates, "Ragdoll" Cemetery, St. Omer Cemetery. As often the case with information online, it was not helpful when it came to locating these places. I was deep into the search for St. Omer Cemetery when, at a cookout outside the University Apartments, a friend introduced me to a young woman named Jennifer. Jenny, a local, was also interested in ghost stories, and she introduced me to Airtight Bridge.

Airtight Bridge was fascinating in its own right, but what happened there—*why* locals talked about it in such hushed tones—remained a mystery. There were the usual tales of phantom automobiles and vanishing or odd characters, but there were also rumors of a murder. After speaking with local residents and professors at EIU, I learned a woman's body had been found near the bridge sometime in 1980. So, I did what any good historian would: I sat in front of a microfilm reel of the Charleston *Times-Courier* for the year in question and scanned the headlines until I came across one pertaining to the Airtight case.

Growing more curious by the day, I browsed through archives of the *Daily Eastern News* and the nearly 700-pages of William Henry Perrin's *The History of Coles County, Illinois* (1879) for other unusual events or stories.

It was the summer of 2003, and I was back home in Prospect Heights working at the River Trails Park District. Picking up garbage at 6:00 a.m. gives a person a lot of time to think, and as I sweat, mowed lawns, and pruned my way through the hottest months of the year, I got an idea for a book of historical fiction stories based on past events in Coles County. I distinctly (if not fondly) recall picking empty bottles of Corona and cigarette butts out of the playground of Willow Trails Park, daydreaming of the stories I would tell in *Tales of Coles County, Illinois* to pass the time.

As 2004 rolled around, I decided to go into the publishing business for myself. I learned how to make chapbooks by dissecting *The Vehicle*—the EIU English Department's publication for student poetry, fiction, and photography. Chapbooks, traditionally, are four to forty-eight pages in length and consist of a regular 8.5 x 11-inch piece of paper folded over and bound together by stitching or staples. They were popular during the 16th and 17th centuries when printing was expensive and time consuming. Today, pamphlets and chapbooks can be printed for a few cents a page at an average print shop, and you can make dozens of pamphlets for very little cost. I sold my first chapbook, *The Distance of Sorrow*, for five dollars. *The Distance of Sorrow* was a multi-part short story I expanded into a "special edition" and hawked to my dad's friends and coworkers. With all the "special features" included, the booklet ran exactly 42 pages. Its special features included author commentary, deleted scenes, and alternate endings. The response was positive.

Next, I set to work writing the stories I imagined the previous summer, and when classes resumed in the fall of 2004, I printed a few dozen copies of *Tales of Coles County, Illinois*. I sold some, but mostly gave them away or left them in coffee shops and laundromats, at Aaron's Barbershop, or at parks. My friend Anna's mother found a copy at Morton Park while eating lunch, so I knew my marketing tactic had been successful. Rather than write fiction as a young and unknown author and attempt to sell it to a general audience, I thought my writing would generate more interest if I wrote on local topics. By leaving out copies of *Tales of Coles County*, I hoped to create a sense of mystery surrounding the work.

Meanwhile, I organized an informal student group at EIU that met every weekend in September and October to explore local haunts and share an interest in the subject. The group, which I referred to as (with tongue-in-cheek) the "Ghost Club," lasted from 2004 until 2009, a year after I left Eastern. A different set of people joined every year, which always kept it interesting. I have many fond memories of field trips out to fog-shrouded Airtight Bridge at night or scavenger hunts in Lafler-Ennis Cemetery. Whether it was the time I accidentally drove into a cornfield, or the time we passed an old man in a nightgown walking his dog along the roadside in the dark, we never failed to have an interesting experience. We talked about our own encounters, toured local sites, played games, and watched horror movies. One year we even told ghost stories around a campfire. The *Daily Eastern News* printed three articles on the group.

In October 2005, Laura Griffith wrote a review of *Tales of Coles County, Illinois* for the *Daily Eastern News*, giving it three out of five stars. "The story follows a group of Eastern students, Tami, Max, AJ and Nancy, as they are stranded in the rain when their car breaks down while looking for a campsite just south of Charleston," she wrote. "They come upon a small cabin in the woods and are invited inside by an old man and woman, who give them dry clothes, shelter and a warm dinner. During the meal, the couple shares stories with the students, stories about the history of Coles County and things they remember from their childhood that went on in the area, in chronological order... The concept of the book is a great one. It makes the history of Coles County a more interesting read, and tricks people into reading history without feeling like they're going through a history book."

Another project I began in 2004 was a website that served as a repository for the stories I collected about Coles County, which was aptly named *Legends and Lore of Coles County*. In 2006, I began writing and publishing a monthly electronic newsletter by the same name. I posted the first issue, on Airtight Bridge, in March, and it ceased publication nine months later in November of that same year. My original intent was to create a photo comic in which I would act as a "guide" to strange or interesting places in Coles County, but that required more creativity than I apparently possessed. The newsletter quickly evolved away from that idea, and by its second issue, it consisted of one or two pages of information accompanied by five or six pictures in a downloadable PDF. Years later, I was delighted to discover that Chad Lewis and Terry Fisk cited the *Legends and Lore of Coles County* in a chapter on St. Omer Cemetery in their book *The Illinois Road Guide to Haunted Locations* (2007).

Not long after I predicted a dismal end to Ashmore Estates in the June 2006 issue of the *Legends and Lore of Coles County*, Scott Kelley contacted me and revealed his plans to rent or even purchase the property. He first became interested in Ashmore Estates around ten years earlier. Scott, a longtime operator of haunted attractions including the local haunts at Elsinore Farm and Rockome Gardens, believed the institution would make an excellent haunted house. He purchased the property from Arthur Colclasure in early August and immediately began renovating. To finance the project, he offered flashlight tours of the interior for five dollars a person, and volunteers helped clean up the property and the interior of the old almshouse. While the risk of arrest always accompanied earlier visits, Scott gave me free run of the building.

That October, for the first time in its history, the doors of Ashmore Estates opened to the general public. People who had swapped stories about the building for over a decade lined up to get a look inside. On June 8, 2007, Scott asked me to come and speak about the history and folklore of Ashmore Estates at an overnight event. That was my first public speaking engagement. I stayed for pizza and the movie *White Noise*, but left before midnight. Thanks to Ashmore Estates and the *Legends and Lore of Coles County*, my reputation grew. On October 22, 2007, I gave a presentation on local ghost stories at the Charleston Middle School and my picture made the front page of the *Times-Courier* the next day. When I first began to explore Coles County, I never thought the interest would take me that far, but there was even more to come.

By that year, I was a graduate student in the history department at Eastern Illinois University, writing a bi-weekly opinion column for the *Daily Eastern News*, publishing the *Legends and Lore of Illinois* and my art & culture zine *Black Oak Presents*, and participating in Coles County Buy Local. In October, I presented a history paper on the Illinois Copperheads at the 2007 Conference on Illinois History in Springfield.

Coles County wasn't through with me yet, however. Although I moved to Rockford in June 2008, Ashmore Estates had become something of a phenomenon in the ghost hunting community, so

I found myself returning to Charleston to be interviewed for several documentaries. The first was the Booth Brother's *Children of the Grave 2*, which wasn't released on DVD until four years later. Philip Adrian and Christopher Saint Booth were known for television specials such as *Spooked* (2006), *Children of the Grave* (2007), and *The Possessed* (2009). The *Times-Courier* covered the story, as well as WCIA Channel 3 News in Champaign. That was the first time I ever appeared on the local news.

I was nervous, of course, and in an effort to say something profound I stuttered out these final remarks: "I think anything that doesn't have to do with [President] Lincoln around Coles County—'cause it's a big thing around here—any kind of other history is good for people to know about." That segment aired on July 2, 2008. The other project for which I was interviewed was an episode of Hart Fisher's *American Horrors* called "Fear in the Flatlands." Directed by a St. Louis native named John Specht and produced by Tyson Reed, the project proved to be controversial. A few years later, in 2011, I briefly spoke about the history of Ashmore Estates in an episode of *Ghost Adventures* on the Travel Channel.

My next project involved getting my stories and research into print. For years I wanted to write a book about haunted places, legends, and odd happenings from east-central Illinois and Coles County in particular. When I heard that Schiffer Books, a publisher based in Atglen, Pennsylvania, was looking for submissions, I pitched an idea to them for a book titled *Legends and Lore of the Ambraw River Valley*. This book would have included ghost stories and even famous murder cases and crime sprees from Champaign down to Vincennes, but Schiffer did not believe that book appealed to a broad enough audience. They rejected it with the caveat that they might consider the idea in the future. In the meantime, I wrote stand-alone articles on Pemberton Hall and Ashmore Estates that I offered in PDF format on my website. For two Octobers, I wandered the streets of Charleston and Mattoon, flyering apartment doors, coffee shops, restaurants, and dorms, advertising "The Legend of Pemberton Hall." That article, as of this writing, has been downloaded over 2,350 times.

It wasn't until I moved to Rockford that a representative at Schiffer Books contacted me, wondering if I wanted to write a book about ghost stories in the entire state. That was an opportunity I couldn't pass up. I made sure that *Paranormal Illinois* (as it came to be called) included three chapters on places in Coles County: Pemberton Hall, Ashmore Estates, and Airtight Bridge, and I made sure my readers would not be left in the dark about the history of those places, as I had been back when I first arrived in the county.

On October 24, 2013, with help from my friends Becky and Lesley and the EIU Creative Writing Club, I gave a presentation on Coles County legends and lore at the Martin Luther King Jr. University Union at EIU. After years of writing about these stories, giving this presentation at my alma mater was a wonderful opportunity. Sitting at Java B&B in the student union, drinking a chai latte and eating a scone as I had so often as a grad student, this time reading an article about my presentation later that night, somehow made me feel like my journey had come full circle. So many people showed up we had to move to a larger room.

Less than a year later, in February 2014, I had the distinction of being a featured speaker at Lake Land College's "Tacos & Tales" event. The event was a huge success, attracting over 40 students hungry for both knowledge of local folklore and tacos. I was told it was one of the best turnouts yet. Lucas Thomas, then Student Activity Board Chairman, was a wonderful host, even delivering the twelve green M&M's I jokingly requested. I returned later that spring to speak at the 150th Anniversary of the Charleston Riot event at the Coles County Courthouse.

It's been many years since I left Charleston, but I felt my work in the county would remain incomplete until I released a final edition of *Tales of Coles County, Illinois*. This edition, which includes the *Legends and Lore of Coles County*, as well as a few other tidbits, is to be my final contribution to the place I called home for nearly a decade. There are other stories to tell, but I will leave those to be discovered by future generations. Perhaps there is already someone like me getting ready to leave home for the first time and start his or her new life at Eastern Illinois University. Maybe they will be inspired by these words and realize that, contrary to the belief of every comedian who ever visited EIU and made a joke about there being "nothing but cornfields," Coles County is a lot more interesting than it first appears.

TALES

INTRODUCTION

Welcome to the final edition of *Tales of Coles County, Illinois*. First, a disclaimer: all places and events in this short book are based on reality, however, it is a work of fiction and not history. When it comes to the history, I have, for the most part, tried to re-create events to the best of my ability with the information I have available to me.

In some instances, like "The Second Battle of the Ambraw," there's almost no historical information about what took place, only a brief mention in *The History of Coles County* (1879). Therefore, all characters, except Samuel Whiteside, lived entirely in my imagination. Samuel Whiteside (1783-1866) was a rugged frontiersman and lifelong soldier who rose from private to brigadier general in the Illinois militia. He also served as a delegate in the Illinois General Assembly from 1819 to 1821. Like many early Illinois pioneers, Whiteside's family came from North Carolina. His father was a Revolutionary War veteran. When he was a child, Samuel and his mother escaped an Indian attack which left his brother dead and his cousin severely wounded.

He spent nearly his entire adult life in the Illinois militia, fighting as an infantryman, mounted soldier, or ranger in Tecumseh's War, the War of 1812, and the Black Hawk War. In previous editions of *Tales of Coles County*, I referred to him as "General Whiteside", but I later learned he wasn't promoted to brigadier general until 1819, a year after the events of the book. He was a colonel in 1818. He died in Christian County, Illinois.

The story of the Charleston Riot was re-created using actual testimony and newspaper articles from the time. It's mostly accurate, although some things have been simplified or tinkered for entertainment. Everyone in the story, with the exception of Oliver and Daniel, were real people (although one account does mention two boys at the scene). I tried to portray them as authentically and sympathetically as possible. If one of your relatives happens to be mentioned in a bad light, it was either an unavoidable fact of history, or important to the story, and no offense was intended.

The origins of the Charleston Riot are complex. During the American Civil War, like any war, civilians on the Homefront were divided between pro-war and anti-war factions. Members of the most radical anti-war faction of the Democratic Party were called Copperheads. They believed President Abraham Lincoln was prosecuting an illegal war with the Southern states, and that the Union should be restored peacefully to what it was before he was elected to office. Central Illinois was starkly divided along political lines, and the war only inflamed those tensions. Some Union soldiers believed these home front critics were little more than traitors, so when the soldiers came home on furlough, they shut down opposition newspapers, made Copperheads take loyalty oaths, and confiscated their weapons. It was in this climate that rioters attacked the 54th Illinois Volunteer Regiment in Charleston in 1864.

Afterwards, many of the rioters fled. Twenty-seven men were arrested in the immediate aftermath (11 released and one died), and twelve were indicted for murder but escaped. Two were exonerated at trial. Sheriff John Henry O'Hair died in 1872 at the age of 37 and is buried in Edgar County, Illinois. Congressman John R. Eden ran unsuccessfully for governor of Illinois in 1868.

"In These Shallow Walls" is a fictional story. Only the location, historical background, and girl who died in the fire are real. Elva Lowduskey Skinner was the daughter of Adam and Lucinda Skinner. Adam was a Civil War veteran who left nothing behind when he died, condemning his wife and three children to live at the Coles County Poor Farm. On Sunday morning, February 15, 1880, Elva slept in while her family ate breakfast (the *Mattoon Gazette* inaccurately reported it was Monday). She rose to dress herself, but stood too close to the fireplace and her dress caught fire. She burned to death two weeks shy of her fifth birthday.

The accident happened in the first almshouse built on that property, a brick and timber building 38x58 feet and two stories tall, with an attached kitchen. Almshouses and poor farms existed as an institution in Illinois from 1839 to 1967, when they were abolished by the Public Aid Code. Coles County's first almshouse was built in Charleston Township near Loxa, but in 1870 it moved to a 260-acre farm in Ashmore Township. That building survived until 1915 when the current building, which became known as Ashmore Estates, was built. Elva died in the 1870-1915 building, not the one standing today, so why do so many people think her ghost lingers there? I don't know for sure, but I never heard anything about her ghost haunting Ashmore Estates before publishing this story in 2004.

Every character in "Innocence" is also made up, although the homicide case was real. I deliberately fictionalized details about who found the body, etc, even though it is public record, because I felt since the people involved are still alive today, it would be in poor taste to include them in a fictional story. On Sunday morning, October 19, 1980, two hunters from Champaign County discovered the body of Diana Marie Riordan-Small, a resident of Bradley, Illinois, on the riverbank near Airtight Bridge. Her identity would not be ascertained until 12 years later, and a suspect would not be arrested until 2017. Prosecutors charged her husband, Thomas A. Small, for her murder. He was convicted and sentenced to 30 years in prison. This was Coles County's most famous unsolved murder, which was finally resolved after 36 years.

"April Embers" is a new story set during the Blair Hall fire of April 28, 2004. I was on campus at the time and took two dozen photos on my film camera—it was the worst physical disaster in EIU's history. Yes, that was the year cell phones became popular in the U.S., and most cell phone cameras were less than one megapixel! That year, as was every year since 2002, the Iraq War was a controversial and divisive topic and sparked protests, vigils, and more than a few arguments. I wanted to show all sides of the debate, from war hawks, to peaceniks, and people who just wanted to serve their country and didn't care about the politics. I attended my share of antiwar protests as a student at EIU, but I later joined the Army and served in Iraq during the fight against ISIS, so I can better understand these perspectives.

Tragically, April 28, 2004 was also the day *60 Minutes* released photos of horrible abuse at Abu Ghraib prison in Iraq. As college students, we were constantly bombarded with news and images from the war, but there was a big disconnect between what was going on over there and life at home. Though tragic, the Blair Hall fire brought the community together in a way that was sorely needed. The outpouring of support from local businesses was incredible. They donated food, coffee, and even trash bags to emergency workers. It seemed like everyone on campus turned out to watch the fire. EIU administrators worked hard to salvage the building, and after two years and $6 million, Blair Hall was painstakingly restored to its former glory.

I disagree with William Henry Perrin, author of *The History of Coles County* (1879), when he wrote "Such incidents are better forgotten than perpetuated upon the pages of history." To those who accuse me of dredging up things better left buried, I say: "the past is the past." We might not always be proud of our history, but it's important to learn about it, and to learn from it. I could have written positive stories about people having summer romances in the heart of Mattoon or picnicking at Fox Ridge State Park, but I don't believe those stories would be interesting or informative. Fiction is a wonderful way to get people interested in their past. I chose these particular events and places because they're so little mentioned in history books. It's that history that needs the most sunlight.

The Old Miller's Tale

The 1990 Dodge Omni's engine sputtered under a torrent of heavy rain that beat against its rusted body. Its driver, a young man in his early twenties named Max, leaned forward and tried to see past the curtain of water tossed around by the painfully inadequate windshield wipers. His heart raced and his eyes frantically darted from the sky to the road. Thick, black clouds swirled dangerously close to the treetops, and visibility was reduced to inches beyond the Omni's headlights.

"Are you sure you know where you're going?" Nancy whined from the backseat. She wore a teal-blue tank top and light gray yoga pants with Old Navy stenciled on the rear. There were two other passengers in the small car: Tami, Max's girlfriend, sat on the front passenger side, while Max's best friend, AJ, sat next to Nancy. The four were heading down Route 130 south of Charleston to a camping spot for the weekend.

Max, who made no secret about his dislike for Nancy, pretended to clean out his ear, earning a scolding rebuke.

"Why don't we just turn back?" Tami suggested, her short, red hair bobbing with each syllable. "We're not going to be able to enjoy our weekend anyway." The weather forecast hadn't predicted rain, but then, suddenly, the radio announced a tornado warning.

"Please don't start, Tami," Max pleaded. "I don't need you against me too."

"No one's against you, hon," she said defensively. "It's just pouring rain, that's all. We can barely see what's in front of us. This is scary."

"It's going to let up any minute," Max insisted while he took the car around a sharp turn. His eyes were so focused on the dark clouds above that he didn't see the black shape in the headlights. It moved too quickly for his foot to react. Nancy, who gripped the headrest, screamed as the animal's body dropped with a thud on the hood before rolling awkwardly onto its four hooves. The Dodge Omni screeched to a halt as Max slammed on the breaks. The deer twitched and shook its spindly legs in fear and confusion for what seemed like an agonizing amount of time before stumbling off the road into the forest. The four students sat in stunned silence while the rain tapped on the hood and smoke poured from a violent crack in the grill.

"What was that?" AJ asked, his voice trembling with adrenaline.

"A deer, I think," his friend Max whispered from behind the wheel. Everyone inside the car was deathly still, and a few moments passed in which the spattering of rain was the only sound the four heard. The smell of old gym shoes, cigarettes, and radiator fluid filled their nostrils.

AJ's hand reached for the door handle. "We need to push the car off the road," he said with uncertainty.

Nancy pulled out her Motorola RAZR and said, "I'm going to call a tow truck." She flipped open the phone and then violently shook it. "Damn!" she yelled in frustration. "There's no reception. Why are we out in the middle of *nowhere?*"

Max put the gearshift in neutral, and his friend and he raced from the car into the rain. As the downpour soaked into their t-shirts and shorts, the two young men pushed the Omni slowly forward with the two girls inside.

AJ cursed, but was thankful that he wore his baseball cap as water dripped down the brim and away from his eyes. "What are we going to do now?" he shouted over the thunder.

"I think I saw a light up there," his friend replied. "Maybe it's a farmhouse. We could go ask for help."

The car slipped from their hands with a jerk and came to a stop in a sloppy ditch along the roadside, where they threw open the passenger doors. "Max thinks he saw a light up ahead," AJ shouted to the girls. "We're going to check it out. Maybe we can get help."

"We're *not* staying here by ourselves!" Nancy shrieked as she grabbed her purse. Tami zipped up her green, loop-terry hoodie for some protection from the storm, while Max helped her out of the car and held an old copy of the *Daily Eastern News* over her head to block the rain.

AJ trudged ahead while his girlfriend struggled to pull herself from the backseat. "Where is this place?" he yelled as raindrops smacked the pavement and thrashed the greenery.

"I saw it just around the bend!" Max yelled back. His eyes scanned the treeline until they fell upon the soft yellow glow of a window in the near distance. A flash of lightning illuminated the small cabin for a moment before it plunged back into darkness. The four left their broken car behind and sprinted toward the dwelling.

"I don't like this," Tami whispered in Max's ear as they rushed ahead. "I don't like just going up to someone's house at night and barging in. We don't even know who these people are."

"We have to," Max replied. "What are we supposed to do, sit in the car all night until someone comes along? We only saw one other car our whole way down here." As the group neared the cabin, they passed a wooden mill set back from the road, its ancient wheel creaking in the rushing waters of the Embarras River. Max thought it looked like it belonged in a Tim Burton film. There were so many holes he thought the wheel would break off at any moment and be carried away by the current.

Before they knew, they were up on the cabin's porch, bracing themselves for the reception they were about to receive from its unsuspecting residents. AJ's hand reached for the door handle, but to his surprise, it jerked away on its own. The four students jumped back with the click of the latch. The door slowly opened to reveal a small man with leathery, creased skin, a lightly trimmed beard, and baggy old clothing. His toothy grin greeted them as warmly as the soft light coming from the lit fireplace and oil lanterns inside.

"Harold, who's there?" a woman's unsteady voice called from somewhere out of sight.

"Come in, come in," Harold instructed the four students, ignoring her question. He grabbed AJ by the arm and guided him into the cabin. AJ looked back at his friends with a worried expression mutually etched on all their faces.

"We're sorry to bother you," Tami cut in with a sympathetic tone. "But our car broke down out there. Something hit us, I mean, and it was pouring, and we saw your place here."

"You needn't explain, dear," Harold's wife, Edith, assured her. "We're glad to have the company." She was a striking woman, with streaks of gray in her otherwise austere hair. Like that of her husband, her face was creased with age and decorated with liver spots.

The elderly couple led the students into their claustrophobic cabin that, for all eyes could see, consisted of a wide front room and one bedroom in the back. The cabin smelled like old cedar, and there was no visible bathroom or closets. A single cast-iron stove sat in the corner opposite the fireplace, near some hand-built shelves. The sturdy, wooden table in the middle of the room was set with dishes, and it looked as though the couple had just been sitting down for dinner.

"Do you have a phone?" Max asked loudly and deliberately. "None of us can get a signal out here."

"A signal?" Harold repeated. "No, I don't think we have one of those."

Max threw up his hands incredulously.

"Oh, you must get dry clothes on," Edith said cheerily. "Harold, see if you can't find something for these boys here." She turned to Nancy. "Oh my, I don't think any of my clothes will fit you, dear. Maybe I have something from when I was a youngin'."

Nancy couldn't hold in the laugh that escaped, and an awkward silence followed while the old couple searched their antique armoire for dry clothes. "Why do they talk like they're from the South?" she whispered. AJ leaned over and gave Max a worried look.

After the four took turns changing into their used clothes, which reeked of mothballs, they were invited to sit down at the dinner table, where they waited in silence for Edith to slowly put food on their plates. Nancy pulled with contempt at the loose sleeves of the faded gray dress she wore, while Max tried not to look like he was scratching his legs, which were getting irritated from the rough cotton pants.

"Where y'all from?" Edith finally asked.

"Oh, we go to Eastern," Tami piped up. "You know, EIU? We were heading to Fox Ridge for the weekend to go camping."

Edith glanced at her husband, a wry smile on her face. "How nice," she said as she dumped a piece of meat on Nancy's plate. Her hands shook, but still moved with nobility.

"Oh, I don't eat—" Nancy started to say, but the elderly woman cut her off.

"Why don't we say grace," she suggested. "Harold?"

Harold and his wife closed their eyes and folded their hands together, and Tami kicked Max under the table and gestured toward him to mimic their hosts. He reluctantly complied, while Nancy and AJ stared straight ahead, trying not to snicker.

"How do you like it down here?" the old lady asked, when her husband had finished the short prayer. "It's beautiful in the fall, isn't it?"

"It's okay," AJ mumbled before anyone could answer. "But it's pretty boring. Nothing ever happens."

The elderly couple froze and Max stared at his friend in disbelief.

"*Boring*?" Harold echoed.

Max quickly tore his gaze away and looked around the room for anything else to talk about. They hadn't been there more than an hour and already his friends were well on the road to getting them kicked back out into the rain. By happenstance, his eyes fell on what looked like a pile of chipped stones on the fireplace mantle. "What are those?" he asked, pointing to the stones.

The old man smiled. "Thems are Indian arrowheads, boy," he coyly explained. "Found 'em on this very property." He turned to AJ. "There's your *boring* history for ye'. I bet you didn't even know a battle had been fought right near our mill."

"No, I didn't, sir," AJ replied, his voice tense with apologetic deference.

Tami perked up. "Why don't you tell us about it while we're eating?" she suggested. "We would all *love* to hear about it, right AJ? We could all use a little break from talking, *right AJ*?"

AJ reluctantly mumbled affirmatively while hiding his face behind his glass of water.

The old man's demeanor brightened. "Yes," he agreed. "Maybe y'all learn a thing or two."

Nancy picked at the piece of strange looking meat on her plate as Harold began his story.

THE SECOND BATTLE OF THE
AMBRAW

The summer sun beamed down through the treetops and illuminated the forest floor, while cicadas buzzed incessantly from hidden branches. A column of men clad in buckskin slowly coiled its way along a well-worn deer path. Most sat on horseback, but some rode in a small supply wagon mid-formation. The year was 1818, six years before the first white settlers would arrive in the area that became Coles County, and a few remaining American Indians, most notably the Kickapoo, refused to leave their lands and join the tribal relocation beyond the Mississippi.

Most of the westward-bound pioneers avoided the wild region of east-central Illinois, but some, like John Parker, would eventually stop and erect cabins near large groves or adjacent to rivers and streams. John Parker and his four sons: Benjamin, Daniel, Silas, and James, would, in a few years, build a mill (later known as Blakeman's Mill) near a ford in the Embarras River to service neighboring farms. It was near the site of this mill that the legendary Indian fighter Samuel Whiteside and his Illinois Rangers camped while in pursuit of a Kickapoo, Pottawatomie, and Winnebago raiding party that had stolen some horses and terrorized settlers a week earlier.

The shallow river sparkled as it flowed around a bend in the trees, and it provided a quick drink for the horses as they crossed. The animal's hooves splashed and clopped on the smooth stones. Colonel Whiteside rode at the head of the column with two men at his side. He was tall with a square jaw, broad nose, and long, thin lips. He raised his arm and the company halted.

"I see a good campsite down yonder," he announced. "This will be a fine place to stay for the night. These ridges will hide our fires. Send a foraging party to search the woods for some grub for supper, and scouts to watch for ambushes." Despite his rank, Whiteside wore a threadbare, brown leather vest over a rumpled white cotton shirt. He had no time for fancy clothes or formality.

"Isn't this whereabouts those surveyors got into that scrap with the redskins three years back?" the man on his right side,

Lieutenant Robert Forester, inquired. Forester, in contrast, indulged in a blue officer's coat and black top hat.

Whiteside paused to think. "I do believe so," he replied, and turned toward the man on his left. "Sergeant Johnson, have the men set up camp."

"Yes sir, colonel," First Sergeant James Johnson replied as he wheeled his horse and picked up his pace. A bird chirped loudly in the distance as he headed off, and the horses grew uneasy.

Farther up river, two scouts, Thomas and Daniel, crawled to the peak of a ridge, one of several carved out of the landscape by small streams draining toward the river. The southern half of what would become Coles County had been spared the last great glacial period, and the terrain was much more like that of Kentucky or Tennessee. It was comforting to the settlers who would eventually venture to that part of Illinois, because it reminded them of home.

Thomas peaked his head over a thick log. "That's a raiding party down yonder," he whispered, referring to a group of six American Indian braves resting about fifty yards away on a ridgeside. One of the Indians, near a tree, bent down and seemed to be digging something out of the weeds. A tall man wearing two feathers and a long cotton shirt cupped his hands over his mouth and whistled. The digging man pulled up a medium-sized turtle and said, "*Maskoteehkeeha.*"

"Those are Kickapoo," Daniel whispered. "You can tell by the whistling. They're the only tribe around these parts that does that."

"What do you think they're up to?"

Daniel angled to get a better look. "Looks like they're finding supper. The fact we can't see the rest of 'em worries me."

"Should we get on back to Colonel Whiteside?" Thomas wondered aloud. "Or maybe we should ambush these varmints now and save us the trouble later." The sun was beginning to set, and the tops of the trees were painted an orange hue.

"Don't get yer dander up," Daniel said, and then, referring to the group of Indians who had attacked the white settlements a few weeks ago, "We don't even know if them are the redskins that done it." One of the braves turned his head in their direction and scanned the ridgeline. His head stopped, and Thomas felt the man's eyes lock with his.

Daniel saw it too. "Now it looks like we don't have a choice," he spat as a cry rang out from the camp.

Thomas went for his weapon, an old Springfield 1795 musket, laying at his side.

"Wait a minute," Daniel frantically said. "No one's done any shootin' yet."

Before he could say anything else, Thomas fired a shot. The heavy lead ball rocketed from a burst of thick smoke and splintered a tree branch. The Kickapoo braves ducked, but collected themselves quickly and gathered their weapons. Thomas uncorked his powder horn and started to fill the rifle barrel, but his friend grabbed his arm and pulled him to his feet.

"There ain't no time for that!" he yelled. "Dang it! You've really stirred up the hornet's nest now!" The two stumbled down the ridgeside with a scatter of arrows whistling above their heads.

The sun had nearly set over the small encampment of the Illinois Rangers. The rangers, made up of volunteers from across the state, were grouped around several campfires. Colonel Whiteside walked among them with his eyes pointed to the sky. He nodded at anyone who approached, but didn't stop to talk or exchange greetings. "It was nice to dig out these three old 'taters," he heard one of his men say in a voice thick with bitter sarcasm as he walked past a campfire.

"At least we're eatin' something other than squirrel," Whiteside heard another reply. He continued his stroll to the edge of camp and looked out over the Embarras River from the top of the short drop-off that led to the water. The river flowed slowly past and carried leaves and other debris from the forest somewhere downstream. A branch snapped, but he didn't show any sign that he heard it.

"Yes, Sergeant Johnson?" he asked without turning to see who it was.

"Not Johnson, sir," the man corrected him with hesitation. "Lieutenant Forester."

"Ah," Whiteside replied. "Any word from those two scouts we sent out?"

"Not yet, sir," Forester informed his commander. "They should've been back by now."

Whiteside shuffled his feet and began chewing on a stem of tall grass. "They may have deserted," he speculated bitterly.

"I don't think so, sir," the lieutenant responded. "That's not like neither of them. Daniel is too loyal and Thomas wouldn't back down from a fight." There was a long moment of silence as Lt. Forester waited for a response. "Should we deploy skirmishers for the night?" he asked when no reply came.

"The redskins won't attack us in the dark," Whiteside finally said. "They'll riddle each other with arrows and be on the run before the sun comes up. I believe those varmints are running for their lives." He nodded his head as if agreeing with himself.

Forester grit his teeth and walked off in frustration.

The woods were alive with the sound of insects buzzing and the crash of heavy footsteps. The two scouts raced through the hills and valleys about a mile from the banks of the river, but Daniel was the first to slow down. His chest heaved and he grabbed his thighs tightly. "Just let 'em get us," he wheezed in desperation. "I ain't used to all this runnin'."

Thomas paced furiously with his rifle cradled in his arms. "They got my horse," he mumbled over and over again. "My Molly is gonna kill me." The two stopped just over the crest of a ridge where they would be hidden, but could easily defend themselves if attacked.

"Forget yer dang horse," his friend shouted to him. "You're lucky we outran 'em."

"Outran 'em, hell," Thomas cursed. "It just got too dark to follow our trail." He stopped pacing and took another look over his shoulder. His anger slowly gave way to nervousness as the adrenaline subsided and their surroundings took on an unfamiliar appearance in the twilight. "I think we're lost," he whispered as he scanned the dark trees.

"We ain't lost," Daniel assured his friend. He stretched out his hand. "Give that pin of yourn here."

Thomas looked down at the silver pin sticking through the breast of his butternut shirt. "Molly gave that to me," he explained. "Don't go losing it." He handed over the pin after some hesitation.

Daniel descended the slope toward a small pool of stagnant rainwater at the bottom of the shallow ravine, and Thomas followed close behind with a worried look on his face. The scout crouched next to the water and grabbed a nearby leaf. He placed the pin delicately on the leaf and then put both in the pool. The leaf floated around a bit and then came to rest with the tip of the pin facing north. "You see," Daniel explained. "That's the way the river runs, north to south. We've been going alongside it this whole time and all I reckon we have to do is walk a ways that way and we'll meet up with the colonel." He picked the pin off the leaf and handed it back to his companion. "For now I suggest we get some sleep. No one's going anywhere tonight. The moon's barely showing and we won't be able to see our hands in front of our faces in a few minutes." The pair picked out a place near a large tree and tried to make themselves as comfortable as possible.

A cricket chirped nearby as Thomas watched the shadows move across the forest floor and let his imagination play with the inky darkness. He thought of home, of the family he'd left in Indiana to find better land to make a homestead. All he found was this God-forsaken territory, the new state of Illinois, with too many forests in the south and nothing but swamp and tall grasslands to the north. Now he was running for his life. Exhaustion overwhelmed him despite his fear of what tomorrow would bring, and he slipped off into an uneasy sleep.

It was still dark when Thomas awoke, and slowly he realized Daniel was shaking him. "What in tarnation?" he exclaimed.

"Shhh!" Daniel whispered. "Look!"

Thomas took a moment to clear his eyes before he rolled over and crawled to the crest of the ridge. It was hard to see with his pupils still adjusting to the dim light, but he could make out a mass of shapes moving through the early morning fog in the holler below.

"*Redskins*," Daniel whispered. "A whole mess of 'em heading right for the colonel, and I bet he's going to be caught with his britches down."

Dark shapes moved silently through the trees. Only silhouettes of feathered headdresses and their distinctive weapons could be seen clearly in the early morning darkness. "Colonel Whiteside will be completely surprised," Thomas agreed with alarm in his already shaking voice. "It'll be a massacre. We have to do something." He pulled out a large knife from his boot and stuck it in the earth next to him. The two readied their muskets and looked at each other in silent agreement.

"Company, form up!" Daniel yelled in his best impression of an officer. The collective mass of men below froze in their tracks.

"Ready!" Thomas added in a voice that echoed through the holler. "Aim! Fire!" The two scouts let their muskets flare. The sparks from the barrels illuminated the ground, and for a brief moment they saw the determined faces of their foes. A cry rang out from the war party below and the two scouts saw a brave drop and writhe on the ground. Daniel and Thomas quickly loaded their muskets for another round while a collective 'whoop' came from the warriors as they sprang into action.

Sweat dripped down Daniel's forehead as his finger squeezed the trigger again. Arrows rained down around the scouts as the Kickapoo braves began to fire back. One arrow sunk into the ground next to Daniel's arm, and he gave it a quick glance before reloading his weapon. The mass of men below started surging up the hill, but the darkness and the steepness of the ridge made any advance difficult.

"I hope this works!" Thomas yelled over the din of shouts and musket fire.

An aid frantically shouting about gunfire coming from somewhere nearby threw aside the cloth flap from the entrance to Col. Whiteside's tent, waking him. "Get Sergeant Johnson!" Whiteside half yelled, half mumbled as he collected his senses. His saw only the shapes of his men frantically running around in the darkness.

After a few moments, First Sergeant Johnson popped his head into the tent. His hair was tangled and his unshaven face was as coarse as an angry badger.

"What's going on?" Whiteside asked while pulling on his pants. "You look like hell."

"Nobody knows," Johnson said frantically, ignoring the comment. "Someone's shootin' down yonder. Those two scouts are still missing. Do you think the redskins got the jump on us?"

Whiteside paused and carefully ran a hand through his greasy, unwashed hair. "Deploy skirmishers," he ordered. "Start marching toward the sound of firing, and I'll follow with the rest of the company."

First Sergeant Johnson nodded and ducked out of the tent. Most of the Illinois Rangers had collected their weapons and stood waiting for orders, leaving their horses tied. Johnson quickly found Lt. Forester and advised him to get the men into line. He then proceeded to pick out twelve rangers, the closest ones he could get his hands on, and pushed them forward. The group fanned out and ran headlong into the woods. The sun had begun its ascent, and it became easier to see when they reached the top of a ridge and spotted the large group of Kickapoo warriors climbing up the side of a parallel ridge. They saw an occasional flash of musket fire at the crest. The Indian braves were perilously close to their prey.

"Let's give those boys some help!" Johnson shouted. The skirmishers gave a yell and opened fire on the Kickapoo, to little effect. Johnson discharged his pistol just in time to see the two scouts on the opposite ridge disappear in a swarm of naked skin, fur, and feathers. Some of the braves, who were armed with muskets, turned and shot back. Others shouted and pointed at the newcomers. An arrow struck the man next to First Sergeant Johnson in the chest, sending the man sprawling onto the forest floor. "Take cover!" the first sergeant yelled, and he found a thick tree to hide behind. The tide of Kickapoo warriors now changed direction and surged toward the beleaguered skirmishers. Johnson glanced over his shoulder to see if the main unit was on its way. To his relief, he saw a line of men clad in brown and tan spilling into the holler below, with Colonel Whiteside at the lead riding his brown and white spotted horse. They were only a few minutes away.

The Native braves changed tactics and swept around to the right, where the ridges gradually came together. They ran at full pace, whooping a war-cry as they came. Johnson motioned his men to follow as he ran to try and protect the Ranger's flank. Whiteside, from atop his horse, saw what was going on and wheeled his men to meet the new threat. He stopped the Rangers on a ridge, which was now separated from the next by only a few feet. The Kickapoo flooded toward them.

Whiteside raised his sword as his men loaded their muskets and readied to fire. The Kickapoo braves stopped in their tracks and waited until Whiteside's arm swung downwards. A burst of fire and smoke filled the gap between them, but the native warriors fell to the ground and avoided the volley's full force. Lead balls smacked harmlessly into trees or spiraled from sight. The Kickapoo got to their feet and raced forward with a war cry—

tomahawks flailing in the air. Whiteside's men, eager for the fight, broke ranks without orders and ran down to meet their enemy.

Birds scattered angrily from the fierce fighting, and their cries mingled with those of the men below, while the summer leaves rained down on the convulsing mob of bodies. Hatchets, knives, and the butts of muskets caught flesh wherever it dared to be exposed. Whiteside stood on his horse and fired his pistol wildly into the fray. "We got 'em, boys!" he yelled over the noise until his voice was hoarse.

Lt. Forester had, until then, kept his remaining men away from the melee. He ordered them to creep down the ridge and position themselves to cut off their enemy's retreat. From this new vantage point, he could see the bodies of the two scouts high on the second ridge with a trail of wounded Kickapoo leading to the top. The sight hardened his resolve to end this conflict right here. He knew Whiteside wasn't in the mood for taking prisoners. He was a breed of man who knew nothing but fighting.

Forester's rangers kneeled in the soft dirt and leveled their muskets. A few minutes later their anxious wait ended and a stream of Kickapoo rushed toward them. Although they had thrown their weapons aside and were running for their lives, a burst of lead balls cut them down as quickly as they came. Lt. Forester closed his eyes and felt the sting of sweat. He whispered a silent prayer for the dead while the cool forest air tickled his clammy skin.

When the smoke cleared, the battle was over. Wounded men limped or crawled to the pools of water at the bottom of the hollers, and their pitiful groans—a language all could understand—filled the air. Col. Whiteside carefully led his horse through the dozens of bodies to where Lt. Forester stood. "It's a hell of a thing," he whispered to the shaken officer. "Once we've taken care of the wounded," he said, straightening himself in his saddle, "we'll return to Fort La Motte and send word to Governor Edwards that the band of raiders has been disbursed and the stolen property recovered."

"It is that, sir," Forester answered. "A hell of a thing." He watched Whiteside nod, turn his horse, and trot slowly back to camp.

* * *

"Wow," Nancy gasped, her mouth hanging open with a radish impaled on her fork. "What happened after that? What happened to the Indians?"

"The last of 'em were forced out of the state in '32," Harold explained, revealing a mouth with less than a full set of teeth, "and Col. Whiteside got himself a county named after him."

"That's not fair," Max interjected.

"Who said life was fair, boy?" Harold asked with a toothy grin.

Max scoffed. "This meat tastes different," he said in a detached, almost bored voice.

"Yeah, it tastes like a rabbit smells," AJ chuckled.

Edith turned toward him and smiled. "Because it is rabbit, dearie. Harold trapped it this morning. Would you like some more?"

Nancy stopped picking at the meat and examined it with disgust. "So tell us something else," she said slowly and deliberately.

Max interrupted Harold as he began to speak. "Has anything else happened like that around here? Any other battles?"

Harold shifted uncomfortably. "Don't you want to hear about anything else, boy?" he snapped. "How about the great freeze of 1836? The streams were frozen in place in seconds, you know."

"Harold!" his wife yelled, a hand resting on her hip as though she was scolding a child. "These are our guests!"

Harold rolled his eyes. "Fine," he mumbled and slurped his soup. "I bet you didn't know our country's civil war wasn't just confined to distant battlefields. There was fighting all over the states. One of those fights happened right in the middle of Charleston, less than a mile from where you youngin's go to school."

"It was a terrible time," his wife added, as though she had witnessed it herself.

The four students chewed slowly and listened with curiosity. Thunder rolled outside the cabin, and the rain beat down on its shuddering roof.

THE CHARLESTON RIOT

The Coles County Courthouse and Charleston's town square buzzed with activity. Farmers, shopkeepers, horse-drawn wagons, and furloughed soldiers dressed in blue uniforms saying goodbye to loved ones kicked up dust in the dirt streets. March 1864 was rapidly coming to a close, but despite Union victories, the Southern rebellion dragged on. It was a presidential election year, with Illinoisans divided over Abraham Lincoln's leadership. Many believed the price paid to keep Southern states in the Union was already too high, and warm weather portended bloody months ahead. These supporters of "peace without victory" were called "butternuts" or "copperheads" by their foes. Each faction—Unionists and copperheads—despised each other.

On that mild spring day of March 28, Oliver stepped outside Huron's Bookstore on the west side of the square, engrossed in that week's issue of the *Plaindealer*. Newspapers were still fresh with news of a February fight between copperheads and Union soldiers in the village of Paris in neighboring Edgar County, which left a young man named Alfred Kennedy dead.

Local copperheads bristled over Kennedy's death, as well as several instances of soldiers confiscating their weapons and forcing some to swear a loyalty oath to the federal government. Now they were raising a stink over the presence of two companies, C and G, of the 54th Illinois Volunteer Infantry Regiment. Many of its soldiers, who had enjoyed a few weeks home after reenlisting, were local boys from the county, so Oliver couldn't imagine anything coming of these idle threats.

Oliver looked up from his newspaper to see clusters of men gathered around the square, many sipping from flasks. He recognized familiar faces, but some, who sat on horses near hay-filled wagons, appeared to be from the countryside. A little more than a dozen soldiers ducked in and out of storefronts or conversed on the street. Only a few were armed. Finally, Oliver recognized his friend Asa, who was standing against a tree near the courthouse, and strode over to him. The courthouse was an unassuming, two story redbrick structure with a white cupola, an extension added in 1858, and two out buildings (one on each side) that served as offices.

"Isn't this exciting?" Asa shouted even before Oliver could reach him.

"Isn't what exciting?" Oliver asked in reply. "What are all these people doing here?" He finally reached the tree, which was in earshot of a group of four men who stood on the courthouse steps. The quartet included James O'Hair, Sr., who alongside Frank Toland had a pistol confiscated by soldiers just two days earlier, and his friend Nelson Wells, who was preparing to leave with a party of prospectors to find gold in California. Their wagons were hitched along Columbus Street (present-day 7th Street) on the east side of the square.

"Democrats is havin' a rally and Congressman Eden is goin' to give a speech," Asa replied.

"I don't like the sound of that," Oliver whispered under his breath. Everyone in the county knew that U.S. Representative John Rice Eden, along with Sheriff John O'Hair, were leaders of the local Peace Democrats. With tensions so high, Eden giving a speech was only asking for trouble. Oliver took note of a Union soldier who walked up to the elder O'Hair. He appeared slightly drunk.

"You call yourselves white men?" he jeered.

James O'Hair and Nelson Wells appeared startled by the soldier's remarks, but James' face revealed a poorly disguised animosity. Asa witnessed the proceedings from his vantage point by the tree and threw a worried glance at Oliver.

"You're no white man," the soldier continued. "No man who's for Jeff Davis is a white man." Jefferson Davis was the president of the Confederacy.

Wells remained calm and stuck his thumbs into his vest pockets. "Look around you, sir," he casually replied. "There is plenty of Jeff Davis men here." A fairly large crowd began to gather around the argument. A man, who Oliver recognized as Robert Leitch, emerged from the crowd and took the soldier by the arm, gently leading him back to a group of his fellow infantrymen. Asa and Oliver watched Mr. Leitch talk to the soldiers in the street but couldn't make out what he said. Leitch returned to the crowd, which for the most part loitered on the courthouse lawn, and then addressed Nelson Wells in particular.

"Sir," he began, delicately turning his hat in his hands. "I have spoken to the soldiers and they say they are heading to the train depot shortly to return to Mattoon. They won't start no trouble if they're left alone."

Wells stared coldly from under the brim of his yellow hat. "Those soldiers have done nothing but pester us all morning, *sir*," he explained with a fiery edge to his voice. "And our own citizens have pointed us out as Democrats so the soldiers may take revenge on us. I say it's about time for us to have revenge in return."

"Revenge is a bad thing," Mr. Leitch replied. "Have you known any man here who is a Democrat or who has been considered loyal, and who has been disturbed by one of these good soldiers?"

Mr. Wells gave no reply, and after a moment of icy silence, Robert Leitch donned his hat and walked toward the train station. Oliver and Asa nodded to each other and decided to follow, confident the situation had been diffused.

The hostility outside was palpable, even inside the courthouse. "Damn it, John," the honorable Judge Charles Henry Constable bellowed, addressing the county sheriff. "It's a mess out there. How are we supposed to conduct the court with this anarchy?"

Sheriff John H. O'Hair turned to Congressman Eden and Orlando Bell Ficklin, a lawyer and former U.S. representative, as if waiting for instructions. When they were young attorneys, Judge Constable and Ficklin, perhaps ironically, won a case on behalf of two slaves who ran away when their master brought them to Illinois. Abraham Lincoln represented the slave owner in court and lost the case.

"I've never seen a crowd like this," Eden said, anxiously scratching his almost snow-white neck beard. "Gentlemen, I think it's best I cancel my speech and return to Washington."

"Don't give it a second thought," Judge Constable replied, shaking the congressman's hand. "That should put the soldiers at ease. Try to urge everyone to go home, eh?"

Eden nodded, said his goodbyes, and left the room while Sheriff O'Hair prepared an accused hog thief for trial.

It only took a few minutes for Oliver and Asa to reach the train station. There they saw dozens of Union soldiers milling around, waiting for the train to take them to Mattoon. Their rifles were stacked like small teepees with pouches, canteens, and coats hanging from the bayonets. There were only a few other townspeople in the area, including themselves and Robert Leitch. Someone they didn't recognize was shouting at the soldiers.

"You're all a bunch of no-good cowards!" the young man yelled. He attracted the attention of a couple of station attendants, who quickly attempted to drag him away, but he resisted. The young man continued to yell as he thrashed his arms, pushing at the men who tried to restrain him. An older gentleman, who Oliver could tell was an officer by the gold stripes on his uniform and the sword at his side, calmly approached the commotion.

"You are drunk, son," he said with a razor's edge. "I suggest you go on and get before trouble starts. As you can see, you are greatly outnumbered."

"Not for long," the young man spat. "We're goin' to clean you out of here today!"

"That's Colonel Mitchell," Asa whispered to Oliver, referring to the Union officer. "Him and my pappy are friends."

Col. Greenville McNeal Mitchell, a Charleston native with a thick, broad mustache, walked past the raving man in the direction of the town square, and two soldiers grabbed their Springfield rifle-muskets and rushed to his side to accompany him. "I'm going to speak with Congressman Eden," he announced. "He'll put a stop to this harassment."

Oliver and Asa followed close behind. A number of others headed in that direction as well, while the man who had been yelling insults was finally pulled away from the nervous and agitated soldiers. It was a short walk to the square, where an even greater number were gathered. The two friends ran to get a closer look at the commotion. The sun slowly descended to the western horizon, signaling the arrival of late afternoon.

"There's a better view over here," Asa called out from the middle of the street. Oliver ran to join him just in time to see another Union soldier stumble into Nelson Wells, who had boasted "By God we have taken all we are going to take from the soldiers." James O'Hair was no longer with him.

The Union soldier, Private Oliver Sallee, apparently didn't recognize Mr. Wells and tapped him on the shoulder. "Are any of those damned copperheads around here?" Sallee asked.

ILLUSTRATION BY KATIE CONRAD

"Yes, damn you," Wells replied while drawing his pistol. "I am one!" Before anyone could intervene, Wells' finger depressed the trigger and smoke exploded from the barrel. The lead ball struck

Sallee in the chest and he stumbled backward. As Sallee hit the ground, he fired his own pistol at Wells, who groaned and staggered past the circuit clerk's office. Wells made it as far as Chambers and McCrory's General Store at the northwest corner of Jackson and Washington streets (today 6th Street and Monroe Ave) before collapsing in a pool of blood.

Oliver's eyes opened wide and he dropped to the ground for cover. The newspaper, which he had been faithfully clutching since earlier that morning, flew from his hands and lay discarded on the ground nearby. Most of the bystanders scattered, revealing only the copperheads and Union soldiers. The copperheads opened fire from all directions. They grabbed loaded muskets and shotguns from underneath piles of hay in several nearby wagons, which had been brought there hours earlier for just this instance. "By God, the town is ours!" one cried.

Oliver, from his new vantage point, caught a glimpse of a neighbor, Marcus Hill, unhitching his horses from a nearby tree.

A man Oliver recognized as John Gilbriath stopped Mr. Hill. "Hill, what in the hell do you think of this?" he asked in a rush.

"It's pretty damned warm times!" Marcus retorted, and he quickly drove his horses away from the firing.

Inside the courthouse, Orlando Ficklin heard shots fired from the square but hardly looked up. "Accidental discharge," he mumbled. Moments later, the shouting and gunfire became general, and Sheriff O'Hair received a painful nick on the chin by a bullet flying through the window. His eyes frantically scanned the room as the judge and jurors ducked for cover.

Colonel Mitchell arrived on the scene as the first shots rang out and marched determinedly up the courthouse steps, but just as he reached the door, a local man named Robert Winkler grabbed him. Both drew their pistols and fired. Colonel Mitchell felt the shot strike his wristwatch and ricochet painfully into his stomach. He pushed his wounded assailant away and fell through the courthouse door. Major Shubal York, regimental surgeon, rushed to his colonel's aid from inside the courthouse, but a fourth man, Green Harke, shot him in the back at such point-blank range the black powder seared his clothes. In February, York's son, Milton, had seriously wounded an outspoken copperhead in Edgar County. Edgar County Sheriff William S. O'Hair, first cousin of Coles County Sheriff John O'Hair, attempted to arrest Milton but was discouraged from doing so at gunpoint.

"Get the doctor," Maj. York pleaded, "I am shot all to pieces."

Sheriff O'Hair grabbed Judge Constable and made a run for the door. He drew both pistols and descended the stairs just as two Union soldiers—rifles at the ready—appeared at the steps.

"There's that God-damn butternut sheriff!" one yelled as they both opened fire. The bullets tore holes in O'Hair's coat, and he fired back with both barrels as he realized how close he'd escaped death. Both of his shots hit their targets, and the two soldiers crumpled to the floor. O'Hair rushed past the groaning men and out the door. Judge Constable and he ran to the east side of the square, where Oliver saw the judge, his face pale and frightened, hide in an alley.

Oliver tried to cover his head as best he could while still getting a view of the bloodshed, but the dense smoke obscured his vision. He saw glimpses of farmer John Frazier riding a horse and shouting, firing his pistol wildly into the air. Someone in a blue uniform came running from the drugstore behind him, but didn't make it across the street before a muzzle flash brought him to the ground.

Just as suddenly as the shooting began, the town square became eerily quiet as gunshots echoed around the buildings for the final time. As the smoke gradually dissipated, Oliver saw Col. Mitchell and Sheriff O'Hair rallying their respective sides. For a moment, all was calm. Suddenly, the sound of rushing feet and a loud battle cry emanated from a company of Union soldiers who just arrived from the train station. The copperheads retreated behind a building on the southeastern corner of the square where some mounted their horses and prepared to continue the fight.

Without warning, however, shots rang out from the buildings around them. Some of the citizens who had ran away only moments ago had come back with their own weapons and were firing at the now outnumbered copperheads. Oliver couldn't make out any faces in the confusion, but Asa grabbed him and pulled him to his feet. "Let's go!" he yelled. "Let's get those rebs!"

Oliver had no desire to run into a melee, but he allowed himself to be dragged forward anyway. The mob of loyal citizenry fell upon the copperheads and took ten prisoner. Among them was a young man named John Cooper. One soldier and one civilian, W.A. Noe, seized him and took him in front of E.A. Jenkins Dry Goods Store, but Cooper wormed out of their grasp and drew a concealed pistol from his belt. "Don't!" Noe cried and fired a warning shot over his head. It was too late. The frightened Cooper began to shoot back, and he was swiftly gunned down from three directions.

The other copperheads, most of whom were on horseback, fled before the remaining soldiers of the 54th Illinois could reach them. John O'Hair was among those who managed to get away. Bodies littered the town square, and the groans of the wounded echoed among the brick walls of the stores. A local physician, W.R. Patton, rushed outside to administer to the wounded.

As Union reinforcements poured into Coles County, the remaining copperheads tried to rally support in the countryside. Federal troops rounded up over forty and dispersed the most rebellious elements, and the feared copperhead insurrection never materialized.

* * *

"Nine people were killed on the square that day," Harold concluded, "including six soldiers and two copperheads. Over a dozen were later reported wounded during the whole fiasco... if my memory serves me right."

Thunder still crashed outside, and the storm hadn't yet exhausted its fury.

"I had no idea," Tami said, her eyes transfixed by the orange glow from the lanterns and fireplace dancing on the cabin walls. "It was like a western movie."

Nancy wiped her mouth with a yellowed cloth napkin with a faint floral pattern on the trim. "I always wondered what that mural painted on the building downtown was about." Then, in reply to her friends' unspoken comment, she explained, "What? I saw it when I was going to the Uptowner."

"Do you know anything about that abandoned asylum?" Tami interjected. "Where is it? Nancy, you've been there, right? It's in the middle a field somewhere. I think it's called 'Ashmore Estates'."

Edith looked at her husband. "As a matter of fact, we do. Lots of folks come by here and tell us stories, and we've heard our share of whoppers about that place. Y'all know it as an asylum, but we know it as the Coles County Poor Farm."

"You see," Harold added, "back then, the government didn't send you a check. If you couldn't support yourself or your family, you was sent to 'the farm', where you was cared for and everyone worked to earn a roof over their head. During the Depression, there was lots of folks around here who didn't have homes or family. Many of them wound up on the county farm."

The four students leaned in closely to hear the old man's enigmatic voice.

In These Shallow Walls

The year was 1934, and the Great Depression and Dust Bowl were ravaging the United States. Downstate Illinois was hit hard, with 412 banks failing between 1929 and 1933. Crops wilted or simply blew away throughout the Great Plains, and farming communities, like those of central Illinois, suffered from this ecological disaster. For individuals and families affected by the Depression, there were only two places to go: the unforgiving streets, or the county poor farm. Almhouses and poor farms were established in the 1800s to support the indigent and infirm. The population of these farms swelled when the stock market crashed. The Coles County Poor Farm, located on 260 acres between the towns of Charleston and Ashmore, was no exception.

That winter, Darby Adare and his daughter Shirley were fortunate to find the Coles County almshouse doors open before overcrowding forced it to turn others away. The two-story, red-brick building in neo-Georgian style with red tile roof was conspicuous on an otherwise humble and ordinary farm. It was the largest building for miles, and stood out even more against the white snow. Inmates cared for livestock in a barn, worked in the smokehouse, tended their own garden, and cooked their own meals, all under the supervision of a superintendent and his family.

Darby and his daughter shared a small room with an elderly woman who had lived her entire adult life in the almshouse. The woman was somewhat feeble minded, but she was pleasant enough and could, for the most part, tend to her own needs. Darby and his daughter shared a cot and stored their meager belongings in an old trunk. The old lady claimed what little furniture they had. Darby's situation was brightened by a nurse named Rose, who lived and worked at the almshouse. His heart leapt when she knocked.

"Come in," he said, waking up from a nap after helping the other able-bodied inmates feed the livestock and mend a fence all morning in the bitter cold. It was early February, and frosty winds swept across the barren cornfields. Only a few small trees and bushes protected the almshouse from the elements, and the farm was only accessible by a rocky, dirt road easily rendered useless by deep snow.

"Time for your medication, Miss Williams," Rose sang as she entered the room holding a wooden tray. "Why, hello Shirley!"

"Hello, Miss Rose!" Shirley replied. She tugged on Darby's sleeve. "Daddy, can I go play with Elva?"

Darby hesitated. For days after being assigned a room, he wouldn't let his daughter, seven years old, wander the imposing brick building on her own. It was, after all, an unfamiliar place with new people, and their experience with day-to-day life on the road made him cautious. Shirley had made friends with several other children in the building, particularly a girl about the same age named Elva, but Darby had never met her or her parents. Still, he dreamed of having a few moments alone with Rose.

"Run along," he said, "but be back by supper."

"Where's Shirley's momma?" Rose once asked him, and he had to tell her the tragic truth; Darby's wife died in childbirth, leaving him a widower at the age of 25. Shirley never knew her mother, and single parenthood weighed heavily on him. He was always looking for a new Mrs. Adar.

"My parents and siblings died of Influenza when I was a young girl," Rose confided. "I grew up here on the farm, and when I was old enough, I volunteered to stay on as a nurse's aide."

That afternoon, Darby sat on his cot watching Rose play cards with the old woman and listened to them talk about how much they both wanted a pet cat. Pets weren't allowed in the almshouse because of the risk of disease and the cost of upkeep, however, there were some strays that managed to sneak in and hunt mice in the basement.

Darby was too engrossed in imagining some clever thing to say to Rose to notice that Shirley had unexpectedly entered the room. His daughter poked around unseen until she jumped up next to him, startling him, and in turn, everyone else. "You scared me half to death!" he scolded her after regaining his composure. "What?"

"Why do we have to sleep in the *cold* room?" she whined. Their single wood-framed window did its best to keep out the wind, but the winter chill still seeped in at night.

"Honey," Darby replied in his best parental voice. He glanced at Rose to see if she was listening. "Everyone's rooms are cold. We're lucky to sleep here instead of outside."

ASHMORE ESTATES - 2002 | PHOTO BY THE AUTHOR

"Elva says it's always warm where she is," Shirley countered innocently.

"Well, you tell Elva she's a lucky girl," Darby said.

Shirley skipped from the room and the adults turned their attention to each other.

"What was her friend's name?" Rose asked as she dealt a new hand of cards. Her voice was largely disinterested, but Darby felt obligated to answer anyway.

"Elva," he replied. "Elva..." He hesitated because he had forgotten her last name. "Skinnly?" He played around with a few more variations of the name before he realized that Rose was no longer paying attention. An awkward pause followed, and Darby stared nervously out the window. Suddenly, he remembered. "Skinner!" he announced triumphantly.

"Hm," Rose replied without turning her attention away from the card game. "Elva Skinner? I don't think I've ever met her."

"Well, I bet there's a lot of people like Shirley and me here," Darby said. "People who are down on their luck and just came for the winter. I'm sure new people come in and out all the time."

Rose didn't respond. Instead, she cleaned up her playing cards and the small wooden tray and medicine cup, and hurried away to continue her rounds.

"Talk to you later!" Darby yelled after her. He sighed deeply and stared at the dirty floor. Soft laughter interrupted his thoughts. At first, he couldn't figure out where it was coming from, but then he noticed the old lady's shoulders heaving up and down. "Oh, you think that's funny?" he spat.

"Little Elva says it's warm," the old lady cackled with a ghoulish smile.

Darby lifted his head. "What did you say?"

"Little Elva dancing in flames."

A confused expression crossed Darby's face. "You're crazy," he said. He shook his head and laid across his beat up, canvas cot.

It was dark when Darby awoke. He couldn't remember falling asleep, but several hours must have passed. As his senses cleared, an acrid smell filled his nostrils. He sat up, rubbed his eyes, and looked around the room. The old lady was sound asleep in her bed, but Shirley was nowhere to be seen. Darby's heart beat rapidly. His daughter knew she was supposed to be back in their room by dinnertime. It was then he noticed an orange glow emanating from the crack under their door. He flew off his cot and tore open the door. Thick, gray and black smoke crept along the ceiling from the end of the hallway, where, to his unbelieving eyes, someone stood consumed in flames.

"Fire! Fire!" he yelled and raced toward the burning figure.

Doors opened and curious inmates poked their heads out as Darby approached the source of the smoke. To his horror, as he got nearer it became clear that it was his own daughter trapped in the flames. "*Shirley!*" he screamed. He ran headlong into a large, heavy shape that stepped in front of him. His vision blurred as he hit the ground, and when it cleared, he saw several people standing over him. "Help me!" he cried as he gasped for breath. "My daughter's on fire!"

"There's nothing on fire," the superintendent, dressed in a bathrobe, tried to reassure him. "You just had a nightmare." The superintendent's comb-over stuck out in all directions, and his eyeglasses slipped down the bridge of his nose.

Darby looked up to see Shirley standing by his side, completely unharmed. The orange glow of the fire had disappeared, and there was no smoke anywhere. He shook his head and tried to get his bearings. *The nightmare seemed so real*, he thought. *It must've been because of what that crazy old lady said.* Several nurses helped him to his feet.

"We're going to put someone outside your room tonight," the superintendent told him. "Just to make sure everything's all right. When you're ready, come to my office tomorrow and we can talk."

Darby rubbed his forehead and took his daughter by the hand. "Come on, Shirley," he said quietly. The two shuffled back to their room while the residents looked on and whispered.

He must have slept all morning and missed his assigned chores, but no one bothered to wake him. Darby paced the floor, casting dirty looks at his elderly roommate, asleep on her thinning, striped mattress. Shirley sat on the edge of their cot, tying her shoes.

"I don't want you playing with that Elva girl anymore," Darby suddenly announced.

His daughter's eyes widened. "Why?" she asked.

"Because I'm your father and I said so," he replied.

"Why?" Shirley asked again. She bounded to her feet and dug her fists into her hips.

"Don't argue with me, girl!" Darby shouted.

Shirley continued to protest, but a knock on the door interrupted her.

From the time of day, Darby knew it was Rose making her rounds, but when he opened the door, instead of her smiling face, a small, blackened *thing* stood in the hallway. The smell of burnt flesh invaded his nostrils. He screamed and stumbled backward.

"Good afternoon, Miss Williams," Rose sang as she walked into the room. She hesitated when she saw the look on Darby's face. "Are you okay?"

"Yea... yeah," he stuttered. The thing was gone. His hands shivered despite his best efforts.

"Maybe you should go outside and get some fresh air," Rose suggested as she brushed past him to wake the old lady. "It's not good to stay cooped up inside all day, especially at this time of year." She wrinkled her nose at the faint aroma of charcoal or burning embers, like Darby had spent the morning working in the boiler room.

"I... I need to see the superintendent," Darby replied. He stumbled over to his cot, tore off the heavy wool blanket, and threw it around his shoulders. Without saying another word, he stepped out of the room and staggered down the hallway.

Near the top of the stairwell, he found the superintendent's door open but knocked anyway.

The superintendent's bespectacled face appeared in the crack. "Ah, Mr. Adare, please come in." He opened the door wide, ushering Darby inside. "How is your little girl?"

"Sh... she's fine," Darby replied. The superintendent's office was sparsely furnished in winter, since his family and he spent most of their time in the nearby farmhouse.

"Still having nightmares?" he asked.

"No... yes... I don't know. It wasn't a nightmare... What I saw was real!"

The superintendent sighed as he offered a cup of coffee. "Darby, this almshouse gets awfully crowded, and inmates get stir crazy in the winter. You know, cabin fever. Being cooped up here for weeks at a time..."

"Our roommate, the old lady, said something about my daughter's friend 'dancing in flames'," Darby interrupted. His eyes grew wide. "Skinner!" he nearly shouted. "Elva Skinner is her name."

"I can't recall any family by the name of Skinner," the superintendent said, sipping his coffee and mulling it over in his mind. "And we haven't had an accidental fire since I've been in charge." He opened a logbook on his desk and quickly scanned the pages. "Your roommate, Miss Williams, came over from the old almshouse," he said offhandedly.

"Could she have known Elva... from back then?"

The superintendent chuckled. "No. That's not possible. It was torn down in 1916!"

Back in their room, Shirley hovered close to Rose. "My daddy's having a tough time," she announced. "He can't find work."

"Tell me about your friend," Rose inquired as she administered Miss Williams' medication. "What was her name? Elva? I haven't met her yet."

"She's nice," Shirley replied. "But she only plays with me. The other kids make fun of her."

"Oh?" Rose said. "I've never heard the other children mention her."

"You can ask her if you want," Shirley said quietly. "She's right here."

A shiver traveled up the nurse's spine. "No one else is here," she said, taking a second look around the room just to make sure.

"Yes she is," Shirley insisted. "She's standing right next to you."

Rose jumped and the medicine cup tumbled to the floor. "Stop it!" she shouted. "There's no one here!"

Miss Williams grinned. "Some places have a way of holding you fast," she whispered knowingly. "Some folks love a place so much, they never leave."

* * *

"Psh," AJ laughed, interrupting the old man. "I don't believe *that*."

Tami gave him a light shove. "*Jerk*," she whispered. "Just let him tell the story."

"I'm afraid there isn't much more to it," Harold said quietly. "But those old walls hide many secrets."

"*Come on*," AJ said. "It's just an old abandoned building. Me and my buddies drove up there a couple weeks ago." He turned to Max. "Remember? When you went home for the weekend? None of the stories you hear about that place are true."

"You never know what a story can teach you," Harold said. "Even a tall tale can contain a little truth." He paused and struggled to lift himself from his chair and grab the tobacco pipe lying on the fireplace mantle. His wife helped.

"You youngins rather hear about something closer to your own time, eh?" Edith asked. "Come sit on the Davenport and enjoy the warm fire." She pointed to a rickety-looking sofa covered with a cushion so thin and worn it made the floor look inviting.

"I think we should be going..." Nancy suggested, looking at her friends for support.

"Harold is a little hard of hearing, dear," Edith explained. "You'll have to speak up."

"Looks like the rain's stopping," Max seconded. "We better get going. So much for camping, though."

Tami grabbed his arm and pulled him to the sofa. "Wait," she said. "I want to hear another story." She turned to Harold and his wife. "What were you going to tell us about?"

The sofa creaked in protest as Max sighed and leaned back.

"Something tells me you'll be interested in *this story*," Edith said with a grin. "It's about a gang of college students going camping, *just like y'all*. You see, during the late 1960s and '70s, there was several unsolved murders. It had everyone scared."

"Then came the most gruesome discovery in this county's history," Harold chimed in. He paused for effect, puffed on his pipe, then added, "This was before you was even born."

"Those were supposed to be the innocent times too," Edith added, "before everyone had to lock their doors and keep their kids in at night." She began her story as the grandfather clock chimed exactly nine o'clock.

INNOCENCE

As Halloween 1980 neared, orange and black decorations appeared in store windows, and pumpkins and fake spider webs adorned porches. For students at Eastern Illinois University, it meant a Vincent Price film festival, the annual Charleston Jaycees haunted house, and of course, renewed interest in the ghost that haunts Pemberton Hall. For one EIU student and Mattoon resident, the upcoming holiday meant nothing out of the ordinary, or so she thought. As Natalie sat on her bed reflecting on the past week, only one thing came to mind: her 29-year-old adjunct philosophy professor, Edward Gillian.

They first met her freshman year during an intro to philosophy class. Professor Gillian had haunting green eyes, an optimistic personality, and an inquisitive mind that challenged her to think about life's deeper questions. Every time they passed in the hallways of Coleman Hall, the building that housed the History, English, Philosophy, and Political Science departments, she blushed and looked at the floor, but he would always say "hi" anyway. She took every class he taught, and he never failed to mention that she was his brightest student. He was the first man who ever really paid attention to her.

Her mother's voice echoed up the stairs, interrupting her thoughts. "Natalie?"

"Yes?" she yelled back.

"I'll be leaving soon."

"*It's about time,*" Natalie muttered under her breath. She slammed her textbook closed and stuffed it in her book bag. Natalie was a sophomore at Eastern Illinois University, but she had lived in Mattoon (pop. 19,293) for as long as she could remember. She decided to go to college to get away from her mom and dad, who were, to use a phrase not coined until ten years later, helicopter parents. *They're so afraid of me getting hurt because I'm their only child*, she thought. She didn't want to be one of those kids who graduated high school and remained in their hometown, getting married and working a minimum-wage job.

Natalie's mother and she were polar opposites. Her mother, Katherine, enjoyed being the center of attention. She hosted parties at their two-story ranch house and sold cosmetics on the side. Her hair was always permed and she wore fashionable tan and brown pantsuits. Natalie preferred the sanctity of her bedroom. She never thought she was attractive and had long ago given up on her appearance. Her auburn hair was long and straight, and her body, as her mother once put it, was as curvy as an ironing board.

The scenery rushed past as Katherine and she drove down Route 16 in a green 1975 AMC Gremlin on their daily trek to Charleston and EIU. Natalie, crammed in the backseat (the safest place if they got into an accident), opened her journal and began writing. It had been months since her mother and she had exchanged more than a few words in the car.

"Is the freedom to choose what makes human beings different from animals?" Natalie scribbled her professor's words even as the rattling car made her handwriting practically illegible. A smile grew across her face.

Katherine's voice quickly removed it. "Remember to call us as soon as you're done with classes," she reminded her daughter for the thousandth time. "Don't talk to any strange kids," she warned. "Drugs and cults are everywhere these days, and I don't even want to think about what all these guys have on their mind." As usual, her mother pulled into the Burger King parking lot on 2nd Street, just two blocks from campus. She ran in to buy coffee, while Natalie headed to class.

"Whatever," Natalie said through her teeth as she slammed the passenger seat forward and squeezed through the door. She didn't look back as she marched past the Physical Science Building and McAfee Gym, across the library quad, past students tossing a Frisbee or sitting under oak trees doing homework. She walked with her head down, holding her books tightly against her faded sweatshirt. It was late October, but still nice enough to be outside without shivering, although gathering clouds indicated it might rain.

"Did you get tickets for the show next Tuesday?" she heard someone ask as she passed a group standing outside the door to Coleman Hall. The band Molly Hatchet was coming to EIU next week, but Natalie had no intention of going.

She arrived outside her classroom a few minutes early, so she stood against the wall and skimmed through her notes. She looked up to see her professor walking back and forth in front of the chalkboard.

Three coeds stood nearby, giggling and chattering loudly because one was trying out for the Coles County Beauty Pageant. Natalie shook her head. "Don't you care about anything else?" she turned and asked them bitterly. "Like the presidential election or the Iraqi invasion of Iran?"

The girls laughed even louder. "Why don't *you* try out for the pageant?" one asked. "Oh, *that's right*," she replied, mockingly brushing aside her hair, which was carefully feathered like Farrah Fawcett's. "Not *everyone* can look like me."

"Oh, that was *so* mean," her friend said, barely hiding a smile. Natalie wasn't paying attention anymore. She was accustomed to the constant insults, and she buried her head in her notebook. Finally, students started to filter out of the classroom.

"Good afternoon, Natalie," a familiar voice said.

Natalie peeked over her notebook. "Hey," she replied. She brushed stray hairs away from her face and tried to smile, but by that time Professor Gillian had gone. Natalie slowly got to her feet and headed into the empty classroom, where she took a seat by the door. The room was small, with only about thirty desks and a large chalkboard behind the podium, which was placed on a desk to bring it up to chest height. After a while, her fellow students strolled into the room. Lana, a 25-year-old woman who came to EIU to finish her education, usually sat next to Natalie and borrowed her notes.

"You always take such good notes," she would say. "You write down everything the professor says."

The clock struck the hour marker and Professor Gillian came into the room holding his coffee mug in one hand and papers and folders tucked under the other arm. He smiled and nodded in his usual manner. "I want to remind you about the camping trip this weekend," he began. "Remember, bring your own tent and alcohol is strictly prohibited." He gave the class a smirk. "But of course, if anyone *was to bring some* they might end up with extra credit." The legal drinking age for beer and wine had only recently been raised to 21, a change widely opposed on campus.

"What if it's *Stag*?" someone shouted from the back of the room, referring to a brand of beer with a reputation for being an old fisherman's drink. The room erupted in laughter. Natalie rolled her eyes.

"I guess that might bring your grade down," their professor replied, using that rebuttal to launch into his lesson for the day.

"Speaking of consequences," he began, furiously guiding chalk across the chalkboard. "Why do we consider the consequences of our actions to go beyond simple cause and effect?"

Natalie began writing intensely too, and before she knew it, the period was over. Professor Gillian brushed past her on the way out the door, and she blushed as their shoulders touched. "I hope you can make it this weekend," he said, baring his white teeth with a broad smile.

Barely squeaking a response, she quickly caught up with Lana and grabbed her arm. "Are you going on that trip this weekend?" she whispered.

Lana looked surprised. "*Are you?*"

"That depends on if I can get a ride."

"You don't have a car?"

"No," Natalie replied, "and I don't think my parents would let me go on this trip, but I really want to."

"Well, heck," Lana smirked beneath her oversized glasses. "I'll take you. A little independence never hurt anyone."

Natalie smiled, thanked her, and they exchanged phone numbers. She then hurried from the room to wait for her next class.

The week went by slowly until, at last, it was Saturday. Students planning to attend the trip were given directions and were supposed to meet at the campsite near Lake Mattoon, 22 miles southwest of EIU. Natalie had no trouble telling Lana where to go. She had fond memories of visiting the lake as a girl, but hadn't been there since junior high.

The drive was short, but Lana bombarded Natalie with questions. "How long have you lived in Mattoon?" she asked.

"Nineteen years."

"Do you play sports?"

"No."

"I like tennis."

"Ok."

"Do you listen to music?"

"Sometimes."

Lana snorted. "This is the longest car ride ever."

"Sorry, I was thinking about something," Natalie mumbled. "Turn left up here."

The sun was beginning its descent as Lana's brown 1971 Ford Pinto Runabout pulled into the gravel parking lot. In the distance, they could see the campfire's orange flames blacken low-hanging branches. Ten students sat on logs around the fire, and Professor Gillian stood to greet the newcomers. Natalie tried to hide her nervousness as he confidently strode toward them. She almost didn't recognize him without his tweed sportcoat.

"Natalie. Lana. I'm so glad you made it."

Natalie was glad it was getting dark. She was wearing a plaid shirt, black jeans, a sweater vest, and a denim jacket. She unconsciously opened another button on her shirt.

"We brought chips," Lana said as she stepped forward and thrust the bag in front of her.

"Thank you," Professor Gillian said with a grin. "Every little bit helps." He set the bag down next to two plastic coolers and an array of snack food.

Lana pointed to a clearing next to a large blue and gray tent. "Do you mind if we set up there?"

"Not at all," he said. "You'll be right next to my tent."

"Perfect," Lana replied, elbowing Natalie.

"Stop," Natalie whispered as their professor took his seat by the fire.

"What?" her friend said. "I see the way you look at him." Sensing Natalie's embarrassment, she changed the subject as they prepared their tent poles. "What did you tell your folks? You know, about where you were going?"

Natalie lied. "I told them I was spending the night at a friend's house." In reality, she told her mother she was studying with classmates at the library. She felt a tinge of guilt, but it was too late. There were no pay phones at the lake—she would have to deal with the consequences later.

They took a seat on a log next to two boys Natalie recognized from several classes, but to whom she had never spoken. The fire crackled and sparked, throwing strange shadows across their hairy mustachioed faces.

"Are you going to see *Misty Beethoven* next Friday?" one of the boys asked his friend in a not-so-quiet whisper, referring to the 1976 adult film *The Opening of Misty Beethoven*, which was being shown in EIU's Grand Ballroom later that week.

Lana snorted. "I *can't believe* the University Board would sponsor that trash."

"Hey," one of the boys yelled back. "If you don't like it, don't watch it."

"No one cares if you watch it at home on Betamax, but at a university? What, you didn't take sex ed in high school?" The gathering erupted in laughter.

Professor Gillian cleared his throat to get their attention. "Remember how we've been discussing free will and personal freedom?" he asked. "Some might argue the UB is just providing college-age entertainment to college students. It's not sanctioning the material, just like how the University of Wisconsin's selling alcohol in their student building isn't an approval of alcoholism."

"But our tuition pays for it," Natalie interrupted. Everyone's attention fell on her and she immediately regretted speaking up.

"Go on," her professor encouraged. "What do you mean by that?"

Natalie hesitated before continuing. Her eyes nervously scanned the faces of her fellow students for signs of approval. "I mean our tuition and fees pay for university sponsored events and activities, and the space to hold them. So we're endorsing it, in a way, no matter what."

"So if you don't like a musician the UB brings to campus, no one else can see them?" the boy next to her asked.

"Sorry," she said, looking at her shoes. "It was a stupid comment."

"No, it wasn't," Professor Gillian interrupted. "The reason for this trip every semester is so that we can talk about things like this outside a classroom, where you won't feel like your answers are right or wrong. This isn't going to be on some test, but it's important to think about. You're students today, but some day you're going to be running schools and colleges like EIU."

Natalie smiled and felt a little better. Lana offered her a hotdog and a can of Falstaff, but she hesitated before accepting. Her parents never kept alcohol in their house and would never approve of her drinking beer. Then again, she was already breaking the rules. A tiny smirk crossed her lips, and she popped open the can. She was free.

"Thata girl," Lana said, knocking her can against Natalie's. "Who knows what you'll do next."

The evening passed with a blur of laughter, wild stories, music from a portable radio, and crackling embers. Natalie couldn't remember what she said or with whom she spoke. A wave of euphoria picked her up and carried her along in its warm embrace. Eventually, however, the night dragged on and exhaustion took over her body. Natalie groped and stumbled her way through the darkness back to her tent and collapsed on the sleeping bag with a smile on her face.

Thirty-three miles northeast of Lake Mattoon, under a brightening sky, two hunters, Ed and Kurt, drove their pickup truck along a well-worn gravel road toward the Embarras River. They slid to a halt on a muddy pull-off near a bridge and notorious party spot for both locals and students from the university. They slammed their dented truck doors and strolled down a path leading to the riverside under the old steel bridge. The orange, red, and yellow leaves of the trees kept them in perpetual shade. "It looks like it's gonna be a nice Sunday afternoon," Kurt said, stopping to take a breath of what should have been fresh Autumn air. Instead, his nostrils caught the scent of something very unpleasant.

"Hey, Kurt," Ed yelled from a few yards downstream. "Come look at this, I think poachers have been here." He cursed and then gagged as he inhaled the putrid smell. "Lord almighty," he yelled. "I don't think that's an animal!"

"What is that?" Kurt choked out as he gazed down at the white torso slopped on the muddy riverbank, about fifty yards from the bridge. Flies buzzed mercilessly around the lump of flesh. "Where's the head?"

"There's no hands or feet neither," Ed added. "Let's get out of here and call the sheriff."

The hunters scrambled back up the bank and grabbed the CB radio in their truck. The sound of farmers harvesting their corn filtered down the road, yet, except for the two men, it was eerily quiet.

Ed furiously wiped off his brown ski jacket with red, yellow, and white stripes on the chest with a handkerchief. "I can't get that smell off."

Kurt hushed his friend and found the CB frequency for the county sheriff, while Ed paced nervously in front of the ancient bridge. "That's right, sheriff," he said. "I don't think it was an accident." A pause. "No, of course you heard right, there's no head, hands, or feet." Another pause. "No, we didn't touch it." The sheriff's voice crackled over the radio and Kurt hung the mouthpiece back on their truck's dashboard.

"Is he coming?" Ed shouted.

"Yeah," Kurt replied. "Like a bat out of Hell I'm sure."

The hunters paced silently along the roadside, suppressing the urge to vomit and trying not to glance at the body. At least twenty minutes passed before wailing sirens pierced the silence, accompanied by the roaring engines of a convoy of emergency vehicles tearing down the gravel road.

At Lake Mattoon, Natalie and her classmates were just waking up as morning light penetrated the canvas walls of their tents. Natalie groaned and rolled over. Her head hurt and kaleidoscopic memories from the night before danced in her mind. The smell of sweat and cheap alcohol invaded her nostrils. "Lana?" she mumbled. "Lana, did everyone leave?"

"Hmm?" a deep voice that sounded nothing like Lana's replied incoherently.

Natalie sat up with a start and examined the person next to her with a growing sense of mortification. His wavy brown hair and muscular shoulders immediately gave him away. It was Professor Gillian. She shoved him violently. "*Oh my God.* Get up!" she hissed. She was suddenly relieved to be wearing the same clothes as the night before.

"Call me Ed," Gillian mumbled as he rolled over. He rubbed his eyes, then blinked several times. "*Natalie?*" he gasped, grabbing his sleeping bag and pulling it up to his neck. "*What are you doing in my tent?*"

"*You tell me!*" she replied. "I can't remember anything from last night."

"I don't either." Gillian wiped his face with his hands. "I must've had more to drink than I thought." He groaned at his colossal lapse in judgment. "Listen, we can't assume anything, you know, *happened*. But everyone is going to assume it did."

"Well, I hope they're wrong!" Natalie protested. Then, she thought wishfully, "Maybe we got up before everyone else." A commotion outside the tent interrupted her.

"Looks like we're too late," Gillian replied as someone forcefully unzipped his tent and thrust their head inside.

"Hey, professor," the young man yelled. "We're going to finish these beers for breakfast, do you want one?" His mouth fell open. "Oh," he stuttered. "S... Sorry to bother you."

Natalie and her professor looked at each other and cringed.

"Okay, there has to be a rational explanation for this," Gillian said as he jingled the keys behind the wheel of his beige 1976 Dodge Dart. "Damn! This is exactly what I was afraid might happen. The department chair told me these trips were a bad idea, but did I listen? I could lose my job over this." His left hand squeezed the steering wheel until his knuckles turned white.

Natalie sat in the front passenger seat, looking out the windshield, at the dashboard, the roof—anything other than her professor's panic-stricken face. "Wait a minute," she said. "Does EIU have a policy against teacher-student relations?"

Gillian stopped jingling his keys and relaxed his grip on the steering wheel. "No," he replied. "But still, I'm supposed to be responsible for you guys on those camping trips. Especially with alcohol involved."

"Hey," Natalie interrupted. "We're all adults. Like you said last night... We're just a group of adults going camping. There's nothing wrong with that. I chose to come here and I chose to get drunk. At least, I *think* I was drunk... I've never actually been..."

Gillian shot her a skeptical look. The whole class had seen them emerge together from the tent, and some even tried—*poorly*—to conceal their laughter.

Earlier that morning, after swallowing her pride and pretending like she couldn't hear her classmates whispering, Natalie told Lana what happened and asked her to leave. Gillian and she needed time to figure out what they were going to say when the rumors started spreading on Monday, but that wasn't the only thing on her mind. Worse, Natalie felt awful about lying to her parents. What seemed like a righteous act of independence, now, in retrospect, seemed more like juvenile rebellion.

"Maybe no one will even care on Monday?" Natalie hopefully suggested.

At their two-story bungalow on Lafayette Avenue, Natalie's parents were glued to the television. A special report broke on WCIA Channel 3 News at Noon about a body found along the Embarras River south of Rardin. Anchor Jerry Slabe's steady voice related events surrounding the gruesome discovery earlier that morning. Natalie's father sat in his recliner, while Natalie's mother, Katherine, rushed to the yellow phone on the kitchen wall and dialed the Coles County Sheriff's Department. Katherine frantically blurted out her worst fears about her daughter's disappearance.

"I'm sorry," the voice on the phone apologized. "Can you describe your daughter one more time?"

"Yes," she yelled into the phone. "She's nineteen years old. She has reddish-brown hair. She's about one hundred and twenty pounds."

There was mumbling on the other end before the deputy came back. His voice was stern but uneasy. "Ma'am," he said cautiously. "There's no reason to jump to conclusions. When did you last see your daughter?"

"*Oh my God,*" Natalie's mother gasped. "My Natalie left home yesterday afternoon with a friend..." She jerked back, dropped the phone, and covered her mouth with trembling hands.

"Ma'am I need you to stay calm," the deputy's distant, electronic-sounding voice said from the floor. "Ma'am are you there?"

Katherine brushed hair away from her eyes and bent down to pick up the receiver. "Are you sure it's not her?" she squeaked.

"That's the problem, ma'am," the deputy said after a short pause. "The victim can't be identified. You're our only lead... The only missing person's report."

"I don't understand," Katherine yelled, regaining her composure. She sat down at the kitchen table and propped her head up with a fist. "What do you mean, *can't be identified?*"

The deputy hesitated, cleared his throat, and stumbled over his words. "The victim's head... was removed. No identifying marks anywhere... except... they say she didn't shave and had auburn colored hair."

"What did he say?" Natalie's father, who had been listening intently to the news program, interjected.

"*Oh my God,*" Katherine gasped. "I don't believe this. I warned her what might happen. Everyday I... I told her not to trust strangers."

"I understand your concern, ma'am. This is the worst case we've ever investigated, and we want to rule out any local missing persons. We've sent the body to Springfield for testing. Those tests should tell us more about what happened. In the meantime, I suggest calling your daughter's friends or relatives. There's a good chance she's perfectly fine and just staying with someone."

"My daughter isn't *fine*," Katherine hissed and violently hung up the receiver.

Natalie's father massaged his wife's shoulders. "She'll come home," he said. "She'll come home."

Back at the campsite, Natalie and her professor finally decided on a plan: telling the embarrassing truth, that Natalie drank too much and stumbled into the wrong tent.

"At least, I hope that's all that really happened," Gillian said with a nervous grin. "You're a nice girl and all, and one of my favorite students, but it wouldn't be appropriate."

"I need to get back home," Natalie whispered. "My parents are probably worried sick."

Gillian scratched his chin, started the ignition, and shifted the gear into reverse. "Come on," he said. "We'll pick up McDonald's on the way. My treat. It's the least I can do after all of this."

As Professor Gillian's car pulled up outside of her house, Natalie blushed and thanked him for the ride. "I'm sure everything will work out," she tried to reassure him. "No one will even remember what happened in a week."

"I hope so," Gillian replied with a roguish grin. He waited until she got to the front door before driving away.

It was Natalie's father who greeted her. "Where have you been?" he shouted, more with joy than anger. His eyes, though exhausted, were wild with excitement. "We've been worried sick about you!"

Natalie felt horrible. "I'm sorry," she apologized. "My class went on a camping trip. I didn't tell you because I wanted to show you that I'd be alright on my own."

Her mother pushed past. "You have no idea what you put us through," she yelled. "I thought you were dead!"

"*Dead*?" Natalie repeated. "How could you think I was dead? That's..."

The grave look on her mother's face quieted her. Natalie and her parents threw their arms around one another and breathed a heavy sigh of relief.

* * *

"Wait, wait, wait," AJ said in disbelief. "There was a Burger King in Charleston?"

"Oh yes," Harold replied. "I reckon it's gone?"

"Harold and I don't get out much, dear," his wife said supportively.

AJ scoffed. "Dude, it hasn't been there for like decades at least."

Max jumped up. "Well, we really have to be going," he announced in a tone with which he hoped no one would argue. "It sounds like the rain stopped."

"Before ya'll leave, won't you repay our hospitality by sharing a story of your own?" Harold asked. "As ya'll can see, we ain't got much. Not much in the way of communicatin'. Everything we know about the outside world, we learn from folks like you."

Tami pulled Max back to the sofa. "My sister went to Eastern a few years ago," she said. "She told me something happened to her roommate's friend. He was there when Blair Hall burned."

"Oh yeah," Nancy seconded. "I remember hearing about that." She waved her arms enthusiastically, no longer bothered by the mothball scent of her borrowed dress. "That's perfect."

AJ sighed. "Got anything to drink, old man? If we're gonna be here a while, I'll need it."

"I know just what you're looking fer," Harold said with a wink. "It'll get ya corned." He motioned to his wife and she retrieved a glass Mason jar filled with corn whiskey from the kitchen. She handed it to AJ, who smelled it, shrugged, and took a drink.

"Ugh!" he yelled, his face contorting in surprise. "This tastes like paint thinner."

Harold chuckled. "Made it myself."

As everyone settled into their seats, Tami began her story.

APRIL EMBERS

Matt had a commanding view of the intersection of 4th Street and Lincoln Avenue from his window seat in the second-story dining room of Jerry's Pizza & Pub. Hardee's empty shell with boarded-up windows squatted on the northwest corner, Positively 4th Street Records stood on the northeast, and directly across 4th Street, Pemberton Hall's gray facade and orange roof like a medieval English manor filled the window. Matt waited for his friends, Chet and Tiffany, as he stared out the window at the cars dancing in the intersection; stopping, turning right, turning left, avoiding pedestrians carrying bookbags heading to and from Eastern Illinois University.

He flipped open his cell phone and took another look at the recruiter's business card. He began to dial the number, then stopped.

"'Sup, nerd?" Tiffany asked as she slid into the booth across from Matt. Chet followed. Both Tiffany and Matt were nearing the end of their sophomore year at EIU. Chet was a senior and a tight end on the football team. His sophomore year, he played on the field and was a member of Sigma Pi with Tony Romo, a fact he never let anyone forget. Despite it being a warm spring day, he wore a blue and gray letterman jacket.

Every Wednesday afternoon, the trio met at Jerry's for the lunch buffet and to plan their weekend, which sometimes started on Thursday night. That week, however, was the week before final exams, a stressful time under any circumstances.

"You're not thinkin' of callin' that recruiter?" Tiffany asked as she saw Matt hurriedly stuff the business card into the pocket of his khaki cargo shorts.

"No, not this again," Chet interrupted as a waitress wearing a white Jerry's t-shirt approached their table. "I want to eat in peace." He turned to the waitress. "Three buffets, as usual."

"And a diet Coke," added Tiffany.

Matt threw up his hands as the waitress walked away. "What do you want me to do?"

"Finish school," Tiffany said. She was short, with straightened black hair, brown eyes, and a light brown complexion. She wore a blue tanktop and jean shorts.

"I know what *I'm* gonna do," Chet said as he got up from the table, "wreck this buffet." Unlike Matt and Tiffany, who grew up in the Chicago suburbs, Chet was from the Illinois side of St. Louis and was such a red-blooded country boy he thought the Dixie Chicks were unpatriotic.

Matt and Tiffany followed him to the buffet line.

"This ain't easy," Matt said as he filled his plate with slices of pepperoni, sausage, and the works. "I want my life to mean somethin'. I want to contribute." As a college town, Charleston had at least a dozen pizza places. It was simple, cheap greasy food that tasted great after a few beers, but Matt couldn't find a decent deep dish south of Interstate 80.

"So stay and graduate," said Tiffany, filling her plate with a mound of iceberg lettuce. "You don't have to die in the desert for some rich old men and those crooks in the White House." Her comment turned a few heads and elicited a noise of disgust from the lady behind her in line.

"Whatever, babe," Chet said dismissively as the trio headed back to their corner booth by the window. He turned to Matt. "Don't listen to her. Pat Tillman gave up a $3.6 million contract with the Cardinals to enlist after 9/11. He was a real American. A hero."

"Yeah, look what happened to him. Killed in Afghanistan last week."

Matt felt his insides turn and he suddenly lost his appetite. Tiffany and he hadn't always argued this much. They both grew up in the south suburb of Blue Island and attended Eisenhower High School. They were seventeen years old when terrorists destroyed the Twin Towers on September 11, 2001, too young to enlist in the military without their parents' permission. Instead, the two friends applied to Eastern Illinois University and turned their attention to college. As the invasion of Iraq loomed, however, Tiffany began attending antiwar meetings and protests, and became more vocal about politics. She called him crying when Howard Dean dropped out of the Democratic presidential primary.

Matt, whose older brother was serving on the aircraft carrier USS *George Washington* in the Persian Gulf, wished he could feel as certain. America overthrew the Iraqi dictator, Saddam Hussein, almost exactly one year ago, but the war was still going on. If anything, it seemed to be getting worse.

"I see our guys fightin' in Fallujah on the news, and here I am, stuffin' my face with pizza," he said. "What's wrong with this picture?"

"What's wrong with it?" asked Tiffany, indignantly. "Everythin'! We shouldn't even be there."

Chet pointed a slice of sausage pizza at Matt, the cheese dripping off. "We're fighting 'em over there so we don't have to fight 'em here."

Tiffany crossed her arms and loudly exhaled. "Who's 'we'? You sittin' here with the rest of us."

"Hey, I got a good thing going," Chet protested. He pushed his plate away, crumpled a paper napkin, and dropped a ten-dollar bill on the table. "I'd rather be dodging bullets in Iraq than listen to you two bicker like a pair o' old hens." He got up to leave.

"We hangin' out tonight?" Tiffany asked, pouting.

"Yeah, yeah." Chet bent down, kissed her, and made his exit.

Matt watched through the window as Chet walked to the parking lot and got into his bright yellow 2001 Jeep Wrangler. "How're you together?" he asked.

"Jealous? He takes care of himself and he got a cool car."

Matt eyed her skeptically.

"He's graduatin' in a few weeks. It ain't like we walkin' down the aisle."

The waitress came by with their check and Matt and Tiffany paid in cash. "I gotta get to class," Matt said as he shoved his hand in his pocket and felt the raised lettering on the Army recruiter's business card. He grabbed his bookbag and slung it over his shoulder.

"Don't be stupid," Tiffany said flippantly as they walked out the door. A strong breeze caught the glass door and slammed it shut.

"I gotta get to class." Matt didn't wait for the crossing signal to change before jogging across 4th Street to campus. He was, in fact, more eager to terminate their argument than attend class. For weeks the only thing he could think about was the war, and his nagging sense that he could make a difference 'over there'. He couldn't escape from it. Footage from the battle for Fallujah and the growing Shia insurgency was even on TV at the Rec Center where he worked out. Then again, he thought, he was almost halfway through his bachelor's degree. Wouldn't graduating college make a difference too?

Before he knew it, he was walking past blooming flowers behind Old Main's crenellated stone walls toward Blair Hall. It was unusually warm for late April, and he was working up a sweat. Soon, however, he'd find relief in an air-conditioned building. Like clockwork, ten minutes before every hour a flood of students filled campus sidewalks going to and from class or took smoke breaks outside classroom building doors. As the temperature raised, layers of clothing disappeared. Sunglasses, boardshorts, tank tops, miniskirts, and halter tops made their appearance. Several students wore Homestar Runner t-shirts.

Blair Hall was a semi-rectangular Neo Georgian-style stone building similar to Pemberton Hall, with century-old wooden walls, doors, and aging tile floors, paint, and fixtures, which was why work crews were diligently making updates. Matt hardly noticed the contractors wearing overalls and tool belts in the human cascade as he climbed the stairs to the second floor for his 3:00 p.m. sociology class.

Matt took out a notebook and shoved his bookbag under a desk in the third row near the window as his professor, Diane Schaefer, paced in front of the chalkboard. His notebook began with notes from the first day of class. As the page number increased and the semester wore on, so did the percentage of sketches, doodles, and scribbles covering the page. It was always more difficult to concentrate near the end of the spring semester, but part of him—the part that wanted to escape the confines of a classroom and run toward danger on the other side of the globe— stopped caring about these lectures weeks ago.

Professor Schaefer was ten-to-twelve minutes into her lecture on contemporary social problems when Matt's mind began to wander. He gazed out the window at the north quad and noticed something odd. A brightly-dressed student was speaking excitedly with two older men, possibly professors, and pointing at the building. He looked at the sanguine faces of his classmates. No one else seemed to notice. Outside, the female student stopped a young man who was walking and talking on his cell phone. The two exchanged words and the man looked up in Matt's direction. Matt frowned and turned his attention back to Schaefer's lecture.

A few minutes later, Matt could no longer see the quad. A thick plume of black smoke swirled outside the windows. Without thinking, he stood up. "There's somethin' wrong," he said, pointing at the smoke-clouded windows. Murmuring and the screeching of metal chairs across the tile floor erupted.

"Ok, everyone, settle down," Professor Schaefer said. "I don't hear the fire alarm. Maybe the smoke is coming from somewhere else?"

As if on cue, the distant wail of a fire engine siren broke the silence. It got louder as it approached. "Stay calm," their professor said in a loud, clear voice. "Don't panic, but let's get out of the building until we figure out what's going on." Many students, including Matt, abandoned their belongings and rushed out the door.

In the hallway, other classrooms were emptying sporadically. A man walked from room to room, pounding on the old wooden and glass doors telling everyone to evacuate. It was only when Matt and his classmates made it to the stairwell that the fire alarms finally went off. Students and teachers flooded the hallways and pushed their way outside. Matt was one of the first. Their professor led them away from the center of campus in the direction of 7th Street and the visitors parking lot next to Park Place Apartments, where a fire crew was unloading Truck 304. From the street, they could see smoke swirling and orange flames licking from charred holes in Blair Hall's roof. As high winds stoked the inferno, a fireman stepped forward.

"I need volunteers to help get this hose off, now!" he shouted over the din of students chattering excitedly about their narrow escape. Other firefighters wearing yellow and orange protective gear ran into the building to make sure everyone evacuated.

Matt and four other young men hesitantly approached the fire engine. Each grabbed six to seven folds of yellow hose from the storage compartment and pulled it toward the closest fire hydrant. His heart raced and the noise and sirens faded into the background. The heavy fiber hose yielded to their efforts and unraveled as they went. By that time, another fire engine arrived on 7th Street alongside two Charleston police cruisers and an ambulance from Sarah Bush Lincoln Health Center. The police officers began cordoning off the east lawn in front of the building with yellow emergency tape. Across the street, students emerged onto their apartment balconies to watch the excitement.

"Thanks, guys, we'll take it from here," the fireman said, waving them away.

Matt felt his cell phone vibrate in his pocket and he flipped it open. It was Tiffany. "Where you at?" he asked, wiping sweat from his forehead.

"Where *you* at?" Tiffany echoed frantically. "Don't you have class in Blair?"

"Yeah, but I made it out," he said. "We all made it out."

"Thank God. I was in psych and the power went out. The whole campus is dark."

"All my stuff was in there," Matt said. "Books. Notes. Everythin'." He stepped over the hoses stretched across the wet pavement and watched a firefighter climb the narrow ladder extended from a nearby fire truck to begin spraying water onto Blair Hall's smoldering roof. He imagined his charred book bag and its contents doused with water. Everything he worked on that semester, gone.

"Stay there," said Matt. "I'm a-be right over." He put his phone away and walked west around EIU's water tower, through the parking lot behind the red-brick Student Services Building to the north quad. He could see a reflection of the firefighter on the ladder in the second-floor windows of Student Services. From his new vantage point on the north quad, the fire damage looked worse. Blair Hall's roof had partially collapsed, and visible flames swirled and sparked in the warm spring breeze. He weaved through the crowd of onlookers, many of whom were taking pictures of the fire with their cell phone cameras. Matt had never seen that many students outside before, not even for EIU's annual Quakin' in the Quad event.

ILLUSTRATION BY KATIE CONRAD

He finally located Tiffany in the crowd near the Physical Science Building. She stood staring, a look of disbelief on her face as flames slowly consumed the third floor of Blair Hall. Its stone edifice, with each corner an upward-pointing triangle, looked like an empty shell. Matt, however, was no longer thinking of the fire or the danger he escaped. He felt exhilarated.

"I'm a-do it," he said.

"What?" Tiffany asked over the noise.

"I'm a-do it," Matt repeated. "I'm gonna call the recruiter and sign up."

Tiffany was horrified. "*What?*"

"This a sign from God," he said, pointing at the fire. "I was sittin' here wonderin' if I should finish school, and that decision was made for me. I have nothin' left. It all burnt up."

"You... you can get an extension for finals. Your professors will understand..."

"Nah," said Matt, resolutely. He hugged his friend, who, still in shock, hardly moved or said a word. "It'll be fine. I'll catch ya later." As he walked off campus, he saw delivery cars for several local restaurants, including Boxa, bringing food for the first responders as they continued to battle the blaze. He pulled the Army recruiter's business card from his shorts pocket and began to dial.

* * *

"What a *wonderful* story!" Edith exclaimed, rising to her feet.

Nancy touched Tami's arm and gave her *that* look, like she had too much to drink and was dangerously close to spending the night on the bathroom floor.

Tami sighed. "Oh, *all right*. It *is* getting pretty late." She rose and approached the elderly couple. "Thank you so much for dinner and all the stories," she said as she squeezed Edith's arthritic hand.

Max thanked the couple as well, but then remembered the clothes his friends and he had borrowed for the evening. "Do you want these back?" he asked.

"Oh, no," Harold replied. "Consider 'em a gift."

"Gee, thanks," Nancy mumbled while feigning a smile. Leading the way, she grabbed her wet clothes and left the cabin. Several more goodbyes were exchanged, and gradually the four friends began the trek back to their car. It was pitch black outside, but the rain clouds had dissipated, and the sweet smell of the night had returned.

"They were such nice people," Tami said as she hurried to keep up with the others.

"Yeah, whatever," AJ replied from a few yards ahead. "I guess they weren't that bad. Let's just get the heck out of here."

Max looked back one more time, but the soft glow of the cabin lights had faded and it was barely visible through the thick, dark trees. As he took out his cell phone to see if he had service, his gym shoes skidded on the slick ground, and he tripped over something hard. His phone tumbled into the weeds. "Damn!" he cursed.

Activating her smartphone flashlight, Tami doubled back to help Max find his phone, but when the light hit the object Max tripped over, she froze. There, side by side, were two faded granite headstones, sunken into the ground and obscured by tall grass and weeds. Tami and Max exchanged glances, making sure they saw the same thing. The lettering was faded, but the names were unmistakable: Harold and Edith. Both died over a century ago. Max put his hand on Tami's shoulder and squeezed. He bent down and retrieved his phone, then without saying a word, the couple rejoined their friends at the car.

At their Dodge Omni, Nancy was holding a flashlight while AJ assessed the damage. The front grill was cracked and the hood bent, but the car appeared otherwise undamaged. "I hope it still works," Max whispered, and he turned the key in the ignition. To his surprise, the engine sputtered and turned over. The four students gave a collective sigh of relief. They sped back to Charleston, their red taillights disappearing into the night.

LEGENDS & LORE

GHOST LORE

ASHMORE ESTATES

O ver the past two decades, Ashmore Estates has gone from obscure local legend tripping destination to nationally-known haunted attraction featured in television shows, books, and documentaries. It survived two storms that permanently altered its outward appearance, but still attracts a steady stream of visitors hoping to encounter the fantastic and otherworldly. Its humble origin as the almshouse on the Coles County Poor Farm could not have foreshadowed this strange transformation.

The Coles County Poor Farm operated in Ashmore Township from 1870 to 1959. Then, for 28 years, between 1959 and 1987, Ashmore Estates served Coles County as a care facility for the mentally or emotional disturbed and developmentally disabled. After its closure, local teens and students from Eastern Illinois University explored its empty corridors and gawked at what was left behind. They came away with stories ranging from the hair-raising to the absurd. It seemed like the 90-year-old building would sit empty, crumbling from disuse. Finally, in 2006, a man named Scott Kelley purchased the building, cleaned it up, and turned it into a commercial haunted house.

This two-story, Georgian-style red-brick building located off County Road 1050N was not the first almshouse on that property. It was built after the first almshouse was condemned by the Auxiliary Committee of the State Board of Charities, who felt so strongly about their decision that they remarked, "our pride and our humanity should make us determined to remove the disgrace of it from us." In January 1915, bids were taken for the construction of a new fireproof building on the farm.

The building contract for the new almshouse was awarded to J.W. Montgomery in March of 1916 for $20,389, and the cornerstone was laid on May 17, 1916. According to the Charleston *Daily Courier*, the metal box in the cornerstone contained a Bible, a book of rules of the county board, the minutes of the supervisor's meeting that authorized construction of a new almshouse, and current copies of three local newspapers. L.F.W. Stuebe was its architect, and it originally boasted two impressive brick porches in the rear, which were later converted into rooms.

The poor farm operated for nearly 90 years, until attitudes regarding public welfare began to change. Ashmore Estates, Inc. opened in February 1959 and had a rocky career filled with financial trouble and controversy. In May of 1979, the Illinois Department of Public Health ordered the building closed after finding twenty-two safety code violations, but it remained open until November after a Coles County judge found progress in fixing the violations. Debris had piled up from renovations and had never been removed, wiring was exposed, fire extinguishers were missing, and there was little in the terms of safety features. The wooden railings seen along the hallway walls were added as a last-ditch effort to keep the institution open.

In the early 1980s, the building reopened under the direction of Sharon Hood and Lynn Davis. The *Times-Courier* described it as a pleasant and caring environment where residents were happy, had their needs taken care of, and even pursued artistic interests.

Ashmore Estates was closed down for the last time in 1987 when the institution ran out of funds. A few years later, in 1990, Corrections Corporation of America wanted to buy the building for use as a mental health clinic for teenage boys, but the Ashmore Village Board denied them a zoning variance. There was also public resistance to the idea. Local residents thought such a facility would devalue their property, and were afraid of what would happen if any of the troubled teens escaped.

From there, the building deteriorated as it bounced between owners and attracted vandals and the curious. In the early morning hours of November 1, 1995, a fire destroyed the small storage building across the driveway from the main edifice. Unclear who was the actual owner, and facing possible condemnation, Ashmore Estates went up for sale at auction in the summer of 1998 because of delinquent taxes going back two years. Arthur Colclasure, a Sullivan resident, bought the building for $12,500 and planned to turn it into his home. After eight years of replacing broken windows, he sold it to Scott Kelley in the summer of 2006.

The new owner opened the building to individuals and groups who were fascinated by its legends. Documentary filmmakers flocked to Ashmore Estates and visitors swapped stories of encountering specters and disembodied voices in its graffiti-covered halls. Stories of the ghost of an adolescent girl and a dapper man named Joe have joined tales of axe-murdering former patients in the litany of legends associated with this fascinating place. Appearances on national television programs followed. In 2011, Ashmore Estates appeared in the fifth season premiere of the Travel Channel's *Ghost Adventures,* and in 2013 it was featured in an episode of the SyFy Channel's *Ghost Hunters.*

In late January 2013, a violent storm devastated the property. It tore off the new roof, which Kelley had installed years earlier, and destroyed several minor structures. Four months later, a four-member partnership purchased Ashmore Estates for $12,700. The new owners planned to raise funds to repair the storm damage and continue conducting tours of the building. After buying out their partners, Robert Burton and Ella Richards planned to add events and programs including a graveyard scene to the front yard, more tours, and a monthly haunted attraction every full moon. After several months of cleanup, Ashmore Estates reopened for paranormal investigations in July 2013.

Robbin Terry, proprietor of the R Theater in Auburn, purchased it in 2014 and has heavily invested in its restoration. Unfortunately, on Sunday, June 7, 2015, a second storm tore through eastern Coles County. Ashmore Estates was directly in the storm's path and sustained heavy damage to its new roof. The damage included a total loss to the portion of the roof over the 1980 addition.

"We were able to salvage about a third of the roof on the original structure last June," Terry said at the time. "The roof on the addition is a total loss. The cost to repair and replace will exceed over $10,000." The community rallied around the building and repairs were made. Robbin Terry continues to own and operate Ashmore Estates to the present day, and interest in this legendary location remains high.

"ANDERSON" FARMHOUSE

In 1982, the *Daily Eastern News* ran a story about an abandoned farmhouse in rural Coles County that neighbors—and visitors—claimed was haunted by the angry spirit of a family patriarch.

In the winter of 1955, the legend goes, the Anderson family sat down to dinner as they had every night before, with their grandfather seated at the head of the table. Without warning, the grandfather died, and in his last moments his face splashed down into his soup. The Anderson family—now only a man, his wife, and their two children—hardly waited for their grandfather's body to be in the ground before they abruptly left their home and all their belongings. They moved to parts unknown, and their farmhouse has sat abandoned ever since... with its table still set for dinner.

Vandals and curiosity seekers soon took over the farmhouse. According to the *Daily Eastern News*, "neighbors say that blue lights sometimes illuminate the inside of the house and that shadows and human shapes can occasionally be seen through the windows." Local teens and students at Eastern Illinois University gleefully trespassed to see all the items the Anderson family left behind, and perhaps to meet a ghost. On more than one occasion, these visitors found themselves locked inside a room as the door mysteriously closed on its own. If you happen to come across this weather-beaten home, be careful that grandpa's ghost doesn't trap you as well.

CHARLESTON COMMUNITY MEMORIAL

HOSPITAL (FORMER)

Driving by this unassuming professional building at 825 18th Street south of Harrison Avenue in Charleston, nothing would alert passersby to anything out of the ordinary. Employees at this former hospital, however, know better. Many insist something from the past remains.

Charleston Community Memorial Hospital opened in February 1953 and operated until 1977, when this hospital and Mattoon Memorial Hospital completed a nine-year consolidation effort by merging into Sarah Bush Lincoln Health Center. After the hospital closed, it was converted into a professional office building and is currently home to the Coles County Health Department and other non-profit organizations.

"Our office was at first what used to be the surgical room," Ellie White told the *JG-TC* in an October 2012 interview. Ellie worked in the building from 1985 to about 1998. "There were no windows and it was all enclosed... There were a lot of mornings I would go in to work and open up, and there would be a strong cigar smell in the area." Fellow employees told her that the ghost of a former cigar-loving doctor was responsible for the strange odor. It was his way of letting people know he was still around.

Other employees heard the sound of children laughing, crying, and running through the hallways. Coffee mugs disappeared and reappeared, and disembodied voices have been heard in the former hospital kitchen.

Becky Guymon worked in the building from 2006 to 2010. She told the *JG-TC* about other strange occurrences. "We would hear some knocking noise that seemed to follow us," she said. "And in the women's restroom, we would have lights turn off and on us, and they weren't the motion sensored lights. You could check the switch and it wouldn't be flipped. And also, the stall doors would open and close."

None of the former employees described the eerie encounters as threatening or malicious, and they continue to this day. Hair raising? Yes, but in their simple way, these ghosts of the past help keep alive the memory of what once was.

MARSHALL-TYCER HOUSE

D ennis Friend Hanks (1799-1892), a distant cousin of Abraham Lincoln, once owned this property and a log cabin near the corner of Jackson Avenue and 2nd Street in Charleston. Hanks was a businessman who, among other things, was a cobbler and ran an inn and gristmill. He died at his daughter's house in Paris, Illinois in 1892 after being hit by a wagon. Col. Thomas Alexander Marshall, Jr. (1817-1873) was a lawyer, politician, and another Lincoln friend. He built a stately Italianate home on Hanks' former property in 1853. During the 1960s and '70s, his house at 218 Jackson Avenue was widely reputed to be haunted by the ghost of Dennis Hanks.

In addition to playing host to Lincoln and his circle, it's rumored the house was used to hide runaway slaves. Its basement contained a dungeon-like room with barred windows and what looked like 12 fasteners to hold shackles.

In 1965, Eastern Illinois University English professor Dr. Marie Neville Tycer (1920-1970) and her husband Forster purchased the home, renovated it, and opened it as the Tycer House Museum. They lived there for five years, furnished it with antiques, and allowed groups to tour the historic home. The Tycers became convinced they shared the property with a lively ghost. Mr. Tycer told the *Eastern News* that he was doing some electrical work in the basement when he lost his balance and almost fell into the wiring. He claimed that unseen hands pushed him away and saved his life.

Mrs. Tycer saw the reflection of the ghost, a tall, dark man wearing a vest and unbuttoned jacket, in a mirror or window as she was painting the porch. She turned around only to find she was alone. She also heard footsteps and claimed the ghost unlocked doors. In one frightening incident, she told the *Herald and Review* she was reading in bed when she heard footsteps in the basement. She checked twice. "I went to see if we had a prowler, but there was nothing," she said. A "tremendous crash" followed, but again, she found nothing out of place when she searched the house. "After 15 or 20 minutes, I couldn't find anything. I decided it was nothing human, so I went to sleep."

The Tycers didn't live in the house long before their lives were cut tragically short. Forster passed away in January 1969. On March 10, 1970, 19 days before her 50th birthday, Mrs. Tycer committed suicide with a .22 caliber pistol in an upstairs bedroom, leaving her 10-year-old daughter orphaned. Their entire antique collection was auctioned off a year later. According to legend, the bloodstains on the floor from Mrs. Tycer's suicide continued to reappear no matter how many times they were scrubbed away.

The next family to live in the home occupied it for quite some time and never experienced anything out of the ordinary, or so they told the *Eastern News* in 1977. It appeared as if the ghost of Dennis Hanks departed along with the Tycers, but no one knows whether Mr. Hanks or Mrs. Tycer still stalk the halls to this day.

MARSHALL-TYCER HOUSE | PHOTO BY THE AUTHOR

HUNT POLTERGEIST

During the 1960s and '70s, paranormal activity plagued an unassuming farmhouse in Pleasant Grove Township between the village of Lerna and the tiny community of Trilla. This farmhouse, though it no longer exists, was once afflicted by a poltergeist that only abated after several exorcisms. The family residing in the home, who remain anonymous, had bought the land in 1960 in order to try their hand at farming. Odd things began to happen, but the family brushed them off as coincidences. It wasn't until they discovered that pounds of rat poison were disappearing without any sign of dead rats that they knew something was wrong.

After that, their youngest son, Joseph, started seeing the ghost of a woman in his room. "She'd be standing in front of his closet and would point outside and tell him to dig," his mother told the *Daily Eastern News*. These incidents attracted attention, and the family asked several local psychics to walk through the house. The psychics said it was haunted by three spirits, including one by the name of Nora Hunt—a previous owner. Locals whispered rumors that, in life, Nora had a cruel streak and used to torture dogs in her yard. After she died, her soul refused to leave.

In the summer of 1980, the family turned to a Methodist minister named Franklin Ogdon, who performed two "exorcisms" on the residence. They prayed together in each room, hoping to dispel the poltergeist. Eventually, the frustrated family moved to Charleston and tore down the farmhouse. The novel *A Family Possessed: A Ghost Story* by L.W. Stevenson is based on these events.

KINGMAN-MOORE HOUSE

When it comes to haunted houses in Coles County, none is more infamous than the Kingman-Moore House at 2701 Western Avenue in Mattoon. Dominating the southwest corner of Western and N 27th Street, this 136-year-old Eclectic Italianate-style house was built by one of Mattoon's most prominent citizens, and its ghostly activity goes back over a century.

As an only child, Caroline "Carrie" Johnson Kingman (1849-1932) inherited large tracts of land from her parents and expanded her real estate holdings from there. She was a patron of the arts who built or owned several theaters in Mattoon, including the Dole Opera House, and was, at one time, the largest landowner and one of the wealthiest citizens in Coles and Cumberland counties. She married Tracy Kingman in 1872.

Her husband and she built the house at 2701 Western Avenue circa 1884 and lived there for an indeterminate number of years. The couple had three children: Charles Dudley (d.1944), Tracy (1881-1970), and Bertha (d.1956). Their life must have seemed blessed, but this small-town Camelot did not last. Sometime around 1904, Tracy Kingman moved to California. Their daughter, Bertha, eloped with a man named Harry Rogers in June 1907 and never returned to live in Illinois (as far as I can determine). Carrie reportedly strongly opposed their marriage. In 1932, Bertha and Harry Rogers were living in Spokane, Washington, and Bertha died on February 9, 1956 in Palm Springs, California.

Carrie sold their house at 2701 Western Avenue to Charles H. Moore in December 1913. None of the Kingmans died there. Tracy died on December 30, 1919 at the home of his niece in Oakland, California. He had been living in California for 15 years. Carrie Kingman died of natural causes on March 6, 1932 at the North Shore Health Resort in Winnetka, Illinois at the age of 82.

Charles H. Moore (1870-1914), the house's next owner, came from a prominent Mattoon family and worked in the lumber business. Charles and his family moved from Mattoon to Alvin, Texas in 1911 but returned in the fall of 1913. They settled into the stately manor that winter, but tragedy quickly soured their homecoming. First, Charles' mother-in-law, Mrs. Eliza Canan, succumbed to cancer in the house at the age of 68 on June 24,

1914. Then, his investment in an apartment building went south. He decided to commit suicide rather than face his creditors.

On the morning of Saturday, November 14, 1914, as the First World War raged overseas, Charles told his wife he would be away on business that day. Between 3:00 and 4:00 p.m., he strolled to his garage, entered the rear door facing away from his home, and locked all the doors. He sat on the floor behind the driver's seat of his Auburn touring car and drank three ounces of carbolic acid. Carbolic acid, also known as phenol, is a versatile antiseptic but highly toxic if ingested. Anywhere from one to 32 grams can kill a human. Charles Moore ingested 85 grams. The *Mattoon Commercial-Star* noted, "although death must have been almost instantaneous, the dead man had suffered horribly." His wife discovered his body while in the garage with a neighbor watering their cow.

After Charles Moore's suicide, the house went through several owners and periods of vacancy. It developed a reputation for being haunted. Many believed the ghost belonged to either Carrie Kingman or Charles Moore, but the earliest report of ghostly activity was in 1912, before Charles committed suicide or any of the Kingmans had died.

KINGMAN-MOORE HOUSE | PHOTO BY THE AUTHOR

In the summer of 1912, J.A. Bell, a railroad mechanic, was renting the house with his family but sent them away due to a diphtheria outbreak. On the night of Thursday, July 25th at around 10:30, Bell returned home to find the upstairs hallway light on when he walked in the front door. Thinking his wife and children had returned prematurely, he called out to them but received no response. The light turned out as he ascended the stairs, so he raced outside to seek help from passersby. On the street, Bell and three other men watched, alarmed, as lights appeared in the second story windows. The posse searched the house and called the police when they came up empty handed.

The four men surrounded the house and waited for the police to arrive. As they waited, the lights mysteriously returned two more times. A Mattoon patrolman named Cox searched the entire home and found all the windows shut and locked. Bell was so shaken by the experience he rented a room that night and did not return.

A woman named Georgia A. Swank, in a letter to the *Journal Gazette*, claimed her parents, Mr. and Mrs. Albert Shores, owned the house in 1945 and 1946 (I believe the second date given in the letter, 1956, was a typo). They lived on the first floor and rented the second. When Georgia's husband was discharged from the Navy, they moved back to Mattoon and rented the top floor from her parents. Georgia described seeing a ghostly figure pacing back and forth down the hallway and staring out the bathroom window. "I knew no one was home but me at the time," she wrote. "I kept telling my husband and he laughed and said I imagined it."

When John and Emily Gehl purchased the house in 1946, they heard stories of it being haunted but remained skeptical. Over the next few decades, the house was divided into four rental units. Its next owners, Mr. and Mrs. Daniel Fuller, bought it in December 1974 and then sold it to Steven Faller ten years later. Steve and his family worked diligently throughout the late 1980s to restore the house to its former glory as a single-family home. The Fallers had many unusual experiences.

First, there were the stories. One woman stopped to ask if they'd "had any experiences." Others told the couple they had seen someone pacing back and forth in front of the dormer window facing east toward 27th Street. Then they tried hanging a painting over the mantel in the parlor, but no matter how hard they tried to secure it to the wall, it would fall off. They moved it to another room and it never fell again. "Carrie and I just didn't have the same tastes," Mrs. Faller told the *Journal Gazette*. In another incident, the hall light fixture upstairs began to move on its own, swaying left to right and back again for nearly 45 minutes.

According to Mrs. Faller, the paranormal activity tapered off and stopped altogether by 1987. Steven and Phyllis Faller still own the house at 2701 Western Avenue, so perhaps the lingering spirits have finally grown accustomed to sharing their home.

LAFAYETTE AVENUE GHOST

In the winter of 1907-1908, a black-shrouded ghost startled residents of Mattoon's west side. It began in December 1907 (formerly a time of year when ghost stories were popular) when residents noticed a diminutive figure dressed head-to-toe in a woman's dress or gown, face covered with a hood, appear on the south side of Lafayette Avenue near 23rd Street around 7:00 p.m. At least three times a week for several weeks, the figure walked west to 24th Street and back before vanishing as mysteriously as it appeared. Then, as now, this was a sparsely-populated neighborhood north of the Peoria, Decatur, & Evansville Railroad.

In the *Journal Gazette*, one man described being followed by the ghost, which emerged from the shadows behind a tree late at night. "I walked about fifty feet past Twenty-third street on the south of side of Lafayette avenue, when the ghost, or whatever it is, stepped out from the shadow of a tree and followed close after me as far as Twenty-fourth street, where it turned around and went back again," he said. Others who were followed claimed the ghost never came within 20 feet.

Residents were so disturbed they formed a "vigilant committee" to watch for the ghost, and if possible, capture it under the assumption it was a man dressed in women's clothing out to scare some unsuspecting victim. By early February, the specter had become so bold it entered one house uninvited and knocked on the door of several others. Mattie Reynolds, who lived at 2213 Lafayette Avenue (today a vacant lot), told the newspaper it knocked on her door one evening. When asked what it wanted, the ghost replied: "It would be past your understanding if I told you what I wanted" before walking away.

Just as sightings of the Lafayette Avenue ghost peaked, residents of Mattoon's north side reported their own specter, this one dressed in a flowing white robe. It appeared in the North Park neighborhood late at night and early morning, chasing unsuspecting passersby. As before, local men took to the streets to capture the mysterious prowler. "Should the spook be found," the newspaper editorialized, "it will likely experience the sensations of being ridden down to town on a rail and locked in the city Bastille until the desire to haunt people will be forever lost."

That spelled the end of the ghostly activity.

Monroe Avenue Mystery House

An old Victorian Style home sits a few blocks east of Charleston's town square, along Monroe Avenue between 10th and 11th streets. Built in 1900, it has weathered years of neglect. From hidden rooms and hideaways in the attic, to disembodied footsteps and doors that slam on their own, to a pile of dusty bones in the basement, one former resident is convinced that its walls conceal a secret history yet to be uncovered.

Lisa (not her real name) was a young girl when her parents purchased the home in the early 1990s. It had been abandoned for nearly 20 years, until an enterprising couple fixed it up and sold it to Lisa's parents. From the moment her family moved in, Lisa knew something was amiss. The previous owners told her mother that during the days of Prohibition, an old man who lived in the house had hideouts in the cross-shaped attic where he would sit and drink his illegal liquor. There they found old bottles and newspapers before safety concerns compelled them to brick up the entry to this attic hideout. A secondary entrance was near the ceiling in the upstairs bathroom closet.

Lisa's bedroom contained three closets, each a different size. In the distant past, someone had carved a note into the wall of one of these closets, accompanied by a girl's name and the date. At one time, Lisa had a rubbing of the note, but has since misplaced it. That wasn't the only thing about her bedroom that sent chills down her spine.

"My mother had a friend who was Jehovah's Witness, and she usually brought her kids over to play," she said. "One night, her daughter was up in my room at the top of the stairs while our parents were downstairs. When you came up the winding stairs, you faced east. If you went down the hall to the north, my door was literally right on your left. So you could not see anyone coming up the stairs, but the way the door opened on the north of the door, you could see if someone opened it inwards.

"We were talking or playing a game or something and all of the sudden, the door flung open. We had those doors with a window at the top and it let light in from the hallway. Both hall and room were lit. The door swung into my room but nobody was there. Then it slammed shut. Now, no windows were open, so that couldn't account for it closing or opening as it had been latched each time it closed. And then it happened again. Needless to say, we ran screaming down the stairs in tears."

The basement was perhaps the scariest part of the old house. With bricked-up windows, sealed antechambers, and a dirt floor, it resembled a catacomb. Once, while exploring a dirt mound in the floor roughly four feet high and 20-30 feet long, Lisa and a friend stumbled upon a grisly discovery. "If you climbed up on there, there was a huge assortment of bones including one that looked like a human femur," she recalled. "My friend took that one home to ask his dad but never gave it back." Later, as an EMT/I and medical lab worker, she was able to retrospectively identify the bone. She was never able to explore the sealed rooms, she explained, "because I knew breaking the brick out of those would lead to something I didn't want to see, if my parents didn't kill me first."

Today, the home sits inconspicuously on a quiet street, and someday Lisa hopes to return. "I've always said if I won the lottery, I would buy the house up and fix it back to its original condition." Adding, "Not because it was my childhood home. I was traumatized a little too much by all of the strange and spooky experiences I had there. I could never spend the night there again. But just to explore all of the undiscovered history of that building."

WILL ROGERS THEATRE

Built in 1938 at a cost of $90,000 in Art Deco style, the Will Rogers Theatre has been a fixture of downtown Charleston for generations. It was named after William 'Will' Rogers, a world-famous actor, humorist, and columnist of the Progressive Era who died in a plane crash in 1935. During the 1980s, Kerasotes Theaters divided the 1,100-seat auditorium and began showing movies on two separate screens. The Will Rogers was added to the National Register of Historic Places in 1984, and designated a Landmark Property by the City of Charleston in 2011.

Like many theaters, there are rumors it is haunted. Since at least the 1990s, employees have encountered strange sounds and surreal events they attributed to a ghost aptly named "Will." Will, however, is just a convenient moniker.

There are several stories behind the identity of this ghost, but no one knows for certain. According to Will Sailor, a former theater employee, the ghost is that of a man who died in the Charleston Riot. Lucas Thomas, who worked at the theater from 1996 to 2000, told the *JG-TC* that he heard it was the ghost of a projectionist who died of a heart attack in the projector room.

In 2007, Will Sailor related an eerie encounter to a reporter from *The Charleston Chew*, a one-shot newspaper created for the Eastern Illinois University Summer Journalism Workshop. "The first time I started working, I remember I had closed all the doors because I was sweeping," he said. "I turned away from the doors to sweep somewhere else, and before even two seconds had passed, I turn back around to find that all four left doors were open... I was the only one in here. There is no explanation for it, and it's not like these doors are easy to open."

Sailor claimed to actually see the ghost on four separate occasions, mostly from the waist down. He described it as a short man dressed in an old-fashioned suit, dark gray pants, shiny black shoes, and a bowler's cap.

Thomas, on the other hand, only heard the ghost's footsteps. This became a weekly occurrence, and he described them as "very distinct" and "as footsteppy as I've ever heard footsteps." He also recalled sensing something moving in the projection office.

WILL ROGERS THEATRE | PHOTO BY THE AUTHOR

AMC closed the Will Rogers Theatre on November 28, 2010. It was already struggling as a result of the new 8-theater multiplex out on Route 16. Katie Troccoli took over ownership in November 2011 and worked hard to renovate the 75-year-old building. Unfortunately, a water pipe burst and flooded the basement and auditorium, hampering repairs. Troccoli fought off the specter of foreclosure, but even by 2017 the prospect of once again seeing its glimmering marquee lights appeared dim.

A non-profit group called the Will Rogers Theatre Project approached Troccoli about working together to restore the historic theater, but she balked at their request to share ownership. "That is never going to happen," she reportedly said.

Despite spending many hours there (including overnight), in 2012 Troccoli told the *JG-TC* she has yet to experience any unusual occurrences. Has the ghost of Will moved on, or is he just quietly waiting until the theater's seats once again fill with patrons? Only time will tell.

EASTERN ILLINOIS UNIVERSITY

BURL IVES

Burl Icle Ivanhoe Ives (1909-1995) was a popular entertainer, radio personality, actor, and country musician, but he's best known in Coles County for dropping out of Eastern Illinois State Teachers College (Eastern Illinois University). While attending Eastern from 1927 to 1930, he was a football player and performed with a banjo on the side. His junior year, he decided academia wasn't for him and left during class, slamming the door so hard it shattered the glass. He went home, gathered his clothes and banjo, and walked away.

Since then, a legend has grown up about why Ives dropped out of Eastern. In *Haunted America* (1994), Beth Scott and Michael Norman wrote that Ives was spotted crawling out a Pemberton Hall window early one morning. Only women, of course, live in Pemberton Hall. An article in the 1986 yearbook led with the assertion "Legend has it that Burl Ives left Eastern after getting caught climbing the ivy on Pemberton Hall," and even a journalist for the *Chicago Tribune* cited a rumor he was "expelled after climbing the walls of a women's dormitory for a peek."

As explained in the 1974 EIU yearbook, *The Warbler*, "Another widely rumored story concerning Pemberton Hall... concerns entertainer Burl Ives, who attended Eastern during the early '30's and was a 250 lb. lineman on the Panther football team. It seems that Ives was visiting a lady-friend up in Pemberton one night when visitation wasn't in effect, and was forced to sneak his large frame out of the building. However, as the story goes, poor Burl didn't quite make a clean escape and was severely reprimanded for his actions when caught."

Is there any truth to the legend? According to an EIU administrator Margaret Allen-Kline interviewed for her 1998 master's thesis, there's a file on Ives and a photo of him climbing out a window of Pemberton Hall. In his autobiography, *Wayfaring Stranger* (1948), Ives himself admitted he was more interested in chasing girls than attending classes, so this story may contain a kernel of truth.

NAPOLEON

O fficially, Eastern's mascot is a black panther nicknamed Billy, but in the 1950s, a golden retriever named Napoleon came close to claiming the title. An etching of the nappy brown and tan dog even graced the cover of the 1959 yearbook. Though thousands of students stroll past his grave marker in the north quad behind Old Main each semester, few know his story.

In 1946, a large golden retriever wandered onto campus. He was a young male, approximately two-to-three years of age, and quickly captured the attention of students at what was then Eastern Illinois State College. They called him Napoleon, or "Nap" for short. As campus evolved with growing enrollment and a new library and dorms, this wandering dog was a reassuring and constant companion for Post-War students, many of whom were veterans attending college thanks to the GI Bill.

For fourteen years, Napoleon reigned over campus and was given free range by students and faculty. He strolled into classrooms, on stage at plays, and was said to attend football games. Napoleon even ran on and off the field with every substitution. All attempts to secure a collar around his neck proved futile. Campus organizations kept him fed, and *Eastern State News* staff held fundraisers called "Nickels for Napoleon" to pay for his medical bills.

In 1953, he appeared in the Homecoming parade riding in the backseat of a convertible wearing a cap and gown. His honorary degree, it's said, was a "Pet-A-Doggy" degree. "He is loyalty in the truest sense of the word," *The Warbler* staff wrote about their beloved mascot. "He is the representative of every high standard for which Eastern Illinois University stands." Professors reported he had a better attendance record than some of their human students.

Napoleon's favorite pastime was chasing other stray dogs off campus. Just before Thanksgiving Break in 1954, Nap and a dog named Sam crashed English 120 and sent students fleeing to the back of the room. They knocked over five chairs and tore up a notebook before some of the boys separated them. He was temporarily banished from the building.

NAPOLEON'S GRAVE | PHOTO BY THE AUTHOR

Napoleon died at 16 years of age sometime over the winter of 1959-1960. He disappeared in November and his body was found beneath a porch at 1410 Seventh Street in Charleston on Tuesday, May 3, 1960, within sight of Old Main. Students took his body to campus, where EIU President Quincy V. Doudna helped bury him in the north quad. Students raised funds and placed a marble marker over his grave and hung a mural in the Student Union.

In 1966, students tried to crown Napoleon II by introducing a new golden retriever to campus, but he only lasted two months before a hit-and-run driver killed him on March 3, 1966. He was buried in the backyard of Rudolph D. Anfinson, dean of student personnel services, where he had been staying.

The Phantom

During the late 1960s and early '70s, while campus protests, panty raids, and streaking were all the rage, a group of pranksters collectively known as The Phantom spread school spirit with a series of baffling capers.

The Phantom made its debut on July 3, 1966, when it perched a 23-pound watermelon and American flag on the tower spire of Florence McAfee Gym (then known as Lanz Gym). Maintenance workers grumbled at the thought of retrieving it, and everyone was perplexed by how the student or students climbed up there. The watermelon sat on its perch for over a month before Eastern hired a contractor with the equipment to remove it. The group also hung a banner from the highest spot on Old Main. The Phantom's next appearance wasn't for nearly two years, when, over the weekend of April 20-21, 1968, a white banner spray-painted with "PHANTOM" appeared fluttering from the spire.

U.S. Marines landed in Vietnam on March 8, 1965, and from there, the ground war accelerated. President Lyndon Johnson increased the draft quota, and anxieties over the draft spread to college campuses across the country. At EIU in May 1969, the Young Republican Club circulated a petition to abolish the draft in favor of an all-volunteer army. On October 15th and November 15th, many students and faculty skipped classes to attend a Moratorium protesting the Vietnam War. During this troubled time, The Phantom's antics added a spirit of mirth, mystery, and frivolity on campus. According to a May 9, 1969 article in the *Eastern News*, The Phantom was a local chapter of a national organization, with a chairman, treasurer, secretary, and even sergeant-at-arms. They communicated with EIU President Quincy V. Doudna so university officials would know which pranks were "official" and which were copycats. Doudna reportedly enjoyed the school spirit.

Other pranks included hanging a "phantom form" over Doudna's portrait in Old Main and a dummy over a statue above the entrance to the Science Building, as well as pennants from the tennis court light posts. They once issued fake parking tickets to all University vehicles.

Phantom activity peaked in the fall of 1969. In early October, it skewered a watermelon on the McAfee Gym spire and erected its name in wood above. A photo of the caper, along with a letter to the editor teasing campus police officers for failing to capture them after hanging a banner at the first home game, appeared in the *Eastern News*. Its greatest prank occurred on Sunday night, October 26, 1969, when The Phantom turned the McAfee Gym clock into an exact replica of a Mickey Mouse watch. The prank featured a six-foot tall plywood Mickey with PHANTOM painted on its shoes and two white-gloved hands wired to the clock hands. Superintendent of the Physical Plant Everett Alms later admitted it was his favorite prank, although it had to be removed to prevent damage to the clock. "It was beautiful," he said.

It wasn't long before The Phantom had to contend with copycats. When a person masquerading as The Phantom sent a letter to the editor declaring his Student Senate candidacy, The Phantom wrote a scathing reply. "We assert again, as we have in previous statements, that we take no stand on any campus issues," they wrote. "The only purpose of our organization is the promotion of school spirit... WE WOULD like to ask our fellow students to refrain from any future blasphemies upon our name."

A group of figures in black, hooded robes drove through the 1970 Homecoming parade before vanishing as mysteriously as they appeared. Phantom activity tapered off in the early 1970s, before culminating in placement of a giant pumpkin and a white, flowing sheet atop Booth Library in late October 1973.

At the beginning of the 1974 spring semester, the *Eastern News* received a letter from a group calling itself The Shadow. The Shadow claimed The Phantom had left campus, and The Shadow was there to replace it. They hung a banner from Old Main welcoming students back to Eastern. "In similarity to the Phantom, we are an a-political organization and wish only for the betterment of the campus atmosphere," they wrote in a letter to the *Eastern News*. Despite promising not to damage property, they broke four locks in their effort to hang the banner from Old Main. "I don't object to what he's doing," Everett Alms told the *Eastern News*, "but when he starts damaging property that's a different story."

The last prank occurred on February 28, 1974, when three roosters bearing nametags that read "Dr. Specter" were let loose on campus. After that, both The Phantom and The Shadow disappeared.

To this day, The Phantom's membership remains anonymous. In 1988, former *Daily Eastern News* advisor and instructor Michael Cordts, who was an Eastern student in the early

1970s, admitted "The Phantom was a group with a ringleader and my roommate was the ringleader." As with President Doudna, the group sent coded letters to the school newspaper to identify their pranks. Retired Campus Police Chief John Pauley once caught several members in McAfee Gym but let them go because, in his words, "They were a good solid group of people." The Phantom might be unknown to EIU students today, but staff and alumni who called Eastern their home from 1966 to 1973 will look back on its pranks with joyful nostalgia.

PEMBERTON HALL

The legend of Pemberton Hall is, by far, the most famous ghost story to come out of Coles County. A variation of a well-known folktale called "the Roommate's Death," it has been passed down by generations of young women at Eastern Illinois University and has appeared in dozens of books. One night, it is said, a deranged janitor attacked and killed a student on the fourth floor. Her ghost, or the ghost of the dorm mother who discovered her body, now haunts the hall. Over the years, Pemberton Hall's own history contributed to this story, creating a unique tale beloved by students and alumni alike.

In 1907, the appropriations committee of the state legislature passed a bill to provide $100,000 to build a women's dormitory at Eastern Illinois State Normal School. The dorm was named after State Senator Stanton C. Pemberton (1858-1944), a strong proponent of the bill. The first dorm director for Pemberton Hall was Mary Elizabeth Hawkins, who served in that position from 1910 to 1917. She immigrated from Shropshire, England in 1901 at the age of 24.

In the early twentieth century, women attending the college and staying in Pemberton Hall would, in addition to their classes, learn basic housekeeping skills and serve dinner to the college deans on some occasions. They were not allowed outside after 7:30 p.m. on weekdays and 10:00 p.m. on weekends. Mary Hawkins personally doled out punishment for any infraction until she left the college in 1917. Perhaps ironically, Miss Hawkins died on October 30, 1918 at the Kankakee State Mental Hospital a year after leaving her position as "Matron" from complications stemming from syphilis.

That's where fact and folklore part ways.

Storytellers allege a crazed janitor murdered a student in Pemberton Hall during the First World War, and missing issues of the college's newspaper, published sporadically to conserve materials for the war effort, lead some to suggest a conspiracy to cover it up. Most versions of the tale say the crime took place on the fourth floor over winter break either in 1916 or 1917, but an October 1984 *Daily Eastern News* article written by Diane Schneidman suggested May, and an article published in 1982 claimed it occurred during Spring Break. Jo-Anne Christensen, in her book *Ghosts Stories of Illinois*, portrayed the crime being committed in the midst of a furious thunderstorm, which also suggests springtime. The *National Directory of Haunted Places*, written by Dennis William Hauck, changed the year of the murder to 1920, long after Mary Hawkins was deceased.

ILLUSTRATION BY KATIE CONRAD

In one version, Mary Hawkins was the name of the unfortunate student, and her ghost acts like a banshee, scratching at doors and leaving behind bloody footprints. In the version told by staff at Pemberton Hall, Mary was the Dorm Mother at the time of the murder, and her ghost has come back to watch over and protect the girls at Pem Hall for all eternity.

The ghost of Pemberton Hall first appeared in an *Eastern News* article written by Karen Knupp in October of 1976. The story, she wrote, had been told for "years and years," and was handed down from veteran Pem Hall residents to incoming freshmen. Some of the eerie encounters she chronicled included a girl who saw a light emanating from a fourth-floor window, a resident assistant who found the lounge furniture inexplicably rearranged, and a strange encounter with a girl in a white gown who went around asking for safety pins before she disappeared. Karen noted that some residents had celebrated their unique heritage by holding a "Mary Hawkins Day" the previous spring.

In November of that same year, Karen wrote a follow up story after she had been contacted by a 1921 resident of Pem Hall named [Estella] Craft Temple. Mrs. Temple told the story of [Euterpe] Sharp, a 30-year-old student who made a habit of scaring the younger girls by jumping out of the janitor's closet. Mrs. Temple, who if she had actually lived there in 1921 could not have known Mary Hawkins (who would have been deceased), claimed that, "no one would tell Miss Hawkins... she was English and very strict." She suggested that Euterpe's strange behavior was the origin of the legend, not a murder.

According to interviews conducted by Margaret Allen-Kline, who wrote her master's thesis on the legend in 1998, several students living in Pemberton Hall connected the crazed janitor in the story to a "local insane asylum," the notorious Ashmore Estates. But as Margaret pointed out, the building that became known as Ashmore Estates was originally an almshouse and not an asylum. Margaret believed the legend of Mary had formed a "folk community" at Eastern because the students always reported the story as if it was true.

Many former residents insist the building is haunted. While living at Pemberton Hall, Alyssa Warner, class of 2009, and her friend had a characteristically unusual experience. "We were both laying on her bed," she told me. "We were watching *Mrs. Doubtfire*, laughing, having a good time and all of a sudden the light went out, the door shut, and the TV went off. I got up fast to check if anyone was in the halls and there was no one. Didn't even hear footsteps, no shadows, just what happened. It wasn't suction, because no one opened another door. You can hear people opening the common doors going floor to floor, especially where her room was located."

Over the years, Pemberton Hall has opened its doors—and the notorious fourth floor—around Halloween as a haunted attraction and fundraiser. According to an October 27, 1978 *Eastern News* article, the tradition dates back to the early 1970s. In October 1984, William M. Michael, a writer for the *Decatur Herald*, spent the night in the fourth-floor piano room, although he reported no encounters with anything unusual. Pemberton Hall resumed its haunted house in 1997, complete with an actress playing the X-Files theme on the fourth-floor piano.

Interest in the legend of Mary Hawkins at Pemberton Hall remains high, and a steady rotation of new students arriving each year guarantees it will continue to be passed down from one generation to the next. For the young women of Pemberton Hall, the spirit of Mary Hawkins will always be there; watching, protecting, and playing pranks.

PEMBERTON HALL | PHOTO BY THE AUTHOR

CEMETERY LORE

BETHEL "RAGDOLL" CEMETERY

Q uaint and unassuming Bethel Cemetery sits nestled among rolling hills, picturesque farms, and new housing developments at the junction of E County Road 1020E and E County Road 600N south of the Coles County Airport. Its legend is little known even to locals, and many merely pass by on their way home or on a Sunday drive through the wooded hills unaware of the strange tale.

Even if they were aware of the legend, they might not recognize this particular cemetery as being home to such a gruesome story. At first glance, much of the cemetery has the same carefully trimmed lawn and identical rows of granite headstones as hundreds of other modern rural cemeteries. But a careful examination of the grounds reveals some interesting features. Off to the right of the main gate, just outside the tree line, lies the old section of the cemetery. Two large oak trees stand guard over the faded or fallen headstones. Many of the remaining markers, as well as an assortment of items left there over the years, lay inside the woods among overgrown weeds. A large collection of stones, having been previously knocked down, is propped up haphazardly against one of the large oaks.

The origin of Bethel Cemetery's folk-name, "Ragdoll Cemetery," varies from person to person. Depending on the storyteller, it will either be simply strange or downright macabre. There once was a little girl of about eight or nine years of age (the year in which the story takes place changes) who loved her rag doll, the typical version goes. The girl died, some say of an illness, others say murder. In the case of illness, she asked to be buried with her doll. In the case of murder, her dying wish went unknown or was ignored.

ILLUSTRATION BY KATIE CONRAD

In all versions, the girl, who was never separated from her favorite toy in life, was eternally separated from it in death. In some adaptations, the doll forever searches for the girl's grave. In others, the girl's ghost forever searches for the doll, which was lost in the cemetery. In a third version, the doll appears every night to look for the girl's killer. The doll is also said to hang from the oak tree near her grave, where it waits to drop down on unsuspecting trespassers.

Elements of the "Ragdoll Cemetery" story do reflect harsh realities. Many children died in the nineteenth century, and local cemeteries are scattered with the graves of those who passed on before their time. The *Coles County Leader* once suggested Sallie T. Hill as a possible candidate for the girl in the story. She died in 1873, when she was only eight years and three months old. Prior to the 1950s, many children perished of diseases like Cholera and tuberculosis, an element in one version of the legend.

Several years ago, Michael Savisky and Joe Lucarelli, an independent filmmaker and former Mattoon resident, chose Bethel Cemetery as the setting for their thriller *Rag Doll*. The movie was filmed at various locations around Mattoon and incorporated elements of the "ragdoll" legend, but it was never released.

CAMPGROUND CEMETERY

Campground Cemetery, at the northern tip of Lake Paradise where it meets the Little Wabash River, is a tranquil rural graveyard with pioneer roots. The first settlers in that area were Methodists who held religious services at large camp meetings. According to *The History of Coles County* (1879), "it was esteemed a blessed privilege to be permitted to ride five or six miles, on horse-back, to engage in hymning songs of praise to God and hear the sweet words of Gospel truth." The Sawyer Camp Ground was started in the 1830s at Wabash Point, and a pioneer Methodist preacher known as Uncle Hiram Tremble constructed a large wooden pulpit for the religious services held there. It was named after Charles Sawyer and his family, who were among the first settlers in that area. For that reason, Campground Cemetery is also known as Old Sawyer Cemetery.

Until the 1850s, it was an informal burial ground for travelers who expired during the camp meetings. Its first formal burial was Willis H. Clark in 1854. In more modern times, visitors and passersby have reported unusual activity said to be reminiscent of those olden days. "About 10 years ago my ex and I went out fishing," Katie [last name withheld] told me. "When we left, we drove past the cemetery and I saw two ladies in 1800 era clothing walking into the woods next to it. I said 'look at how weird they are dressed', but they had already gone into the woods. Didn't think much about it till a couple years later when looking at ghost stories and read about those ladies walking around the cemetery. Never was a believer but I sure am now."

Chad Lewis and Terry Fisk, in their book *The Illinois Road Guide to Haunted Locations* (2007), also claimed travelers on Lake Road have seen figures dressed in Victorian mourning attire flickering among the headstones. A local woman told them that in the 1950s, Girl Scout leaders told ghost stories about the cemetery around the campfire, in particular, about the ghost of a Catholic nun named Sister Mary Worth.

LAFLER-ENNIS CEMETERY

Lafler-Ennis Cemetery, northeast of Charleston in Ashmore Township, is surrounded by woods along the Embarras River and is accessible by way of a gravel path announced by a hand-painted sign. A layer of white dust from the Charleston Stone Quarry covers the plants and trees. Many graves in the long, rectangular burial ground are simply indicated by upturned rocks or cement markers, but a row of three identical granite stones stand out. The name "Mary Hawkins" is chiseled into one, but it is not the Mary Hawkins of Pemberton Hall fame.

The three headstones shaded by trees mark the graves of three sisters: Mary, Jane, and Laura, daughters of Oliver D. and Mary Hawkins. Mary and Jane both died in 1851 at the age of a little more than a year, and Laura died in 1846 when she was only a year and seven months old. Oliver D. Hawkins was born in Kentucky and moved to Coles County with his family in 1841. There he married Mary Lafler, a progeny of the family for whom the cemetery is named, and the two lived in Ashmore, where Oliver served as a judge for 25 years. Oddly enough, he was also the chairman of the finance committee at the time Coles County bought the land on which the poor farm was built.

He then became the superintendent of the poor farm (the predecessor of Ashmore Estates) for three years. According to county records, Oliver owned the land around Lafler-Ennis Cemetery in 1893. His three deceased daughters (three out of fifteen children) will always be remembered at their final resting place thanks to a strange coincidence, and the efforts of preservationists who diligently maintain their headstones.

St. Omer Cemetery

S t. Omer Cemetery and the defunct village of the same name probably would have been forgotten a century ago had it not been for one unusual family monument and a misprinted date. As is often the case in Coles County, these peculiar circumstances gave birth to an obscure but enduring legend. According to local lore, Caroline Barnes, one of four people buried under the massive stone, was put to death for practicing witchcraft. It is said no pictures can be taken of her monument, and that it glows on moonless nights.

The Barnes family monument is difficult to describe. Some say it looks like a crystal ball mounted on a pyre. Conventionally, orbs in cemetery art represent faith, and logs, or tree trunks, are fairly common imagery representing growth and enduring life. This particular gravestone is rare, but similar monuments can be found in several central Illinois cemeteries, including Union Cemetery in northeastern Coles County.

Why do some people believe a witch is buried here? The only evidence for the legend seems to be the gravestone's dramatic design, the way local citizens grow nervous whenever the story is mentioned, and most strikingly, Caroline's impossible date of death chiseled in the granite: February 31. The monument also faces north-south, while most headstones are oriented east-west.

Of course, these things can be explained without appealing to the supernatural. A mistaken date would have been difficult and expensive to correct on such a large monument. As for the reaction of locals: vandalism as a result of the legend has been a very real and present danger. The cemetery trustees have had to hoist the stone upright several times after vandals knocked it down. Perhaps the last time it was righted, no one checked which direction it faced.

Still, theories abound. In 2003, Maria Kelley, then a Lake Land College student, told the *Coles County Leader*, "They tried to kill [Caroline] by hanging her but that didn't kill her so they buried her alive... When they went back to see if she was dead, they said she was gone. That's why people say she was a witch."

Historically, the Barnes family suffered a tragic fate. According to local historian Carolyn Stephens, Marcus Barnes (Caroline's husband) died in a sawmill accident in December

1881. Caroline Prather Barnes, only twenty-three years old, died two months later of pneumonia on either February 26 or 28, depending on which document is consulted. The couple had one child: a girl named Minnie Olive, who married Charles William Kearns and died in 1971 at the age of 89. She was born on August 9, 1881, just a few months before her mother and father died.

There is no documentary evidence supporting the notion that Caroline Barnes was accused of witchcraft, let alone put to death for it. In the harsh world of rural life in the nineteenth century, many people died at an early age of a wide variety of what are now easily treatable illnesses. Such a death might be less fantastic, but it is more likely what actually happened.

Whatever you believe, few can deny that the fascinating story of St. Omer Cemetery has captured the imaginations of generations of Coles County residents. Offerings in the form of flowers or coins make regular appearances at the grave, and the tiny cemetery has found its way into nationally-published books and local newspapers.

If nothing else, Caroline Barnes and her family's unique monument has kept their memory alive for future generations.

ST. OMER CEMETERY | PHOTO BY THE AUTHOR

Union and Knoch-Golladay

Cemeteries

Morgan Township contains two cemeteries of interest. The first, Union Cemetery, rests at the edge of the timberland along Greasy Creek, across County Road 1950E from the former location of the Union-Cumberland Presbyterian Church. Aside from an antique outhouse, this cemetery boasts some impressive monuments. Visitors familiar with the St. Omer "witch's grave" might be surprised to discover an identical monument in Union Cemetery. As if to preempt any similar rumors, an inscription on this particular monument reads: "He died as he lived—a Christian." Union Cemetery is also the final resting place of nineteenth century murder victim John Mason and his family.

The second, Knoch-Golladay Cemetery, sits along County Road 2080 E, a meandering, rugged road, on ridge overlooking the Embarras River. Some of the oldest graves in the county are located here, but the most interesting one is more recent. A lone headstone belonging to Emma Knoch sits at the extreme right-hand side of the cemetery. Shortly before she died of an illness in 1952, Emma dug her own grave about a foot deep so that it was certain where she would be buried. The reason: she wanted to greet visitors from the afterlife.

Mad Gasser of Mattoon

I t was September 1, 1944, the fifth anniversary of the opening salvos of World War 2. American GIs had been fighting their way across northern France for three months. Across the nation, the press churned out lurid accounts of Nazi rocket attacks on London, and comic books depicting Nazi thugs battling super heroes with space age weapons were sold at dime store counters. In Peoria, Illinois, the search for a German prisoner of war who had escaped from nearby Camp Ellis ended that afternoon in a local tavern.

At a nondescript home on Marshall Avenue in Mattoon, Elsie Kearney and her three-year-old daughter Dorothy readied for bed. Her sister, Martha, occupied the living room and two young children were asleep in other parts of the house. As Mrs. Kearney lay with her eyes closed, she began to smell an overpowering, sweet scent she assumed came from the flowers outside her window. It seemed harmless at first, until she felt her lower body go limp and her legs became unresponsive. "Martha!" she screamed. "Martha, help!"

After a few agonizing moments in which the paralysis slowly climbed up Mrs. Kearney's body, her sister burst into the room. "What's wrong?" she asked, frantically throwing on the light.

Mrs. Kearney explained that she was unable to move from the bed. Martha noticed the unusual smell, determined it must be coming from outside, and closed the window. She then rushed over to a neighbor's house and told him to call the police. The neighbor, Karl Robertson, searched the Kearney's yard, but failed to find anything out of the ordinary. The police had similar results, and Mrs. Kearney recovered the use of her limbs shortly before midnight. Her daughter was also ill, and remained so until the next morning.

Meanwhile, a friend had gone out to find Mr. Kearney, who was working late as a taxi driver. He was unable to return home until 12:30, when he noticed a man lurking near his wife's bedroom window. He later described the man as tall, wearing dark clothes and a knit cap. He shouted and rushed at the intruder, but the intruder disappeared into the darkness. Mattoon police officers were again summoned to the home, but found nothing.

Unbeknownst to either the Kearneys or the press, Mr. and Mrs. Urban Reef had suffered a similar attack the previous evening. The *Daily Journal-Gazette* proclaimed that an "anesthetic prowler" was on the loose, and that Mrs. Kearney and her daughter were its first victims. Their symptoms were consistent with exposure to either chloroform or diethyl ether, both organic compounds that depress the central nervous system and produce a loss of consciousness. Chloroform is the more hazardous of the two, and has a sweet smell consistent with Elsie and Martha's description. It can be dispersed into the air using a hand pumped insecticide sprayer that was commonly used at the time.

The phantom anesthetist struck again five nights later, after many believed he fled Mattoon for parts unknown. The next "attack" was much less direct and involved a rag that was left on the front porch of the Cordes residence on N. 21st Street. Mr. and Mrs. Cordes arrived home at 10:00 p.m. and entered through the back door. As they were winding down for the evening in their living room, possibly listening to radio news reports from Europe, they noticed through the screen door a white cloth basking in the soft glow of the porch light. Curious, Mrs. Cordes picked up the cloth, which she described as being larger than a man's handkerchief, and smelled it.

A jolt suddenly shot through her body, and her throat burned. She dropped the cloth. Her husband helped her back into the house and called a doctor, then the police. Mrs. Cordes began to spit up blood. The next day, she showed her injuries to a reporter from the *Daily Journal-Gazette*, who wrote that "her throat and mouth were so badly burned by the fumes she inhaled that blood came from the cracks in her parched and swollen lips and her seared throat and the roof of her mouth."

As in the previous incident, police found no evidence of the prowler, but they did pick up and later released a man in the neighborhood who claimed to be lost. Mrs. Cordes said that she had found a well-worn skeleton key and a used lipstick container on the sidewalk.

ILLUSTRATION BY KATIE CONRAD

Over the next three days, dozens of people—mostly women—reported strange smells, paralysis, and other unusual occurrences they attributed to the "mad gasser." Panic seized the town, but as time went on the police department became increasingly skeptical. On Tuesday, September 12, Chief of Police C. E. Cole issued a statement in which he blamed the reports on mass hysteria resulting from odors emitted by local industrial plants. "Chemicals used in coloring leather, bleaching broom straw and cleaning clothing have fumes which may have been carried to any part of the city by changing winds," he said.

Representatives of Mattoon industry responded by denying that any such gasses had escaped from their factories. Their employees had not reported becoming sickened that month, nor had there been one instance of sickening in the previous four years. Furthermore, the State Department of Health had inspected the factories and said there was no possibility of chemical vapors escaping "in any amount of concentration that would even closely approximate a toxic condition."

Never-the-less, mass hysteria fueled by the climate of the Second World War has been given as the official explanation for the "phantom anesthetist" ever since. But mass hysteria did not paralyze Mrs. Kearney, sicken her daughter, and make Mrs. Cordes' throat bleed. Mr. Kearney actually did see someone lurking outside of his wife's bedroom window. Despite the lack of concrete evidence pointing to a particular suspect, the reality of these events cannot be disputed.

In his book *The Mad Gasser of Mattoon: Dispelling the Hysteria* (2003), Scott Maruna theorized that the attacks, at least some of them, were real and were perpetrated by a University of Illinois chemistry student named Farley Llewellyn, who was disgruntled by the treatment he received at the hands of his peers. Llewellyn grew up in Mattoon, and Maruna discovered that several of the victims lived near his home and had attended high school with him.

Were the strange attacks in Mattoon in September 1944 an act of revenge, or were they caused by over active imaginations fed by years of stories of bizarre Nazi plots and chemical weapon attacks? The victim's testimony overwhelmingly pointed to a human perpetrator, but without more concrete evidence, it is unlikely that perpetrator will ever be found. One thing is certain: after that strange summer, the residents of Mattoon kept their windows closed for a long time.

Roads Less Traveled

Airtight Bridge

A irtight Bridge is one of Coles County's best kept secrets. Located along Airtight Road between Ashmore and Morgan townships, it is the only direct route between the village of Ashmore and the unincorporated towns of Bushton and Rardin. The location is isolated, and most people do not come upon it by accident. The bridge, which even 40 years ago was described as "old" and "creaky," already had an unsavory reputation, but the 1980 discovery of a woman's dismembered body in the Embarras River ignited local imaginations. Since that time, visitors have returned from nightly excursions with many unusual tales to tell.

Designed by Claude L. James, Airtight Bridge was built over the Embarras River in 1914 by the Decatur Bridge Company. Some say the bridge earned the name "Airtight" because of the unnatural stillness encountered while crossing it. Others, that the name came from a design flaw in early automobiles that caused them to stall when driving down the steep slope approaching from the east. Thanks to its remote location, it became known as a drinking spot for local teens and students from Eastern Illinois University. In 1981, it was added to the National Register of Historic Places.

One common legend about the bridge is that cars parked nearby will fail to start. In 2013, Michele Watson and two friends experienced this phenomenon firsthand. "We drove for what seemed like ages, and finally over the last hill sat the bridge..." she said. "We stopped the car, turned it off, and got out to walk the bridge. We were taking pictures, laughing, looking down the waterway, and remarking on the sound the bridge makes when you walk on it. I had assured them, I totally believed this bridge was just a legend, and we'd find nothing here.

"We'd been there about five minutes when I started to get very uneasy and felt watched. I said to the girls, 'Hey, let's get out of here, I just don't feel right.' So we headed back down the bridge toward the car. As my companion turned the key to start the car, my heart dropped. Click. Click. Click. Nothing. The car would not start. She tried several more times, but the car was dead. We were stuck.

"I panicked. Scenes from every bad horror movie flashed through my head. We found flashlights, grabbed what we needed to carry with us, and headed up the hill. Eventually we called 911 and the wonderful young man who answered was calm and reassuring and sent a sheriff's deputy to meet us. He met us at the car, and after reassuring us, he says 'I know where they found the body, would you like to see?' He showed us using his flashlight. We talked for hours, then he drove us home.

"Monday morning, we went to retrieve my friend's car and have it towed back to her hometown. She got into her car to see if it would turn over and it started like nothing was wrong! She drove it home. What I have blown off for years as a silly teenage urban legend is true."

In 2010, the Coles County Highway Department replaced the crumbling steel and concrete deck with wooden planks, reverting the bridge to its original appearance. But those rusted, burgundy trestles spanning the Embarras in rural Coles County will always elicit a tingle along the spines of visitors.

AIRTIGHT BRIDGE | PHOTO BY THE AUTHOR

DEAD MAN'S CURVE

Many communities in Illinois have an intersection or stretch of road to avoid where it's said car accidents frequently occur. Northwest suburban Des Plaines has "Suicide Circle", Spring Valley has "Help Me" Road, Henry County has "Death Curve", and the tiny town of Towanda has a "Dead Man's Curve" on Historic U.S. Route 66. Coles County's is unique, however, because its name predates the road itself. When settlers first crossed the wilderness of East Central Illinois, large groves of trees became important landmarks. One such grove, in LaFayette Township on the north branch of Kickapoo Creek, was originally known as Island Grove. It was two miles in diameter and filled with hackberry, elm, and oak trees, and supplied a neighboring village of Kickapoo Indians with firewood and wild game.

In March 1826, a man named Samuel Kellogg discovered the frozen body of a Sand Creek settler named Coffman sitting upright against a tree with his horse bridle thrown over his shoulder. Kellogg hoisted the dead man onto his horse and took him to a nearby settlement for burial. Since then, Island Grove has been known as "Dead Man's Grove."

In 1918, nearly a century after Coffman's frozen body was discovered in the grove, Illinois Route 16 opened to motorized traffic between Mattoon and Charleston. The road curved at a 90-degree angle in front of Oak Grove schoolhouse near the grove, which by that time had been reduced to a fraction of its original size. By the 1930s, news articles referred to it as "Dead Man's Grove Corner" or "Dead Man's Grove Curve." In the 1940s and '50s, the younger generation began to simply call it "Dead Man's Curve" because, they believed, numerous fatal accidents had occurred there.

One of the earliest and most dramatic accidents happened in the wee hours of Friday, February 1, 1935. Nineteen-year-old Harold Conard of Sullivan was joyriding with his brother and two friends when their sedan side-swiped a stopped truck as they headed west into the curve. The truck, they said, had unusually bright headlights. Rather than make the turn, they continued straight onto the road in front of the schoolhouse (today E County Road 900 N), where the accident occurred. Harold's passengers received only minor injuries in the rollover, but flying glass severed Harold's jugular vein and he died as passersby took them to the hospital. Originally, it was reported the truck fled the scene, but an investigation later exonerated the driver, Leland Kerans of Ashmore, who stopped to help pull Harold from the wreckage before driving off to summon an ambulance.

When a 4-lane highway, the present-day Route 16, was constructed between Mattoon and Charleston in 1962, the stretch of road containing Dead Man's Curve was re-named Illinois Route 316. Despite its reputation, county officials insisted the curve was nowhere near as dangerous as its reputation suggested. In 1984, Coles County Coroner Richard "Dick" Lynch told the Decatur *Herald and Review* there had only been five fatal accidents at the curve in the past 70 years. "Altering the curve won't change anything," he said. "Actually, it's not the curve that is unsafe and causes the accidents, it's the drivers."

Dead Man's Grove is gone today, replaced by a concrete mixing plant. The old Oak Grove schoolhouse is gone too, but the legend of "Dead Man's Curve" lives on. The curve is located along Illinois Route 316, at the intersection with E County Road 900 N, approximately five miles northeast of Mattoon.

DEAD MAN'S CURVE | PHOTO BY THE AUTHOR

HIDDEN HISTORY

CRIME

FRONTIER CRIME

From the beginning, Coles County was no stranger to violence and crime. Two battles between Illinois Rangers and American Indians, in 1815 and 1818, and the Charleston Riot in 1864 are just the most dramatic examples. According to *The History of Coles County* (1879), the early settlers of Wabash Point in Paradise Township had no tolerance for law breaking. One man was caught stealing cowhides and potatoes, and a swift trial and conviction followed. His punishment was 29 lashes with a whip and banishment from the settlement.

Morgan Township, which hugs the Embarras River, was named after David Morgan, a Kentuckian who arrived in Coles County in 1834. American Indians populated that section prior to his arrival. According to *The History of Coles County* (1879), a number of Indian burial grounds are scattered around Morgan Township, although none have been excavated by archeologists. In 1877 or '78, a man named Henry Curtis dug up a human skull and a few other bones. The skull possessed a small, round, bullet-like hole in the back. Curtis, shocked by his discovery, quickly reburied the skeleton and covered the site with rocks. It was never determined to whom the skeleton belonged, but this may have been Coles County's first murder mystery.

At least one geographic feature, Greasy Creek, got its name from the acts of notorious criminals. Under cover of darkness, a father and son, Jesse and William Chastene, allegedly stole their neighbor's hogs, dressed them alongside the creek, and discarded the innards into the water, making it greasy with fat and entrails. In the course of their thievery, they severed the animal's heads to prevent identification (the hogs were earmarked by their owners), then threw the heads in Greasy Creek. Jesse and William also sold a plot of land containing apple trees to David Morgan, removed the trees during the night, and carried them off to a new claim. David Morgan, incidentally, was also the area's first Justice of the Peace.

LYNCHINGS

In the nineteenth century, "lynch law" reigned. The most infamous incident in Coles County occurred in the early morning hours of Friday, February 16, 1856 when convicted murderer Adolphus Monroe was lynched by a mob of angry citizens. In October 1855, Adolphus got into a drunken altercation with his father-in-law, Nathan Ellington (who was the first county clerk), and gunned him down. Ellington and his wife, Fannie, strongly disapproved of their daughter Nancy's marriage to Adolphus, who had a reputation for drinking. Ellington confronted Adolphus about mistreating Nancy, and according to local historian Nancy Easter-Shick, Ellington struck Adolphus with his cane. Adolphus drew a small smoothbore pistol, shot him twice, and the two antagonists continued their mortal struggle on the floor. Adolphus was convicted of murder and sentenced to be hanged on February 15, 1856.

Thousands turned out to witness the execution, but Illinois Governor Joel Aldrich Matteson granted Adolphus a 90-day stay of execution. Sheriff John R. Jeffries printed 400 copies of the governor's order and distributed them among the crowd. This inflamed passions, a mob formed, and enraged Coles County citizens surrounded the brick jail in Charleston, which was then located on the west side of 6th Street between Madison and Jefferson streets (where the old post office building is today). The sheriff tried to calm them, but stood aside when it became clear his efforts were in vain. Inside the jail, Adolphus wrote: "I also leave my deep and bitter curse upon all who have either directly or indirectly anything in part to do with the mob who have basely murdered me... I summon them to meet me up there before that awful and final judge."

The mob broke through a wall on the north side of the jail, dragged the prisoner out, and strung him up from a large white oak tree 200 feet north of what is today the Jackson Avenue bridge over Town Branch. He was hoisted onto a wagon, reeling from the morphine smuggled to him by a friend, before the noose was slipped around his neck. Before he died, he reportedly told a man in the crowd: "I die, and if I go to hell, you will go to the same place, for you it was that sold me the whisky that has brought me to this terrible fate." Since 1962, the pistol Adolphus Monroe used to murder Nathan Ellington has been on display in the Coles County Circuit Clerk's office.

One of the darkest episodes in Coles County history came on Tuesday, June 26, 1888 when a mob lynched an African American man named William Moore for allegedly assaulting a teenage girl named Mary A. Bumgardner.

Nineteen-year-old Mary Bumgardner (also spelled Bingardiner or Baumgardner), daughter of Robert Bumgardner and Samantha Byers, was what we would today call a "troubled teen". She lived with her mother near the village of Altamont in Effingham County, Illinois. According to *The Chicago Tribune*, Robert deserted his wife and daughter several years prior, and since then their behavior had created "a scandal". In May, a neighbor's barn burned down, and suspicion fell on Mary. The village marshal told her to leave town or she would be arrested. On Saturday evening, June 23, 1888, Mary boarded a train to Shelby County, where her uncle, Frank Byers (Buyers) worked on a hay farm.

After midnight, the train rolled into the station at Mattoon, where Mary had a two-and-a-half-hour stopover. There she met William Moore, a 38-year-old African-American who, she said, was wearing a porter's badge. Moore was born in Virginia in 1850 and came to Mattoon in January 1887 with his wife and four children. Moore had most recently been employed as a porter at the Dole House Hotel, but was a bit of a ne'er-do-well who worked odd jobs to make ends meet.

Mary asked William Moore where she could get something to eat at that hour, and he offered to show her. She left her bag on the bench and followed him outside, where he led her up Union Street north of the Essex House to the outskirts of town. There, she alleged, she became suspicious and tried to run away but he overpowered and raped or sexually assaulted her. She escaped when he left to purchase food and made her way to the home of Mr. and Mrs. Jack Shea, who then took her back to the train depot and informed the police. Moore was quickly arrested. On Monday afternoon, both Moore and Mary Bumgardner appeared before Judge Robert H. McFadden (1834-1914) for a closed-door preliminary hearing to investigate the alleged assault. Moore was held on $1,000 bond and taken to the county jail in Charleston.

The story spread that a black man had "outraged" a young, innocent white girl. Early newspaper reports described her as a German immigrant, 16 years old, and a "young girl just budding into womanhood... her general appearance indicated her lack of acquaintance with the great world and its mysteries and sins..." Other, less flattering accounts described her as "not very bright", and "ignorant and innocent." Later, as reporters inquired into her background, they began to question her story. She was, her neighbors said, an untrustworthy fugitive with a bad reputation.

On Monday, June 25, Republicans in Mattoon and Charleston were celebrating the previous day's nomination of Benjamin Harrison and Levi P. Morton for president and vice president. The 1888 Republican National Convention was held in Chicago that year. Although Harrison won on the eighth ballot, former abolitionist Frederick Douglass became the first African-American to have his name included in a major party's roll call vote for presidential nomination. Bands played, cannons fired, and local Republican leaders gave speeches.

Meanwhile, conspirators gathered inconspicuously among the crowds. Among them, it was said, was a large contingent of strangers from Effingham and Shelby counties. When indictments for the ringleaders were later handed down, however, all were from Mattoon, including former Mattoon mayor John Byron Benefiel (1847-1938). J.B. Benefiel, a Democrat, was an entrepreneur and meat-market proprietor who was elected mayor c.1880 as temperance candidate. Some newspaper reports hinted that politics may have played a role in what happened next, since William Moore, a Republican, had days earlier gotten into a confrontation with a Democrat named Hoffman that was so forceful police had to intervene. According to the Decatur *Daily Republican*, "The Charleston and Mattoon people assert that the lynching was prompted largely by political feeling..."

That night, Coles County Sheriff Salem Wallace McClelland (1861-1941) let his guard down. His deputy, Dowling, shrugged off talk of a lynch mob as another empty threat and didn't bother informing the sheriff. After midnight on June 26, a mob of 150 to 200 masked men overwhelmed the two night watchmen in Charleston and surrounded the jail. About fifty men armed with revolvers appeared at the sheriff's office and escorted the jailer out, while others broke into William Moore's jail cell with chisels and sledges. Finally informed of what was happening, Sheriff McClelland and State's Attorney Samuel "Sam" Marion Leitch (1853-1889) hurried to the scene and pleaded with the mob to disburse. Leitch appeared to be making headway when he was roughly ejected from the jail at gunpoint.

The mob seized Moore, who "made no resistance whatever... he seemed to realize that he was in the hands of a merciless crowd, and from the time he left the jail until his place of execution was reached uttered no word of protest." They tied his hands behind his back and threw a rope around his neck. McClelland and Leitch followed, waiting for an opportunity to rescue the prisoner or plead for his life. The mob stopped beneath a telegraph pole in front of Richter's Hotel, but someone suggested a nearby water tank north across the railroad tracks opposite a freight depot.

They hauled Moore to the water tank, where they surrounded him and gave him an opportunity to kneel and pray, which he did. As they threw the rope over a cross-beam, State's Attorney Leitch stepped forward and asked Moore if he had committed the crime. "As I hope to be in Heaven in a few minutes, I did not," Moore replied. The mob hesitated. Seeing his last opportunity, Leitch swore he would prosecute Moore to the fullest extent and appealed to their sense of civic pride, saying what a disgrace another lynching would be to Charleston and Coles County. Finally, a man seized Leitch from behind and carried him off, and the mob hung William Moore by his neck from the water tank. After his body went limp, he was taken down and a few local residents attempted to resuscitate him. It was too late.

Moore's body was returned to the jail, where his wife, two grown step-daughters, and two young children tearfully took custody of his remains in a coffin provided by the county. "Many a deed of darkness would be abandoned in its conception could the perpetrator but know the effect its commission would have on innocent parties," wrote a reporter for the *Mattoon Gazette*. Moore was buried in Dodge Grove Cemetery's potter's field.

The lynching drew widespread public condemnation, and Coles County authorities promised to bring the perpetrators to justice and acted quickly to investigate. "No law-abiding citizen sanctions the work of the mob which hanged Moore," newspapers proclaimed. On July 11, the Coles County Board of Supervisors passed a resolution empowering Judge James F. Hughes (1839-1906) to call a special session of the circuit court and empanel a grand jury. Horace S. Clark (1840-1907), a city police magistrate and judge of the Common Pleas Court, and State's Attorney Samuel Leitch were tasked with prosecuting the offenders. Clark was also acting as Moore's widow's attorney and threatened a civil suit for damages of $5,000 against the perpetrators.

The grand jury was empaneled on August 4 and worked diligently for over two months when, on October 7, it handed down nine indictments for the lynching of William Moore. According to *The Daily Press* of Plainfield, New Jersey and other newspapers, the indicted mob leaders were all Mattoon residents: H.M. [Hans Marcus] O. Thode, L.D. Weaver, John Byers, William

Kincaid, R. Brewer, S.H. Kirkpatrick, Adolf Walker, Eli Myers, and J.B. Benefiel. Several of the accused were placed on bond, while others fled the area. Evidently none were successfully prosecuted, because in his 1905 *History of Coles County*, Charles Edward Wilson noted "his [Moore's] executioners have escaped punishment, except as their consciences could inflict."

What really happened in the early morning hours of June 24, 1888? Did politics play a role in what happened next? What led to the charges against the ringleaders being dismissed? The answers to these questions may never be known, but one thing is certain: the failure of Coles County authorities to hold anyone accountable for the lynching of William Moore was a dark chapter in the county's legal history.

JOHN MASON

In 1880, the cold-blooded murder of an elderly German-American farmer and shopkeeper named John Mason shocked Coles County residents. Though two suspects were arrested, they were acquitted at trial. To this day, the person or persons responsible for Mason's death remain a mystery.

John Mason was born in 1807 in Württemberg, Germany and came to the United States sometime prior to 1840. He married Christena Fogle (1815–1870) and the couple had four children. They lived in Ohio before coming to Coles County sometime in the late 1850s. There his son Henry married Theressa Louisa Raser (spelled Theresa Reasser in the marriage record), daughter of Frederick and Johanna Henryette C. (Henrietta) Raser, recent immigrants from Saxony, Germany, on January 18, 1870. John's wife, Christena, died at the age of 54 on February 26, 1870. Three months later, John and 45-year-old Henrietta were wed.

For the next ten years, the couple were prosperous farmers in Seven Hickory Township and owned a grocery store eight miles north of Charleston along the plank road. His property stretched outward from the northwest corner of the intersection of what is today State Highway 130 and County Road 1600N to County Road 1700N. John Mason's thrift and distrust of banks was widely known, and he lent money to his neighbors. The Chicago *Inter Ocean* reported he was worth $30,000, which would be over $800,000 today. This considerable stash was thought to be the motive for what transpired late one spring evening in 1880.

According to local newspaper accounts, John and Henrietta closed their store and retired to bed around 9:30 p.m. on Monday, April 19th. A knock at the door shortly followed, and a man's voice inquired about tobacco. John Mason, age 72, rose and walked into the store, which was adjacent to their bedroom. "You are late tonight," Henrietta heard him say. "What kind of tobacco was wanted?" Then came the report of a pistol and the sound of someone running.

When Henrietta rushed into the room, she saw her husband lying on the floor across his loaded shotgun, bleeding from a .32 caliber gunshot wound to the right eye. He was clinging to life but unable to speak. Henrietta ran outside to seek help. Jesse O'Hair, a neighbor, brought a doctor to the scene, but John was dead by the time they arrived.

Strangely, Henrietta had not heard any argument prior to the gunshot, and no cash was missing. Tracks were found leading to and from a nearby pond. The marshal arrested Noah Scott and Joel Towles (Joseph Toles/James Tales), "two hard characters", on suspicion three days later after they were found wandering Charleston with mud on their clothes, but evidently, they were let go.

In November 1880, a grand jury indicted two other men, Erastus McKee and Benjamin Kelly, for the crime. The trial began on November 27th and lasted only two days before a jury returned a verdict of not guilty due to conflicting testimony. The prosecution's witnesses were, reportedly, of low character, while the defense called several "respectable citizens" who saw McKee and Kelly in Charleston the night of the murder.

John Mason was interred near his first wife in Union Cemetery north of Rardin. Henrietta moved to Arcola in Douglas County and married a third time, to a man named Jacob Kramer. She died on March 8, 1918 at the age of 90. No one was ever convicted of John Mason's murder, and the perpetrator, or perpetrators, took their secret to the grave.

THE STRANGE DEATH OF CORA STALLMAN

Cora Stallman stood out. She was approximately six feet tall and 175 pounds, physically larger than average. She was a 45-year-old unmarried former schoolteacher, a college-educated woman from Cincinnati, Ohio who routinely rode a horse into town. Some neighbors described her as eccentric, odd, and even "stuck up" or "demented." Others that she was kind and benevolent, especially toward children. When Cora's brother-in-law discovered her body mostly submerged in a cistern on his wife's farm in Humboldt Township, it ignited a mystery that remains unsolved.

It was 1925, the year F. Scott Fitzgerald published *The Great Gatsby* and the battle between evolution and creationism was waged in the "Scopes Monkey Trial". On a 600-acre farm two miles southeast of Humboldt, Illinois, a village of approximately 330, in the early morning hours of Saturday, August 1, 49-year-old Tom Seaman went to check on his sister-in-law, Cora, but she was not at home. He sought out Boston Martin "Bos" Lilley (1886-1972), a tenant farmer on his wife's land, and together they searched the property, including a small cottage where Cora kept her belongings. Tom's wife, Anna, was away on a Mississippi River cruise.

"Then as we walked north my eyes fell on the cistern," Tom later testified. The wooden planks covering the opening were slightly ajar. "It was then about 5:30 o'clock. I remarked, 'I hope she ain't in there.' Then I looked down in the water and saw something like a coat. I got the clothes line prop and reached it down in the water and discovered then it was Cora down there." According to Coles County Coroner Frank Stephen Schilling (1881-1953), Cora was fully clothed and sitting in three-to-four feet of water, mostly submerged except for part of her face and back, with minor scratches on her forehead. A few nearly-illegible letters were found in the water.

Newspaper articles initially reported Cora Stallman's death as a suicide, but as authorities investigated, they found no easy answers. Her lungs were not filled with water, ruling out drowning, and there were no visible wounds on her body severe enough to cause death. Examination of her internal organs later found no evidence of poison or severe illness. The case only got stranger from there.

Thomas Ellison "Tom" Seaman (1876-1941) married Anna Stallman (1877-1962), his second wife, on August 16, 1919. Anna, from Cincinnati, had inherited the adjacent Lane Bogart farm. Shortly after marriage, the couple had a falling out and drew up a contract in which they would reside separately on their respective farms during the busy season, although Tom came to Anna's for one meal a day. Cora Stallman moved to Illinois about 1920 to act as her sister's business manager and lived in a small cottage on her sister's farm, where she had daily interactions with both Tom and Anna. Owing to their unusual arrangement, tongues wagged that "something" was going on between Tom and Cora, although both Tom and Anna denied it.

Then there were the letters. In the months preceding her death, Cora received dozens of threatening, often lengthy anonymous letters apparently written by multiple persons, including one signed "KKK". They described visceral, nasty disdain for Cora on behalf of local townspeople. "You are as common as dirt, and a regular snob. Impudent when you shop in Humboldt. Your horse is a nuisance, keep him where he belongs," one said, and "We know you are from a common family. You drive into Humboldt like you smelt a stink. If you don't like us, stay out you snot nose. You need not think you are so much either..." said another. Bos Lilley and his wife, Edith, and Tom Seaman also received threatening letters, some of which came after Cora's death. Cora and Anna had taken to wearing whistles for fear of being attacked.

At around 10:00 a.m. on Friday, July 31, Bos Lilley was speaking with Tom's nephew, Oscar Seaman, Elmer Howard, a tractor salesman from Arcola, and Howard's 14-year-old nephew, Keith Dixon, when they heard a sharp whistle coming from the direction of Anna Seaman's house. There they found Cora, who told them a strange man dressed in overalls and a straw hat had come out of Anna's house, struck her and knocked her down, and told her he would kill her if she told anyone what happened. The four men searched a nearby cornfield and found a straw hat and overalls.

That evening, Cora was seized by a fit of delirium, tossing and turning in bed. She raved about "nasty medicine" the man who attacked her made her drink. Tom, who called Oscar and his wife to come over to help, offered to send for a doctor, but Cora said she didn't need one. At around 10:00 p.m., she settled down and ate bread and butter and drank tea. After another hour, she told Oscar and his wife to go home. Then, at around midnight, she told

Tom, who slept in his clothes on the porch in case something happened, to go to bed. Later, Tom said he awoke that morning at 5:00 a.m. to what he thought was the sound of Cora moving around the house. He left to milk the cow, and when he returned, she was nowhere to be found.

That was when Tom sought Bos Lilley's help and the two men pulled Cora's body from the cistern. A short time later, after Coroner Frank Schilling arrived, they found a large piece of cardboard on the porch with "We have got your sister" painted in crude lettering.

Both Anna Seaman and Edith Lilley suspected Cora had written the threatening notes and letters herself, although the handwriting did not match her's. Both thought she was disturbed. "Of course, she committed suicide," Anna, who contradicted herself several times, said. "She had been unbalanced for a long time." Edith hesitantly agreed, testifying, "I never thought Cora crazy until the last week or two, when she was always watching the road and then coming in and reporting she had seen curious acting people no one else had ever seen. It looked queer to us." Cora's diary was filled with codes and cryptic symbols.

The anonymous letter writers were never found, nor was the stranger who attacked Cora on the Friday morning before she died.

Was Cora Stallman murdered? Did she commit suicide? Or did she die of fright, hiding from imaginary pursuers? Almost exactly one month after Cora's body was found, after interviewing over 45 witnesses, the coroner's jury determined that she died of "unknown causes." It recommended her case be taken up by a grand jury, but to this day, no one has ever been held responsible for her death.

THE COX MURDERS

"Violence is the greatest obscenity against man," the *Journal Gazette* editorialized. "We are stunned. We are shocked. We are appalled. But we can't tell you why such things happen." Any murder is a tragedy, but murders involving children are particularly horrifying. In the spring of 1968, Coles County experienced its worst mass murder before or since when a young man from Texas took the lives of five children from the Cox family on a warm but windy Saturday afternoon.

Thomas Charles Fuller II was a below average student, 5-feet, 8-inches tall with dark hair and brown eyes, "very quiet and polite," but "a loner" and "sullen as a preacher." The 18-year-old senior at Mattoon High School had recently moved from Texas to Mattoon with his parents, William and Lucy Fuller, and three siblings. He was a member of the junior ROTC program and dated 16-year-old Edna Louise Cox, a pretty girl with brunette, bubble flipped hair.

The Cox family lived in a two-story, white clapboard farmhouse eight miles northwest of Mattoon in North Okaw Township. William Junior (1923-2010) and Lydia Mary (1929-2006) Cox had a large Catholic family with nine children at home: Kenneth Winford, Theresa Jean, Edward Louis "Louie", Mary Katherine "Cathy", Gary Lee, Edna Louise, Billie Colleen, Timothy Leroy "Timmy", and Patricia Ann "Patty". The children had two married half-sisters: Marie Rose Cline and Christine Beahl, and two adult half-brothers: Robert Joseph and William George. Christine and Robert lived elsewhere in Illinois, and William was serving in the U.S. Navy.

The trouble began around Christmas when Fuller asked William Cox, a construction worker for R. R. Donnely & Sons, permission to marry his daughter. William declined, citing Fuller's age, his lack of employment, and a desire for Louise to finish school. Fuller, who believed Louise's family was persecuting her with burdensome chores while they were "always laying around," fumed. "Perhaps I've always wanted to kill..." he later wrote in his diary. Among other wild fantasies, he planned to kill her entire family, then the couple would flee to Canada. According to Fuller's friend and classmate, Sammy Lee Davis, Fuller contemplated the plan for weeks.

On Saturday, April 27, 1968, around six months after Fuller and Louise began dating, Fuller hitched a ride to the Cox farmhouse and arrived around 11:00 a.m., but did not eat lunch with the family. He was wearing a green Army jacket with a PFC rank sewn on the sleeve, a gray t-shirt, khaki pants, and brown suede boots. A pocket knife was tucked into one boot and a .22 caliber pistol in a leather holster. After lunch, Fuller claimed that a sibling struck Louise. When she chased her assailant upstairs, four others followed and ganged up on her, kicking and beating her. Lydia Cox, her mother, would not let Fuller run upstairs to help. Fuller stepped outside, he said, because he couldn't stand to hear Louise screaming. Louise testified at trial that her siblings had "pulled her hair, hit her and tickled her".

Shortly after, William Cox took Timmy, 15, to help fix a truck at his brother's house while Lydia heated up two pies for an afternoon snack. When 14-year-old Patty accidentally leaned too close to the gas stove, her blouse caught fire and burned her back. Lydia frantically called Marie to come take them to Mattoon Memorial Hospital, which she and a neighbor did around 4:15 p.m., leaving the remaining children alone. According to Fuller, Louie, 16, and Gary, 7, bugged him to go outside and shoot birds with his .22 caliber pistol, and he reluctantly agreed after Louise told him Billie Colleen, 12, would help her with the dishes. Fuller took the boys past an old wooden double corn crib approximately 200 feet from the house. Five-year-old Kenneth, the youngest, followed, and Theresa and Cathy went to play outside.

Fuller later described watching himself commit the murders as though he was having an out-of-body experience. Louie egged him on to shoot the birds. "Go ahead, shoot, shoot," Louie said, but Fuller turned his gun on the boys instead. He shot Louie first, then Gary, and then Kenneth; all three in the head. Kenneth died instantly, he said, but he had to return to Louie and Gary to finish them off. The boys' bodies were later found outside the northwest corner of the corn crib. Kenneth lay west of the crib. At that point, Fuller returned to the house to get a drink of water.

"Where's Louis?" Louise asked.

"Out back," replied Fuller.

Fuller then lured nine-year-old Theresa and eight-year-old Cathy to the corn crib by asking them if they wanted to shoot rats. Instead, he shot Theresa twice and Cathy multiple times in the head just inside the crib's southern entrance. He then returned to the house for another drink of water. "Shot some birds," he told his girlfriend. Billie later recalled him saying, "I've killed five little birds. Come on out and see."

COX FAMILY GRAVES IN CALVARY CEMETERY | PHOTO BY THE AUTHOR

It was 5:00 p.m. when Marie and Lydia returned home. Without saying goodbye to Louise, Fuller asked Marie for a ride back to Mattoon. She dropped him off at the corner of 33rd Street and DeWitt Avenue around 5:20, and Fuller wandered the streets until he ran into his 17-year-old friend Samuel Lee Davis near the Penn Central train yard near Moultrie Avenue. There, Fuller confessed to murdering the Cox children "Because he [Davis] knew it was going to happen."

As the sun went down at the Cox home, Lydia sent Louise to holler for the other children to come inside. The yard was eerily silent. Louise and Billie saw their sisters lying on the corn crib floor and ran back into the house. "Theresa and Cathy must have fallen from the rafters," they frantically reported. Lydia phoned her husband to come home right away. As William pulled up to the driveway, he saw Billie trying to flag down help. It was worse than he feared. The girls' bodies were cold and lifeless. He discovered the three boys nearby. Unable to comprehend what happened, the Cox family first called the Mitchell-Jerdan Funeral Home and George Jerdan arrived at the house before the police.

Shortly before 7:00 p.m., Samuel Davis and his mother walked into the Mattoon police department and reported that an acquaintance told him five Cox children had been murdered.

Within minutes, Coles County Deputy Sheriff David O'Dell was on his way to the Cox residence. This triggered a chain of events culminating in a massive manhunt involving over 100 officers and volunteers. Roadblocks stopped traffic at all roads leading into Mattoon, but Thomas Fuller had slipped away. He walked all night along the railroad tracks until he ended up twelve miles away in Charleston. George Bosler, an Eastern Illinois University security guard, and Jack Turner, a Charleston police officer, saw Fuller at the intersection of 4th Street and Lincoln Avenue around 6:30 a.m. and took him into custody. Fuller surrendered without incident. In a matter of hours, he appeared before a judge and Coles County State's Attorney Ralph D. Glenn (1929-2018) charged him with five counts of first-degree murder.

Funerals for the five children were held at Immaculate Conception Catholic Church and they were interred in identical white coffins at Calvary Cemetery on 19th Street in Mattoon. Sister Rosita, principal of St. Mary and St. Joseph parochial schools, cancelled classes the day of the funerals.

When asked how she felt about Fuller now, Louise replied, "I hate him, I hate him, I hate him."

At first, Fuller pleaded not guilty to the murder charges, but after hearing damning preliminary testimony, he decided to change his plea. On October 24 at around 2:30 p.m., his public defender told the judge, "The defendant, Your Honor, wishes to withdraw his previous plea of not guilty and enter a plea of guilty." The decision shocked members of the press, who had prepared themselves for a long and sensational trial. The *Journal Gazette* had to stop their printing press and recall delivery trucks in order to get a story about the change of plea into Thursday's evening edition. On Tuesday, December 10, 1968, Circuit Judge Harry Ingalls Hannah (1890-1973) sentenced Fuller to two consecutive sentences of 70 to 99 years in the Illinois State Penitentiary at Joliet. William Cox was outraged, believing that Fuller's crime warranted the death penalty. "Why in hell can't he die the way my babies did?" he shouted as he was escorted to the elevator after being restrained by two sheriff's deputies.

After the murders, William Cox struggled to come to terms with what happened, became a Jehovah's Witness, and wrote about his family's experience in *Awake!*. Thomas C. Fuller is currently prisoner #C10244 at Graham Correctional Center in Hillsboro. All his attempts at early parole have been denied, and members of the Cox family have fought to keep it that way. He is not scheduled to be released until 2056.

The Tragic '70s

T he 1970s were a difficult time in the United States, with economic slowdowns, high inflation, soaring crime rates, political scandal, and civil unrest. A general sense of pessimism pervaded the country, and for residents of Coles County, frustration mounted over a string of brutal homicides. In a span of less than five years, between 1972 and 1977, there were at least eight murders and one suspicious death in and around Coles County. Many of these cases were never solved or the perpetrators escaped justice. Public sentiment was so inflamed, a rumor circulated that someone erected a billboard in Florida saying "Go to Coles County if you want to commit murder and get away with it." Over 45 years later, the cases may have gone cold but the victims' families still pray for answers.

Kenton Gene Ashenbramer

C larence W. "Jack" Ashenbramer (1909-1996) and his wife Helen Grace returned from a weeklong vacation to their home at 920 Piatt Avenue in Mattoon at around 2:30 p.m. on Sunday, August 27, 1972. Their son's red 1967 Ford Fairlane with a white stripe was not parked outside. When they entered the back bedroom where their 34-year-old son Kenton Gene Ashenbramer was staying, they made a sickening discovery. He was lying across his bed with multiple stab wounds, a knife nearby. The horrified parents called police and an investigation was launched.

Kenton Ashenbramer was a former Marine with three children who worked at the Firestone Tire and Rubber Company and had lived in Mattoon since 1955. On Saturday evening, August 26, 1972, he met two 26-year-old women, Ann Cole and Shirley Mae Moutria, at a bar called Club Oasis, 1406 Broadway Avenue in Mattoon. The previous day, Ann Cole and Shirley Mae Moutria left East St. Louis, Illinois and traveled to visit Moutria's mother in Watson, south of Effingham. Ann and Shirley then went to Mattoon on Saturday to find Shirley's ex-husband and two kids. They checked into a motel, then went bar hopping. At Club Oasis, Kenton and Shirley hit it off. Shirley was described as having shortly-cropped blonde hair and masculine features.

At around 1:00 a.m., Kenton and Shirley decided to go back to Kenton's house while Ann returned to the motel. Eyewitnesses saw Kenton and Shirley on his parent's porch at the corner of Piatt Avenue and N 10th Street around 2:00 a.m. That was the last time he was seen alive.

Shirley later confessed the couple drank, took drugs, and had sex. In a letter to her parents, she said she became sick and wanted to leave but Kenton tried to persuade her to stay. She blacked out, and when she regained consciousness, Kenton was dead. She claimed she was abused as a child and raped by a truck driver the previous summer, and her encounter trigged a violent reaction. Coles County Coroner David Swickard had determined Kenton died from a deep stab wound to the abdomen at approximately 8:00 a.m. Sunday morning.

Shirley stole Kenton's car and fled west with Ann Cole, triggering a nationwide manhunt. After two months on the run, the FBI apprehended the two women on October 31 in El Monte, near Los Angeles, California. Ann voluntarily returned to Coles County to face charges of vehicle theft, while Shirley Mae Moutria was extradited to face charges of theft and three counts of murder. She initially pleaded innocent, but later changed her plea to guilty in exchange for a reduced charge of voluntary manslaughter. On Thursday, March 8, 1973, Judge Carl Lund sentenced her to six to 18 years in prison and recommended psychological treatment.

SHIRLEY ANN RARDIN

At around 12:30 a.m. Monday morning, July 3, 1973, Shirley Ann Rardin, a 20-year-old sophomore art major at Eastern Illinois University, finished her shift at Hardee's at the corner of 4th Street and Lincoln Avenue in Charleston, changed clothes, and said goodbye to her coworkers. She was 5 feet 7 inches tall, 125 pounds, with shoulder-length blonde hair and blue-green eyes. She was wearing wide flare jeans, a black halter top, and blue tennis shoes, with $5 in her pocket. Shirley was a local girl, having graduated from Charleston High School in 1971, and a young divorcee. She had been previously married to a former manager at Hardee's named Rich DeWitt.

Shirley was renting Apt. 203 in the Lincolnwood building at 2210 9th Street, exactly one mile from the Hardee's, and was believed to be heading there after work. She usually rode her bike to and from work, but that night she walked. If she ever arrived, no one knew. Medication she needed to take four times daily for a serious medical condition was later found in her apartment.

Her boyfriend, David Thomas, a fellow EIU student, reported her missing to Charleston police at 1:14 a.m Tuesday. The search dragged on for almost a week, but police were hampered by the fact that Shirley was a legal adult and could do as she pleased. As the days passed without any leads, however, they began to assume the worst.

On the afternoon of Saturday, July 7, four teenage boys were camping in Barrett's Woods approximately five miles south of unincorporated Logan, northeast of Paris, in Edgar County not far from the Indiana state line. At around 4:00 p.m., they were tubing in Brouilletts Creek and decided to cut through the woods back to their campsite. About 15 yards from the creek, near an isolated party spot, they stumbled upon Shirley Ann Rardin's nude body lying face down across a rough trail, partially decomposed in the summer heat. She was later identified by a ring she wore and other personal items found at the scene.

The Rardin case caught local law enforcement by surprise. Charleston Police Detective Ed Kallis told the Decatur *Herald and Review* "I don't think in 16 years of police work in this area that I've ever seen anything like this involving a girl." EIU's Head of Security John Pauley agreed, saying, "In my experience as a law enforcement officer of more than 20 years in the Charleston area, I know of no Eastern student being murdered..."

After initial confusion over her cause of death, forensic specialists in Springfield determined she had been shot in the head at close range, but the bullet was never found. Because of the crime scene's isolated location, police believed her killer must have been familiar with the area. They interviewed several people but there were no suspects. In 1982, Shirley's name was mentioned in the trial of Randy Wright, who was accused of murdering Edgar County Deputy Sheriff George Redman, Jr. in 1974. Several witnesses testified that Wright had bragged about killing Shirley for being a "narc". Wright, however, was acquitted and the judge threw out testimony about Shirley's murder because it was irrelevant to that case. To this date, no one has ever been charged with Shirley Ann Rardin's murder.

BARBARA SUE BEASLEY

As the summer of '73 dragged on, Coles County suffered the loss of another daughter at the hands of an unknown assailant. At around 10:00 a.m. on Friday, August 3, 1973, 11-year-old Barbara Sue Beasley of Mattoon disappeared while riding her white Stingray bicycle near the Cross County Mall. She was approximately 5 feet tall, 95 pounds, with blonde hair and green eyes, wearing slacks and a blue blouse. She lived on E. DeWitt Street, and her father, Warren Beasley, worked at the nearby General Steel and Metals plant. Her parents reported her missing on Saturday.

On the evening of Tuesday, August 7th, exactly one month after Shirley Ann Rardin's body was found, two teenage boys left the Cross County Mall and headed to hunt turtles in a drainage ditch one-quarter mile north of the railroad tracks. At around 6:00 p.m., they stumbled upon the badly swollen nude body of a girl lying on her back in two inches of water under a pipe that ran across the ditch west of Columbia Machine Company. The girl's blouse was beneath her body, pants wrapped around her left arm, and her other clothes, alongside her bicycle, were strewn along the drainage ditch approximately 35 feet south. The boys ran back to the mall and called the police.

Though Barbara had no dental records, there was enough other evidence to identify her body. Investigators, however, found no obvious marks or wounds to indicate a cause of death.

Barbara's 14-year-old brother, Tommy, later testified he last saw Barbara with a 6-foot tall, 38-year-old man named Clarence L. Foster near the railroad tracks. He left to get something to eat at a nearby root beer stand, but when he returned, his sister was gone. Foster, who also lived on DeWitt Street, worked at the same General Steel and Metals plant as their father. He had been charged with a residential burglary earlier that spring. Another witness, Randall Trader, claimed Foster confessed to him while drunk.

Cross-examination, however, found holes in their testimony. Tommy Beasley was developmentally disabled, and Trader, a convicted felon, changed his story several times. Coles County State's Attorney Bobby Sanders dismissed all charges against Clarence Foster on April 11, 1974 due to lack of evidence. Foster later briefly escaped from jail but was recaptured and incarcerated on the burglary charge. The murder of Barbara Sue Beasley remains unsolved.

JOE CARL PLUMLEY

The discovery of Barbara Beasley's body was still in the headlines on the morning of Friday, August 10, 1973, when a passing motorist on Illinois State Route 16 saw a truck parked alongside the road near the Moultrie/ Coles County line one mile east of Gays, Illinois. A man's body, later identified as 34-year-old Joe Carl Plumley, was lying face down in a nearby ditch, his wallet missing. Plumley, from Tupelo, Oklahoma, was a foreman for Morrison Construction Company working a temporary job and staying at Carroll's Motel in Mattoon. He had been shot twice—once in the back with a shotgun and again in the back of the head with a .22 caliber pistol.

Police suspected Plumley had been lured to that spot by a late-night phone call to his motel room. Around 9:40 p.m., a witness described seeing Plumley's truck and a light-colored car along the roadside where his body was discovered the next day. Eventually, two men, 24-year-old Buford Hobbie of Hendrix, Oklahoma and 23-year-old Oliver Harold Morris of Commerce, Texas, were charged with his murder. Three women, including Plumley's widow, Phillis, his mother-in-law, Joyce Hackworth, and his sister-in-law, Linda Hobbie Sims, were charged with conspiracy to commit murder.

The Plumley murder trial got underway at the Coles County Courthouse on June 19, 1974, nearly a year after his body was found. The prosecution's case, however, quickly collapsed when several key witnesses refused to testify. There was no physical evidence tying the men or women to the crime, and the murder weapons were never found. "We have no case," State's Attorney Bobby Sanders reportedly told the court. Sanders wanted the opportunity to charge them later if more evidence emerged, but Judge Carl Lund sided with the defense, ruling that Hobbie and Morris could not be charged twice for the same offense. They were both released into police custody due to other unrelated criminal charges.

Citizens were outraged, and the Mattoon *Journal-Gazette* editorialized: "The all-too-true and often heard remark that 'if you want to commit murder and get away with it do it in Coles County' must be disproved." But the body count continued to rise.

JAMES R. FRYER

Shortly after midnight on Monday, October 1, 1973, 16-year-old James H. Fryer, a junior at Mattoon High School, was working alone at the Owens service station at 720 Charleston Street in Mattoon when two robbers burst through the door, cleaned $488 out of the back room, shot him several times, and took off. A coworker, who happened to stop by, found James lying on the floor in a pool of blood. The teen languished for several days at the hospital before dying on Wednesday afternoon. He had been shot five times in the head, once in the jaw, and once in his hand.

In the last week of November 1973, police arrested 24-year-old Stephen M. Watson and 20-year-old Michael W. Beavers, both Mattoon residents, for the crime. Watson had been implicated in several other burglaries. The case never went to trial because Beavers agreed to testify against Watson in exchange for prosecutors dropping the charges against him. On June 3, 1974, Watson reached a plea bargain with State's Attorney Bobby Sanders, and the judge sentenced him to 17 to 27 years in prison.

LINDA DIANE SHRIVER

Twenty-three-year-old Linda Diane Shriver belonged to a church-going family. She graduated from Mattoon High School in 1970, worked at Horn's onion ring factory in Mattoon, and was engaged to a Decatur man named Robert Gilbert, Jr., with a wedding date set for June 7th. At around 8:30 p.m. on Saturday, March 9, 1974, she left her home at 1828 Maple Avenue in Mattoon, telling her parents she was going out for a Coke. A Mattoon policeman named Archie Armer later recalled seeing Linda driving east on Broadway Avenue between 9:30 and 9:40 p.m. That was the last time she was seen alive.

At around 10:00 p.m., a passing motorist stopped to investigate an abandoned car approximately 2.5 miles west of Mattoon on Dole Road, a quarter-mile north of Western Avenue. The car was still running, a woman's purse was inside, and a pair of shoes were nearby. The items belonged to Linda Diane Shriver. The discovery touched off a wide-ranging search involving Illinois State Police and sheriff's deputies from Coles and neighboring counties that lasted throughout the night and into the next day. At around 3:00 p.m. Sunday, a family friend found Linda's nude body southwest of Lake Paradise in a culvert under a bridge along E County Road 250 N, one mile west of Zion Hill United Methodist Church. The site was approximately seven miles south of her car.

THE RIDDLE 1970 YEARBOOK PHOTO OF LINDA DIANE SHRIVER

Coles County Coroner Richard "Dick" Lynch later determined Linda had been raped and strangled. He also found damage to her nose, mouth, and lower jaw, but could not determine what caused it. Investigators found no fingerprints inside her car, and Linda's clothes, aside from her shoes, seemed to vanish. The discoveries, or lack thereof, raised more questions than answers. Where was Linda between the time she left home and the time policeman Archie Armer saw her on Broadway? If Linda was driving east on Broadway, why did she turn around and head west outside of town? How did her body end up seven miles from her car?

"And there is one final question which no one appears to be willing to face," reporter Harry Reynolds wrote in the *Journal Gazette*. "Will it happen again?"

Though Coles County Sheriff Paul Smith increased nighttime patrols, police had no leads.

"What does it take to open our eyes?" Linda Shriver's family asked in an open letter to the *Journal Gazette*. "It can happen to you! It has to us as a family and as a city and unless we do something it can happen again, maybe even to you! What can we do about it? ...We cannot remain mute while the very foundation of decency is crumbling around us until we cannot discern what is decent and what is not, what is right and what is not."

A $10,000 reward offered in the summer of 1977 failed to solicit any new leads, and the case went cold.

DARWIN RAY WEBB

Thirteen months after Linda Diane Shriver's murder, the frozen body of a 29-year-old man from Lancaster, Texas named Darwin Ray Webb was discovered in a deep ditch along Illinois State Route 316, three-quarters of a mile west of Loxa Road. A work crew was patching the road when they discovered Webb's body shortly before noon on Tuesday, February 11, 1975. The 5-feet 6-inch tall Webb was wearing brown shoes, bluejeans, a flowered shirt, and gold corduroy jacket, and was laying on his back parallel with the road. His chest and neck bore wounds from two shotgun blasts at close range.

Darwin Ray Webb and 30-year-old Russell Lee Roberts of Warrensburg, Illinois were suspected of robbing an IGA store in Mattoon the previous Friday. At approximately 7:06 p.m. on February 7th, two gunmen wearing ski masks and ponchos armed with shotguns cleaned out the front registers and a safe at Taylor's IGA at 1316 DeWitt Avenue. One customer, a man named Joe Mitchell, tried to intervene and grab a shotgun from one of the men. It went off in the struggle, blowing a hole in the ceiling. The second gunman struck Joe on the back of the head with the butt of his shotgun and the pair fled. Before they took off, a bystander wrote down their getaway car's license plate number.

At 12:20 a.m. Saturday morning, police arrested 5-foot 9-inch, 170-pound Russell Lee Roberts at the intersection of 21st Street and Western Avenue, approximately one mile southwest of the store. He was driving a white and blue 1969 four-door Chevrolet. At some point, Roberts may have switched plates because according to the *Journal Gazette*, his car did not match the description of the getaway vehicle given by eyewitnesses. Prosecutors charged Roberts with armed robbery.

Coles County Coroner Richard Lynch theorized based on local weather and evidence at the crime scene that Darwin Ray Webb had been killed sometime between late Friday night and early Saturday morning, February 7th or 8th. An inch and a half of snow fell on Saturday, and there was no snow underneath Webb's body. A corpse would not produce enough heat to melt that much snow, he reasoned. Because of the freezing temperatures, however, it was impossible to precisely determine time of death.

There was no evidence directly tying Webb to the IGA robbery, or to Russell Lee Roberts. Webb and Roberts were both at the Macon County Jail in Decatur from January 30 to February

3 and were released on bond within days of each other, but otherwise, investigators could not establish any relationship between them. Was it a coincidence both men ended up in Coles County, or that Webb was killed by the same type of weapon used in the IGA robbery? If not, what would lead one accomplice to murder the other?

In 1975, Roberts pleaded guilty to a reduced charge of robbery and was sentenced to one year in prison. To this date, no second person has been charged in the IGA robbery, and no one has been charged with the murder of Darwin Ray Webb.

ANDY LANMAN

A t around 12:30 a.m. on Wednesday, February 23, 1977, 29-year-old Andy Lee Lanman was last seen leaving the house of Dr. Andrew Griffiths, a local dentist, on 18th Street in Charleston and getting into a car with several unidentified people, saying he was going to a party. He was wearing a green, military-style coat. Lanman, a senior theater major at Eastern Illinois University and student art teacher at Mattoon High School, belonged to a local family and served as a parachute rigger in the U.S. Air Force in Vietnam. He lived in an apartment building at 1624 University Drive in Charleston, was 5-feet 5-inches tall, weighing 150 pounds, with brown eyes and curly brown hair.

Harold Lanman reported his son missing on March 2, over one week after Andy allegedly got into an unidentified car and disappeared into the night. On March 5, Les Easter and Mike Lanman, Andy's cousin, and their fraternity brothers from Sigma Pi led a wide-ranging search coordinated with local law enforcement involving two airplanes and a boat. After several days, the volunteers came up empty handed. Then, at approximately 4:00 p.m. on Sunday, March 20, 1977, two hunters stumbled upon Andy's body 150 to 200 feet from the road in tall grass near a wooded party spot known as "The Cellar" five miles south of Charleston between the Embarras River and 18th Street (S. Fourth Street Road). His green jacket was missing, and the only things in his pocket were a set of keys and a nickel. The Cellar was an old concrete storm cellar north of the intersection of 18th Street and E. County Road 420 N. Today it is on private property, but in the 1970s it played host to numerous keggers and wild parties.

Deepening the mystery, Andy had no visible wounds or markings that would indicate cause of death. A toxicology screening later determined his body contained six to ten times a lethal dose of morphine. For that reason, investigators would not rule out homicide. "If as suspected, foul play was responsible for the tragic death of Andy Lanman, we hope Coles County authorities will be able to improve on their performances in past slayings and solve the case," 'Mat' Toon, a cartoon character personifying the *Journal Gazette* editorial board, said on March 21. "At least four murders have occurred in recent years and not a single conviction has been obtained."

Dr. Andrew Griffiths, Terry LeMay, and Gary Stuffle were the last known people to see Andy Lanman alive. Gary Stuffle was the brother of Illinois State Representative Larry Stuffle (1949-2016) and a close friend of Andy. Larry Stuffle represented the Illinois 53rd District from 1977 to 1983. According to Charleston Mayor Robert L. "Bob" Hickman (1938-2016), Stuffle repeatedly accused local law enforcement of harassing him and trying to frame him for a drug crime. "If you pigs don't quit harassing me and my employees I'll have your jobs," he allegedly shouted at officers sent to his office on 6th Street. Stuffle denied the allegations to the *Journal Gazette*, but did accuse local police of following his brother, pulling his brother away from Andy's funeral for questioning, and planting a suspicious package at his office door.

At an April 14 inquest into Andy Lanman's death, Dr. Griffiths refused to answer any questions and invoked his Fifth Amendment right against self-incrimination. According to the *Journal Gazette*, he then collapsed outside the room in City Hall where the inquest was being held. The inquest jury requested the Illinois Department of Education and Registration investigate Griffiths for failing to keep adequate records of drugs used in his dentist office over a two-year period. Similar charges were eventually filed against Griffiths' father, Dr. Robert H. Griffiths (1921-1995), also a dentist, but a judge cleared him in September 1979. Andrew Griffiths moved to Watertown, New York, where he continued his dental practice.

No one was ever held criminally liable for Andy Lanman's death, although his parents filed a civil suit in 1979 against Robert and Andrew Griffiths, Terry LeMay, and Gary Stuffle. The individuals Andy left with after midnight on February 23 have never been identified, and the events leading to his morphine overdose remain a mystery.

SUSAN REDDICK

Clear skies and a temperature above 60 degrees sent mushroom hunters combing through the woods of east central Illinois that Sunday, April 24, 1977. Honeycombed heads of morel mushrooms soaked up the sunshine after steady rain for the previous two days. At 10:55 a.m., a Cumberland County mushroom hunter stumbled upon the body of 19-year-old Susan Reddick lying face down under a bridge in the Fulfer Branch of Muddy Creek in Cottonwood Township. She was barefoot, wearing blue jeans and a t-shirt, and had suffered severe head trauma.

Susan Reddick's body was identified thanks to a birth certificate she kept in her pocket because she didn't have a driver's license. Becky Sanders, Susan's sister, told authorities she last saw Susan at a Charleston bar on the night of Friday, April 22 with a 27-year-old Mattoon man. A toxicology screening reportedly came back negative for drug use, and Cumberland County Coroner Charles E. Hiles determined she died of head injuries and skull fractures from a blunt object. Though police interviewed several persons of interest, the case seemingly went cold.

Then, in February 1978, an inmate at the Vandalia Correctional Center named Jerry Lynn Ross was paroled into the custody of Coles County law enforcement on charges of arson and burglary. A parole board member tried to stop Ross' parole when he discovered another inmate alleged the prisoner had confessed to Susan Reddick's murder, but because Ross had never been charged with that crime, the parole board could not revoke his parole. If not for the pending charges in Coles County, Ross would have walked free. "It is rare that the alleged violation is such a serious one and there was no arrest," Parole Board Chairman James Irving remarked.

Frustrated with a lack of progress in the case, Susan's sister-in-law wrote a letter to the *Journal Gazette*, published on March 24, 1978. "Miss Reddick was a young woman and she was brutally killed almost a year ago," she wrote. "I find it inconceivable that this murder plus the other four that have happened in our area is unsolvable. ...There are possibly five murderers running loose and the police still don't have enough evidence to make an arrest?"

Finally, on April 6, 1978, a Coles County grand jury indicted 32-year-old Jerry Ross for Susan Reddick's murder. Ross lived in Mattoon and was a career criminal, having been convicted of multiple armed robberies in Coles County and at one time escaped from an Indiana penal institution. He was on parole at the time of Susan's murder. It seems Susan spent all Saturday, April 23, 1977, with her boyfriend, 30-year-old Fred A. Fasig (1947-2004). Late in the afternoon, Fasig introduced Susan to Jerry Ross at Pat's Lounge in Mattoon, where Fasig elicited Ross' help in selling drugs. They spent some time in Cumberland County before returning to Mattoon, where Fasig and Susan passed out in Fasig's car after midnight early Sunday morning at the intersection of 13th Street and Broadway Avenue. Police officers later testified to seeing Fasig and a young woman sleeping in his car at that intersection, as well as stopping Jerry Ross for a traffic offense nearby.

Fasig's mother testified that he came home, alone, between 1:30 a.m. and 2:00 a.m. Sunday morning. According to an inmate named Glen E. Leonard, Jerry Ross confessed that he had met Fasig and Susan at the intersection of 13th Street and Broadway and offered to given Susan a ride home. He then took her to an abandoned farmhouse near Janesville at the border of Coles and Cumberland counties, seven miles north of Toledo and about 1.5 miles from where Susan's body was found. According to Leonard, the two drank and smoked pot. When Susan rejected Ross' sexual advances, he became enraged, and bludgeoned her to death. Blood on a baseball bat later taken from Ross' home had the same uncommon blood type as Susan Reddick.

Ross maintained his innocence, but the matching blood type and other testimony was enough to sway the jury in the opposite direction. On October 3, 1978, after less than six hours of deliberation, the jury found Ross guilty of murdering Susan Reddick. He was sentenced to 20 to 60 years in prison, in addition to a five to 15-year sentence for arson and burglary.

AIRTIGHT BRIDGE MURDER

I t was a pleasant Sunday morning on October 19, 1980. William and Tim Brown, two brothers from rural Urbana, were on a deer hunting trip when they took the road down to Airtight at around 11:00 a.m. As they crossed the bridge, one of the brothers noticed something unusual in the shallow waters of the Embarras, so they pulled over to the side of the road. At the same time, a local farmer named Victor Hargis was on his way to assist his son in digging a well. Seeing both the men and the partially decomposed remains, he stopped and joined William in going down to the river's edge to take a closer look. The two could hardly believe their eyes.

Victor sprang into action. He drove home and called the Sheriff's Department. Darrell Cox, a deputy at the time, was at the firing range when he got the call. It took him nearly 20-minutes to navigate the back roads from Charleston to the bridge, but he was familiar with the route because it was one the Sheriff's Department routinely patrolled. Recalling his first impression of the crime scene, Mr. Cox, who later became county sheriff, told the *Daily Eastern News*, "I could tell from when I got there that [the body] was missing its head and feet... I remember when I first saw it standing on the bridge, it didn't look like a person."

As police cordoned off the crime scene and word spread of the discovery, reporters and television crews descended on the remote location. Police worked into the evening using scuba divers to scour the river for clues, but the missing body parts, which had been severed "fairly cleanly," were never found. The cause of death was also never determined. Coles County Coroner Dick Lynch described the woman as being in her 20s, "rather flat-chested," "not in the habit of shaving," about 5 feet 9 inches, weighing around 130 pounds, with dark auburn hair. He deduced that she had not been dead more than a day or so, and that she had been killed somewhere other than at the bridge. Her remains were immediately shipped to Springfield to be examined by pathologist Dr. Grant Johnson at Memorial Medical Center, but he was unable to uncover anything conclusive.

In Dr. Johnson's initial examination, he determined that the woman had an uncommon "A-positive" blood type. She did not have any major scars, birthmarks, or tattoos that might have given a clue as to her identity, nor was it easy to determine the time of death. Aside from trace amounts of aspirin, there were no drugs, poisons, or alcohol in her bloodstream, and no evidence of rape or abuse. Without the head or hands, and without any abrasions on the body, it was impossible for the coroner to even determine if a struggle preceded death.

Investigators heralded the determination of the blood type as an important clue in a case that was rapidly going cold. Coles County Sheriff Charles "Chuck" Lister told the *Journal Gazette* that it "could narrow things down significantly." Unfortunately, he also revealed that checks of missing persons reports "failed to produce any substantial leads." By Thursday, October 23, the Sheriff's Department suspended the search for clues in and around the river.

Nearly a year after her discovery, the unidentified body was laid to rest in Charleston's Mound Cemetery under the name "Jane Doe." Those who remembered the case occasionally traveled to her grave and left flowers or other tokens of their sympathy. Finally, in 1992, 12-years after the discovery of the body, there was a break in the case. On November 20, the Sheriff's Department held a press conference in Charleston, this time to announce that the identity of the Airtight victim had been ascertained. Her name was Diana Marie Riordan-Small, a resident of Bradley, Illinois, who disappeared from her home a short time before her remains were found over 100 miles away in Coles County. The revelation was the result of cooperation between Coles County Sheriff's Detective Art Beier and Detective Steven Coy of the Bradley Police Department. Slowly but surely, a picture of what happened to Diana Small began to emerge.

The reason no one matching the description of the body found at Airtight turned up in the missing persons reports was that Diana was never reported missing. "Her husband... told police he wasn't all that concerned because Small had left home on occasions before," the *Journal Gazette* reported. Diana's mother and sister had moved out west, where they became disconnected from Diana and her husband. After nearly a decade, her sister, Virginia, moved to North Carolina. Virginia decided to get in touch with the rest of her family and learned of her sister's disappearance, at which point she filed a missing persons report. According to Dave Fopay of the *Journal Gazette*, "Detective Art Beier saw the report on a national listing, realized Small's descriptions matched that of the Airtight Bridge victim and contacted Bradley police." A DNA test confirmed the match.

In October 2008, the anonymous headstone that had marked the grave of Diana Small was replaced with one bearing her name.

On Thursday, March 2, 2017, after re-opening their 36-year investigation, police arrested Diana's husband, Thomas A. Small, for her murder. Kankakee County State's Attorney Jim Rowe told reporters Small had confessed. The indictment alleged he killed his wife during an argument four days before her body was discovered in Coles County. He drove to Airtight Bridge with his young daughter in the car, dismembered his wife's body with an ax, and disposed of her missing body parts in the Vermilion River. He intended to keep his crime a secret until his death, but guilt overwhelmed him.

Small initially pleaded not guilty to the charges, but later changed his mind to spare his family the heartache of a trial. He was sentenced to 30 years in prison and is currently prisoner #Y25760 in Hill Correctional Center in Galesburg, Illinois.

THE MILLENNIUM MURDERS

As the year 2000 approached, the Dot-com bubble had yet to burst, personal computers and the World Wide Web had opened an exciting new frontier, social attitudes were loosening, and war seemed distant. Eastern Illinois University students and faculty could look forward to growing enrollment, improvements to Booth Library and the food court, a 24-hour computer lab, air conditioning in Lincoln and Douglas halls, internet access in dorm rooms, a commemorative courtyard, and card readers on vending machines. In the spring of 1999, Carol Surles became EIU's first female and first African American president. But four cold-blooded murders in four years shook the community to its core, spreading fear and uncertainty during this otherwise optimistic time.

ANDREA WILL

It had been over 24 and a half years since sophomore art major Shirley Ann Rardin's body was found in a wooded area northeast of Paris, Illinois. For more than two decades, students at Eastern Illinois University enjoyed a sense of safety and security. That all changed on the morning of Tuesday, February 3, 1998. At around 10:00 p.m. the previous evening, 20-year-old Justin J. "Jay" Boulay descended the long wooden staircase to his downstairs neighbor's apartment door and asked to borrow his car to pick up his girlfriend, 18-year-old Andrea Will, from Lawson Hall. Brian Graham, his neighbor, happily obliged. "I've been up to his place a couple of times by myself and I didn't notice anything weird about him," he later told the Decatur *Herald and Review*.

In a letter Justin later wrote and left in his apartment, he described getting into an argument with Andrea that evening when she told him she was dating other men. According to Andrea's mother, Patricia, Justin called Andrea several times over winter break, but Andrea, a freshman marketing major with long blonde hair and cherubic smile, wanted to end their relationship and see other people. "I lost it," Justin, a sophomore history major, wrote. "I couldn't let go of her neck." Coles County Coroner Mike Nichols later determined Justin strangled Andrea with a telephone cord. At around 3:30 a.m., Justin's downstairs neighbor and his neighbor's girlfriend, Michelle McVey, heard loud but "soothing music" coming from Justin's apartment. They knocked on the ceiling and it stopped.

At some point after midnight, Justin called his parents, Raymond and Marcie Boulay, told them "something terrible has happened," and asked them to drive down to Charleston. It's roughly 213 miles, or a three hour and 13-minute drive, from St. Charles to his apartment at 114 1/2 Jackson Avenue. Justin met his parents outside his apartment and they drove to the town square, where he broke down into tears and said Andrea was "injured or worse." Shortly after 5:00 a.m., they went to the Charleston Police Department. When police officers entered his apartment a few minutes later, they found Andrea's lifeless body lying in the bedroom.

The case was particularly disturbing because the couple involved seemed so normal. Friends described Andrea, a 1997 graduate of Batavia High School, as polite, shy, and well-liked. She was a member of Sigma Kappa sorority at EIU. Justin, a 1995 graduate of St. Charles High School, had been a student athlete who played on his high school basketball and football teams. He had no reported discipline problems and his neighbors in Charleston described him as a "nice guy" and "shy." They were all-American kids, yet, in the early morning hours of February 3, a dark, violent impulse bubbled to the surface.

Although Justin Boulay admitted to killing Andrea Will, he pleaded not guilty to first degree murder on grounds of temporary insanity. The defense argued that Justin had no memory of the murder, and was an otherwise nonviolent, mild-mannered young man with no criminal history who had simply "snapped." Circuit Judge Ashton Waller rejected the defense's argument and found him guilty, but took into consideration his clean record and remorsefulness. On Tuesday, May 18, 1999, Judge Waller sentenced Justin to 24 years in prison, four years more than the minimum sentence for first degree murder.

It was a sentence with which Andrea's family strongly disagreed. "Mr. Boulay got away with murder today," Patricia Will (today, Patricia Rosenberg), Andrea's mother, told reporters after the sentencing hearing. In the years that followed, Patricia advocated for what became known as "Andrea's Law." The law, which created the Illinois Murderer and Violent Offender Against Youth Registry, went into effect in January 2012. It required anyone convicted of first-degree murder to add their names, addresses, and other information to a public database for ten years after their release. Justin Boulay was paroled in 2011 after serving only 12 years of his sentence, married a professor who was one of his character witnesses at his trial, and moved to Hawaii. The apartment house at 114 Jackson Avenue where Andrea died was recently torn down.

The tragic case of Andrea Will was only the second time in EIU's history that a student had been murdered, but it wouldn't be the last.

AMY WARNER

At approximately 10:20 a.m. on Tuesday, June 29, 1999, a friend of 23-year-old Amy Denise Warner became concerned that he hadn't seen or heard from her since the previous day. He went to her home at 17 7th Street in Charleston, just north of Jefferson Elementary School. There he found Amy, a single mother and a manager at Elder-Beerman in the Cross County Mall in Mattoon, lying half-way on her couch in the living room, blood covering the floor. Her two children, a 4-year-old girl and 7-month-old boy, were home but not physically harmed. Investigators said there was no sign of forced entry. Amy died from a stab-wound to her neck, and she had defensive wounds on her hands. Investigators estimated her time of death at around 12 hours before her body was discovered.

Amy, a 1993 graduate of Charleston High School, was well-liked, an avid reader, and quick to smile and laugh. She worked tirelessly to provide for her children. Who would do this to her, and why? Her friends and family, and the broader community, struggled to make sense of the senseless brutality.

After months of painstaking investigation with help from the Illinois State Police, including interviews with over 30 friends, family members, and neighbors, Charleston police came up empty handed. Amy's family, along with the *Times-Courier* and *Journal Gazette*, initially offered a $3,500 reward for information leading to the arrest and conviction of the person or persons responsible, which grew to $10,000 by October 20, 2000.

In 2001, police arrested 25-year-old Anthony B. Mertz for the murder of fellow EIU student Shannon McNamara. During his trial, two friends of Mertz testified that he bragged about killing Amy Warner, as well as setting fire to an apartment building, but there wasn't enough evidence to charge him with either crime.

Tara Hofer, a former girlfriend, testified that Mertz had been asleep with her the night of Amy's murder, and she would have awakened if he left, but many remain unconvinced. "I am satisfied with the fact that they have the right one in prison," Linda Walker (1944-2019), Amy's mother, told the *Journal Gazette*. Though Coles County State's Attorney Steve Ferguson never charged Mertz with the crime, upon retirement, he admitted "The evidence points that way."

Charleston Community Unit School District 1 purchased the house at 17 7th Street and eventually tore it down to make way for an expanded Jefferson Elementary campus. To this day, no one has been charged with Amy Warner's murder, and the case remains open.

AMY BLUMBERG

As Eastern Illinois University let out for winter break in December 1999, sorority sisters at the Gamma Mu chapter of Sigma Kappa were still grieving from the loss of Andrea Will less than two years earlier. Twenty-year-old Amy J. Blumberg, a junior family and consumer sciences major, joined Sigma Kappa in the fall of 1998, so the two young women never met, however, she undoubtedly heard stories and shared many mutual friends. She lived with around 40 other members in the Sigma Kappa sorority house in EIU's Greek Court and served as activities chairman.

Amy Blumberg returned home to Collinsville, Illinois, a Metro East suburb of St. Louis, to stay with her parents, Ken and Sue, over the holidays. They were devout members of St. John's Evangelical United Church of Christ. She worked at her uncle Dennis' store, On Stage Dance Apparel at 138 Eagle Drive in nearby O'Fallon, to help out and earn extra money for school. The store, a cottage-like brick building just east of the I-64 and U.S. Highway 50 interchange, was tucked away between a gas station, railroad tracks, and an empty field. On Friday, December 31, 1999, Amy was working alone until closing at 6:00 p.m., anticipating ushering in the new millennium with her friends later that night. It was a calm, snowless evening, with a temperature around 50 degrees Fahrenheit and falling.

Amy never came home. Her parents began to worry when Amy's friends called to ask about her whereabouts. At around 9:00 p.m., they drove to the store to re-trace her route, thinking her car might have broken down on the way home. Amy's car was still in the parking lot. Ken, her father, went inside, where he discovered Amy's body lying on the floor, wearing only a dark blue shirt pulled up to her armpits, near the restroom in a pool of blood. Later, the cash register showed the last purchase was for a $29.96 pair of black leotards at 2:25 p.m. The coroner estimated her time of death at 4:00 p.m., which left two hours between the murder and the time the store was supposed to close. Did any potential customers see her body, and if so, why hadn't they called the police?

There was at least one witness. Edward S. Phillips, then 32 years old, was working as a truck driver delivering food to prisons for the Illinois Department of Corrections and lived with his wife, Dawn, and young daughter in Mount Sterling, Illinois. He was five foot, eight inches tall, roughly 210 pounds with brown hair and hazel eyes. Phillips did not deny finding Amy's body. He bought something for his daughter, he said, and later followed a trail of blood to Amy's body when he went to return the purchase. Rather than call police, he panicked and drove back to Mount Sterling, over 130 miles away, disposing of an unregistered pistol along the way. He told his wife he had blood on his clothes from moving a dead animal off the road.

There appeared to be no motivation for the crime. No money was missing from the register, and Amy hadn't been sexually assaulted. O'Fallon police officers were so befuddled they sought help from the Major Case Squad of Greater St. Louis for the first time since 1982, as well as an FBI behavioral science unit. Within days, detectives from the Major Case Squad arrived at Eastern Illinois University to interview Amy's friends, classmates, and professors. When classes resumed for the spring semester, Amy's parents and several hundred students held a candlelit memorial service in the Grand Ballroom inside the Martin Luther King Jr. University Union.

Four years later, in January 2004, St. Clair County State's Attorney Robert Haida charged Edward Phillips with first degree murder while Phillips was in prison serving time on unrelated charges of burglary, perjury, and obstructing justice. After Phillips and his wife Dawn got divorced, they were embroiled in a heated child custody battle, and Dawn told police about the blood on his pants the night of December 31, 1999. Phillips' ex-wife, prosecutors said, also bore an uncanny resemblance to Amy Blumberg as a young woman. At trial, prosecutors showed jurors an empty box for a .380 caliber pistol found at Phillips' home, which fired a small caliber bullet similar to the one that killed Amy Blumberg. The murder weapon, however, has never been found.

Prosecutors admitted their case was circumstantial, but Assistant State's Attorney Jim Piper asked jurors to "Use your common sense." Phillips' defense attorney claimed the prosecution's case rested on the testimony of a bitter ex-wife and that other suspects warranted consideration. The jury deliberated for over 24 hours before returning a guilty verdict. On Tuesday, May 29, 2007, Phillips was sentenced to 55 years in prison without parole for the murder of Amy Blumberg. At sentencing, Phillips, who declined to testify at trial, turned to Amy's parents and told them "I didn't kill your daughter."

Ken Blumberg, Amy's father, was not convinced. "There's no doubt in my mind that Ed did it," he told the press.

Phillips' conviction brought closure to the case, but nothing would bring Amy back. Amy's friends and sorority sisters continue to keep her memory alive. Phillips, currently prisoner #S01121 in Menard Correctional Center, will remain in prison until December 9, 2060.

SHANNON MCNAMARA

On Tuesday morning, June 12, 2001, Eastern Illinois University's campus was deserted. The temperature was in the low 70s and rising with rain clouds overhead. Most of EIU's 10,531 students had returned home for the summer, but several hundred remained behind for summer classes. In a three-story apartment building near the corner of 4th Street and Taylor Avenue, 21-year-old Shannon McNamara's roommate discovered her strangled and brutalized body on their living room floor. Shannon, from Rolling Meadows, Illinois, was a physical education major and sorority sister of the Zeta Alpha chapter of Alpha Phi.

Police found a credit card belonging to someone named Anthony Mertz in Shannon's apartment, and a bloody knife in a nearby dumpster. Mertz, a former Marine who lived across the street from Shannon, was soon arrested for the crime. Shortly after the murder, witnesses saw Mertz, 25, hide a .22 caliber handgun in the ceiling of the Student Rec Center, where he worked.

The murder shocked EIU's close-knit community. When the fall semester began, over 1,500 students and faculty marched in a candlelit procession from Lantz Gymnasium to Greek Court in honor of Shannon's memory. In the nearly 100 years between Eastern Illinois University's opening in 1899 and the murder of Andrea Will in 1998, one student, Shirley Ann Rardin, was murdered (although Andy Lanman's death was suspicious, it wasn't officially a homicide). Now, in a span of four years, the typical length of an undergraduate degree program, three students, all young women, were dead. One male student was in prison and another was the chief suspect in two homicides. It's difficult to describe the psychological impact this had on students and faculty at this small Midwestern university.

During his trial, two friends of Mertz testified that he bragged about killing 23-year-old Amy Warner, a mother of two, in her Charleston home on 7th Street in June 1999, as well as setting fire to an apartment building at 4th Street and Buchanan Avenue, behind E.L. Krackers, in February 2000.

There was not enough evidence to charge him with those crimes, which remain unsolved.

On February 12, 2003, a jury took less than three hours to pronounce Mertz guilty of aggravated sexual assault, home invasion, and the first-degree murder of Shannon McNamara. Two weeks later, a Coles County judge sentenced Mertz to death.

After the guilty verdict, *Daily Eastern News* editor Nate Bloomquist wrote poignantly, "Mertz bloodied Charleston and Eastern's standing as a Mayberry. Residents will deadbolt doors now. They'll look over their shoulders a few more times, or maybe they won't go out at night. The area's innocence was lost through Mertz's guilt."

The Illinois Supreme Court affirmed his sentence on appeal. In 2011, however, Governor Pat Quinn signed legislation abolishing the death penalty in Illinois and commuted the sentences of 15 convicts on death row, including Mertz. Shannon's mother, Cindy, was understandably outraged. If anyone deserves to die for their crimes, it's Anthony Mertz, who is currently serving a life sentence.

We grow up believing "you get what you deserve," but that seldom reflects reality. Shannon McNamara was a model college student with a bright future ahead of her. What did she do to deserve such a brutal and humiliating end? Her murder taught a whole generation of fellow EIU alumni, you can be intelligent, popular, athletic, and happy, and evil might still find you.

DISASTERS

SUDDEN FREEZE OF 1836

An obscure historical weather event blew through central Illinois in the 1830s known as the "Sudden Freeze." It appeared without warning on December 20, 1836. The weather had been relatively warm in the proceeding days, and a light rain turned the snow to slush. In the early afternoon, a dark cloud traveling about 25-30 mph descended from the northwest "accompanied by a roaring noise."

What happened next was described by William H. Perrin in *The History of Coles County, Illinois* (1879):

> As it passed over the country, everything was frozen in its track almost instantly. Water that was running in little gullies or in the streams was suddenly arrested in its career, blown into eddies and small waves by the wind, and frozen before it could subside. Cattle, horses, hogs and wild animals exposed to its fury were soon chilled through and many frozen in their tracks. Where a few moments before they walked in mud and slush, was now frozen, and unless moving about they were frozen fast.
>
> In some instances where individuals were exposed to the fury of this wave and unable to reach shelter, their lives were lost. One man was found afterward standing frozen in the mud, dead, and still holding the rein of his horse in his hand. He had apparently become bewildered and chilled, and freezing fast in the mud and slush, remained standing.

Three residents of Coles County reportedly froze to death.

There are several stories of pioneers who were unfortunately caught outside and instantly froze to death. According to *History of the Early Settlers of Sangamon County, Illinois* (1876) by John C. Power, in the western part of Douglas County near the border of Piatt and Moultrie counties, "two brothers by the name of Deeds had gone out to cut a bee tree, and were overtaken by the cold and frozen to death. Their bodies were found ten days later, about three miles from home."

Anecdotal accounts put the cloud near Springfield, Illinois around 12:00 p.m., and Lebanon, Ohio (in southwestern Ohio) around 9:00 p.m., covering that distance in nine hours. Its width reportedly stretched from Ottawa, Illinois to a short distance below Coles County, or about 140 miles. The freezing storm cloud exhausted itself somewhere over Ohio. To this day, there is no explanation for this strange event.

1907 INTERURBAN COLLISION

It was a balmy Friday morning, August 30, 1907. The Coles County Fair was in full swing, and passengers packed the interurban trolly to make the journey from Mattoon to the Coles County Fairgrounds near Charleston along the Central Illinois Traction Company line. No one suspected their routine and pleasant journey would suddenly erupt in horror. What happened that morning would be the worst transportation-related disaster in Coles County history.

At approximately 10:40 a.m., Mattoon City Railway Interurban Car #14 (initially reported as #11), loaded with 100 passengers weighing a total of 40 tons, was speeding east 15 to 20 miles per hour slightly downhill at a curve one-half mile from a cloverleaf crossing west of Charleston. It was being driven by motorman Charles Botts and conductor Frank Gucker. The lightly-loaded express line, driven by motorman Ben F. McClara and conductor Grover McCartney, was heading west, uphill, at around four or five miles per hour.

C. R. Curtis, an employee on the express car, saw Interurban Car #14 as it rounded the curve east of Cossell Creek approximately 600 feet away. There was no time to apply the brakes. Both Botts and McClara jumped before the collision, but their passengers were not so lucky. One man, Samuel Royer, said he saw the express car coming and could have jumped, but expected the cars to stop before impacting.

Under normal conditions, the two cars would have been level with each other and their impact not as deadly, but because the Interurban was heading downhill and weighted down by passengers, it sat slightly lower on the tracks. When they collided, the floor of the express car slid over the floor of the Interurban, causing it to "telescope", crushing bodies and mangling limbs. Twelve passengers were reportedly killed outright. The wounded were laid out under the hot August sun to wait for medical aid.

"The scene upon the arrival of the physicians was one which will never be forgotten by those who witnessed it," the *Journal Gazette* reported. "The forms of many of those killed were horribly mangled and torn, limbs broken, skulls crushed in, and their features so defaced in many cases that recognition is almost impossible." The *Paxton Daily Record* added, "The dead and dying were jammed together in a mass. Women were shrieking with pain and children were crying for mothers who were thought to be among the dead."

Dozens of passengers were injured, many seriously, and the final death toll was 18.

Both Charles Botts and Ben McClara were charged with criminal negligence for their roles in the wreck. Six leading figures in the Mattoon City Railway Company were indicted for manslaughter, including company president E.A. Potter and director Francis M. Peabody. Judge M.W. Thompson, however, sustained a motion by the defense attorneys that the grand jury had been adjourned and reconvened illegally, so the charges were thrown out. The company settled individual damage lawsuits with generous cash payments.

TORNADO OF 1917

In late spring 1917, more than a month after the United States formally entered the First World War, the Midwestern United States was hit by the largest and longest sequence of tornadoes on record. The storms appeared for seven consecutive days and ranged over eleven states. For seven hours on May 26, a series of tornadoes tore a path through central Illinois, from the Mississippi River to the Embarras River. Coles County was hardest hit, suffering close to 100 deaths, hundreds injured, 800 families homeless, and over $2 million in damages.

On the afternoon of Saturday, May 26 around 3:15 p.m., the sky grew dark, the wind howled, and the air filled with a greenish hue. "I thought the end of the world had come," said D.S. May of 701 DeWitt Avenue in Mattoon. The storms moved west to east, so Mattoon was hit first. A funnel cloud appeared suddenly, hardly giving those in its path time to flee. It struck a lumber yard, hurling wooden boards and planks through the air like missiles. Reporters compared the limbless trees and flattened buildings to a scene in war-torn Europe. Invoking images of the desolate, cratered Argonne Forest in France, S.A. Tucker of the Decatur *Herald* said Mattoon's swath of destruction looked like a "shell-swept plain."

The Decatur *Daily Review* reported the tornado tore a path through Mattoon's north side two miles long and four blocks wide, avoiding the business district but devastating a residential area. A series of hail storms followed into the evening, battering the survivors and hampering rescue efforts. That night, the city was plunged into darkness, save for the lanterns carried by volunteers digging through the rubble.

Newspapers reported many odd occurrences, including a dog being picked up and thrown against a woman walking several blocks away, neither of which were hurt; a piece of lumber passing above the heads of a family sitting at their dining room table; a woman and her two children standing untouched in a doorway while their entire house was carried off and smashed to bits; and a horse and cow picked up from one field and deposited unharmed in another a quarter-mile away. Houses stood intact on one side of a street but were totally demolished on the other.

The tornado leap-frogged between Mattoon and Charleston, leveling telegraph poles, barns, and farmhouses, overturning cars, and killing horses and livestock. Like its sister city, the cyclone struck Charleston's north side, where property loss exceeded $1 million. In proportion to its size, Charleston suffered greater damage. In terms of human life lost, however, Mattoon suffered considerably more. The tornado killed 64 and injured 467 people in Mattoon, destroyed over 496 homes and severely damaged another 168. Thirty-four died in Charleston, with over 100 injured. Four hundred-eighty-six homes were damaged or destroyed north of Monroe Street. The Coles County Fairgrounds was wrecked.

In the tornado's aftermath, dozens of citizens were deputized and the National Guard called in to keep order, and no looting was reported. The outpouring of support from surrounding communities was rapid and overwhelming. Doctors, rescue workers, volunteers, and supplies of every variety poured in to help clean up and care for the injured and homeless. The town of Paris, Illinois sent 10,000 sandwiches, and families in Shelbyville packed food from their dinner tables into baskets and sent them to Coles County. Local towns sent help as well. One-hundred volunteers came from Ashmore, and another forty from Oakland.

Both Mattoon and Charleston eventually rebuilt and recovered. A tornado struck Mattoon again on March 28, 1998, but the damage wasn't anywhere as bad. Fortunately, only three people were injured and no one was killed in that storm. To this day, the tornado of 1917 remains the worst natural disaster in Coles County history.

BLAIR HALL FIRE OF 2004

On Wednesday, April 28, 2004 at a little after 3:00 p.m., the temperature was 72 degrees and rising, the sky was fair, and wind gusted south-southwest up to 32 mph. Humidity was low. By all accounts, it was a beautiful spring day, and Eastern Illinois University's spring semester was quickly coming to a close. Students crammed for final exams, which would begin the following Monday.

At 3:14 p.m., someone had called 911 from inside Blair Hall, an ivy-covered Gothic Revival building directly southeast of Old Main. Smoke billowed from the third-floor windows. Police and volunteer firefighters from Coles County and neighboring counties arrived around 3:30 and made sure everyone was evacuated. They quickly sealed off 7th Street in front of the building, and water hoses snaked across the pavement. Curious residents of Park Place Apartments watched the commotion from balconies just down the street.

There were so many students and other onlookers standing around taking pictures and recording the event with their cell phones, the *Daily Eastern News* devoted an entire article to the phenomenon.

After an hour battling flames inside and out, an alarm sounded at 4:35 p.m. and firefighters evacuated the building. The outpouring of support from local businesses was incredible. They donated food, coffee, and even trash bags to emergency workers. Firefighters continued to fight the blaze until sundown. In the end, it was determined a blowtorch used by construction workers to remove paint accidentally ignited combustible material in the wall and caused the fire. Thankfully no one was hurt.

Blair Hall is the third oldest building on campus. It was constructed in 1913 and originally called the Model School, then renamed after football coach Francis G. Blair in 1958. It completed the triad of buildings that made up the old campus, including Old Main and the fabled Pemberton Hall. In 2004, Blair Hall was home to the Anthropology, Sociology, and African American Studies departments.

EIU administrators worked hard to salvage the building, and after two years and $6 million, Blair Hall was painstakingly restored to its former glory. It's strange how a disaster can bring people together. For one spring afternoon in 2004, it seemed like the whole campus came out to support and encourage the volunteer firefighters who fought that terrible blaze, and witness and record the worst physical disaster to hit Eastern Illinois University in recent memory.

THE BLAIR HALL FIRE | PHOTO BY THE AUTHOR

GHOST TOWNS

DOG TOWN/DIONA

Dog Town, on Clear Creek in Hutton Township, straddled Coles and Cumberland counties (Cumberland County separated from Coles in 1843) and was among Coles County's earliest settlements, getting its nickname from the large number of dogs kept there. Among the first white children born in the county was a son of James Nees, a resident of Dog Town, in March 1827. When Abraham Lincoln's family first entered Coles County in 1830, they came through this quiet hamlet before ultimately settling west of Decatur. Nicholas McMorris was appointed its first postmaster on October 12, 1869.

FORMER ROTHROCK'S GENERAL STORE | PHOTO BY THE AUTHOR

According to *The History of Coles County* (1879), Dog Town was "an accidental collection of houses" with a store, post office, shops, and a Presbyterian church. It was also known as Diona. The L.D. Rothrock General Store, a two-story brick building with a meeting hall on the second floor, was erected in 1880. The post office closed in 1904. Today, the remains of Dog Town can be found approximately 1.9 miles south of Fox Ridge State Park off Route 130 at County Road 1800 E and 1400 N (GPS coordinates 39.37572, -88.14027). Rothrock's General Store building is still standing alongside a handful of homes.

BACHELORSVILLE

Bachelorsville (aka Batcheldorsville or Dudley's Settlement) in Ashmore Township was one of the first settlements in Coles County. Its postmaster, Laban Burr, was appointed on May 14, 1830. As its name implied, its first settlers were all single men. Guilford Dudley, who lent his name to a nearby creek and schoolhouse, opened a store where he sold cakes and pies, leading to the nickname "Pietown". Guilford and his brothers James and Moses were originally from New Hampshire. When they raised their first barn, they christened it "The bachelor's delight, and the pride of the fair."

Batcheldorsville appeared on maps of Illinois in 1838 and 1842, but like Hitesville and St. Omer, it died out when the Indianapolis & St. Louis Railroad went through Ashmore. Bachelorsville was approximately eight miles east of Charleston and three miles south of Ashmore along what is today N County Road 2420 E, south of the Dudley School. The old Dudley School is located on E County Road 860 N near GPS coordinates 39.503924, -88.031147.

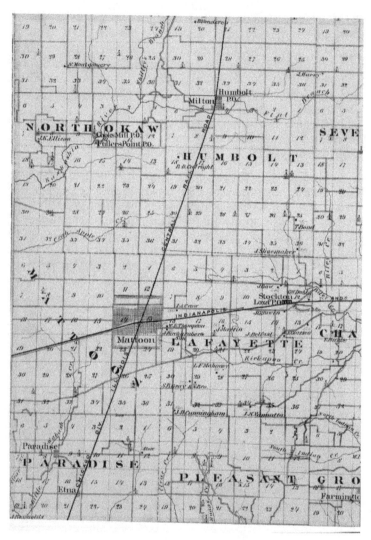

FROM *ATLAS OF THE STATE OF ILLINOIS.* CHICAGO: UNION ATLAS CO., WARNER & BEERS, PROPRIETORS, 1876.

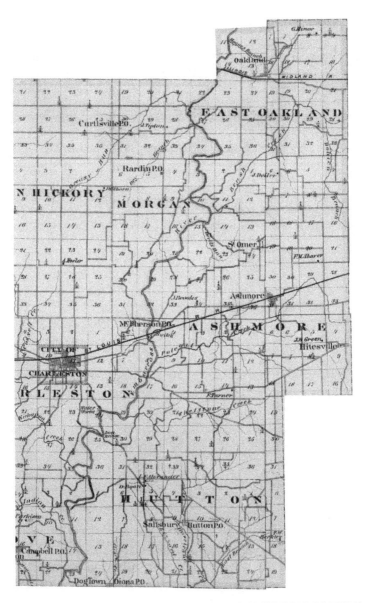

NOTE THE LOCATION OF HITESVILLE, DOG TOWN,
ST. OMER, FARMINGTON, AND CURTISVILLE

String Town

" String Town" is another vanished settlement in Hutton
Township. Never a formal village or town, *The History of Coles
County* (1879) described it as a "thickly-settled
neighborhood" with mechanic-shops, a saw mill, church,
and store owned by Thomas Goodman. By 1879, only the church
and a handful of houses remained. Stringtown Cemetery is
located at the intersection of County Road 300 N and 1920 E (GPS
coordinates 39.41996, -88.11565).

HITESVILLE

James Hite, who immigrated from Kentucky to Coles County in 1831, created this village in Ashmore Township and named it after himself in April 1835. He was appointed postmaster on August 24, 1835. A stone marker at the location, however, says that Hitesville was founded in 1837. Whatever the year of its establishment, at its peak it contained several shops and houses. *The History of Coles County* (1879) stated that the village was "swallowed up" by new villages that appeared when the Indianapolis & St. Louis Railroad was built. Ashmore, which was plotted in 1855, was the most likely culprit.

James Hite and some of his neighbors also built a nearby Presbyterian church. A man by the name of Reverend John Steele presided over the congregation until the building was sold when James Hite moved out of the area. The parishioners, many of whom were from the St. Omer area, then attended a different church. Hitesville lasted long enough to appear on a county map alongside St. Omer and Ashmore, but shortly after, both Hitesville and St. Omer ceased to exist.

Hitesville was located about 3.5 miles southeast of Ashmore at the intersection of county roads 820N and 2780E, not far from Route 49 (GPS coordinates 39.5082, -87.96634). The old Hitesville Cemetery (no longer in use) was approximately one-half mile south along 2780E. The former Greenwood School, now a museum on the Eastern Illinois University campus, once stood west of Hitesville.

FARMINGTON/CAMPBELL

T he long-lost village of Farmington was, for a time, the only village in Pleasant Grove Township. Today, only a few structures remain of this once bustling community. It was laid out on April 25, 1852, at the request of John J. Adams, who owned the land. His wife, Caroline, named the village Farmington, after a town in Tennessee. Unfortunately, the U.S. Post Office refused to change the name of the nearby post, because a Farmington already existed in Fulton County. It remained known as Campbell's Post Office, and soon after the village's official name became Campbell.

In 1853, residents erected a brick schoolhouse, which doubled as a school and Presbyterian church until 1857. According to *The History of Coles County* (1879) it was called Farmington Seminary and operated as a school until the building became too small to accommodate the growing village. It was then sold and repurposed as a general store. Reuben Moore was a wealthy resident of the community. After his first wife died, he married Matilda Johnson Hall, Abraham Lincoln's stepsister. The State of Illinois acquired their home in the 1920s and it has been restored several times, most recently in 1996.

By 1879, Farmington/Campbell was home to around one hundred people, who were served by four stores, a carriage shop, blacksmith shop, steam flour mill, school, and two churches. According to a historic marker outside the Reuben Moore Home, "The boom days, however, were short lived. When the railroad passed up Farmington in favor of Jamesville a few miles to the south, local residents moved elsewhere. Today, only a few houses and a church remind passersby of the village." The Moore Home is located at 400 Lincoln Highway Road, one mile north of Lincoln Log Cabin State Historic Site (GPS coordinates 39.39569, -88.21111).

THE MOORE HOME | PHOTO BY THE AUTHOR

CURTISVILLE

istory of Coles County, 1876-1976 tells us that Morgan Township contained some of the first land to be settled in Coles County because of a prevalence of good forests and freshwater springs. The first schoolhouse was constructed in 1839, probably in an area known as "Greasy Point," but its exact location has been lost to history. It was about a mile or so southwest of that point that settlers attempted to build Curtisville, the first village in the township.

Curtisville originally contained a store owned by a man named Cutler Mitchell, a blacksmith shop, as well as a few houses. The village was never officially platted, but it was featured on early maps and a post office opened there on July 11, 1867. According to the *History of Coles County*, "the post office was simply an office for the convenience of the neighbors, and whoever went to town brought out the mail-bag. It was not a regular office, nor was the mail brought regularly, but as it suited the convenience of some one who had other business at town."

Curtisville was located at the intersection of what is today N County Road 1820 E and E County Road 1700 N, approximately two miles north of Bushton and Rardin (GPS coordinates 39.62346, -88.13355). Aside from an old, crumbling barn, all traces of this village have disappeared or were plowed over a long time ago. Only windswept corn and soybean fields remain.

St. Omer

T oday, St. Omer is mostly known for the cemetery of the same name (see St. Omer Cemetery in Cemetery Lore), but during the mid-nineteenth century it was a thriving settlement. It has been defunct for over a hundred years, and any remains, aside from a few trees, patches of grass, and old fence posts, have disappeared. The settlement itself was located south of the cemetery near the intersection of what is today N County Road 2380 E and E County Road 1300 N (GPS coordinates 39.56479, -88.03103), approximately 2.2 miles north of Ashmore.

St. Omer was officially founded in 1852, although it was previously known as Cutler's Settlement (after John Cutler, who immigrated from Ohio in 1829). Its first postmaster was J.W. Hoge (or Hogue) on October 7, 1852. According to *The History of Coles County* (1879), the village was a collection of around six houses, a store, post office, and a blacksmith's shop, but the *Coles County Map & Tour Guide* says that forty to fifty families once lived there.

St. Omer disappeared in the 1880s. The community of Hitesville, formerly located a few miles southeast of Ashmore, suffered a similar fate. Families living in the two villages packed up and moved to Ashmore when the railroad was built. In 1893, a schoolhouse and Presbyterian church still stood, but nothing remains of either building. The church burned down in the 1950s.

KU KLUX KLAN

*"ATTENTION BOYS—Ages 12 to 18;
for information concerning the Junior Ku
Klux Klan write P.O. Box 212." - Classified
advertisement in the Mattoon Daily
Journal-Gazette and Commercial-Star,
June 28, 1924.*

In the early decades of the twentieth century, D. W. Griffith's silent film *The Birth of a Nation* (1915) revived public interest in the Ku Klux Klan, a domestic terrorist organization founded to resist Reconstruction in the South after the Civil War. The original Klan was stamped out in the early 1870s. The "Second Klan" of the 1920s was centered primarily in the Midwest. Though officially a secret fraternal organization, its members sometimes engaged in intimidation, vigilantism, and fought with anti-Klan organizations. Its White Anglo-Saxon Protestant members preached nativism, supported Prohibition and racial segregation, and opposed Catholics and Jews.

The KKK in Illinois is most infamously known for its war on bootleggers in Williamson County, but there were chapters in east central Illinois as well, particularly in Shelby, Coles, Champaign, and Edgar counties. Its mysterious rituals and regalia, mass meetings, and torch-lit parades attracted a lot of attention in the press. According to numerous articles in the Mattoon *Daily Journal-Gazette*, the Mattoon chapter's most visible spokesperson was Rev. Jesse Forrest McMahan of the First Christian Church in Mattoon. Throughout the early 1920s, Rev. McMahan gave speeches and appeared at Klan rallies across the region.

In late May 1922, the *Daily Journal-Gazette* reported that 100 charter members, including "many business and professional men" had organized a chapter of the Ku Klux Klan in Paris, Illinois. By July, they were making their presence known in Coles County. On Saturday, July 29, the Knights of the Ku Klux Klan made a large donation to Rev. Jesse F. McMahan (1880-1957) accompanied by a letter wishing him "good wishes for the speedy recovery of your dear wife." It closed, "Our creed is for America and 100 per cent Americans. 'God Give Us Men'. Yours for better citizenship in Mattoon."

A week later, rumors circulated that a Klan meeting would be held, similar to the one held in a grove near Mahomet, Illinois the previous Sunday, in or near Mattoon. That Sunday, August 13, 1922, Rev. McMahan, who moved with his wife from Missouri to Mattoon three years earlier, delivered a lecture titled "The Unvarnished Truth About the Ku Klux Klan" to a large crowd at a theater in Mattoon. The KKK had gone public in Coles County.

The arrival of the Klan in central Illinois alarmed many public officials, including Mayor Charles M. Borchers of Decatur. He bristled at the suggestion that the vigilante organization was needed to curb crime in town. "We will enforce the law, and we are not going to dress up in nightgowns doing it, either," he declared. "When we need help, we'll call for it, and we're going to be open and above board about it."

Rev. McMahan continued his speaking tour, extolling the virtues of the "invisible empire" to a crowd of 100 people in Charleston on Friday, October 13, in Springfield on October 14, and before a crowd of 350 at the Playhouse in Shelbyville on Sunday, October 15. There he acknowledged he was a member and said the Klan was "against all forms of violence, but support law and order."

In the fall, the central Illinois Klan appeared in force on the streets of Shelbyville and Paris. At around 11:00 p.m., Monday, October 30, a procession of 150 to 200 cars "composed almost entirely of Mattoon members" drove through Shelbyville dressed in full regalia. Journalists estimated as many as 1,000 Klan members attended. The parade reportedly followed a secret initiation of 200 members from Shelby, Coles, Moultrie, and Douglas counties. Another procession drove through Paris the following week, erecting signs at polling places that read: "Vote sellers, vote buyers, beware: the Invisible Eye is on you."

The KKK intervened on Rev. Jesse McMahan's behalf during a financial dispute with his congregation in December. McMahan and his supporters wanted to build a new church, but not everyone was on board. During a December 4th meeting, several white-robed Klan members burst into the hall and demanded a letter be read. "We wish to pledge you, Rev. McMahan, our loyal support, morally, spiritually and financially, and in any other way you may need... Your enemies are our enemies," it said.

The appearance of the interlopers caused an uproar among older, conservative church members. One man rose and demanded the Klan members remove their masks. "From infancy I was taught to bare my head when entering a church," he later told the *Daily Journal-Gazette*. "...And for those hooded, robed figures, defying all precepts of the teachings of Jesus Christ to enter that church arrogant, bold, heads covered, a veiled threat, I wanted to rise up and invoke the almighty wrath of the Supreme Being on them, for it was a godless act."

When later asked if he had repudiated the Klan, as rumored, Rev. McMahan replied to the contrary. "The statement that appeared in several papers that I had withdrawn from the Klan was erroneous," he said. "I am still a member of the Mattoon Klan, and I am for it, stronger and more firmly than I ever was. I believed in it, and still believe in it." McMahan's activities continued into 1923, giving speeches in Paris and Champaign in January and attending a Klan pageant in Valparaiso, Indiana in May.

On Saturday, May 26, 1923, the Klan held its first and largest procession through the streets of Mattoon. It was estimated 100 cars and 500 Klansmen took part, assembling at Peterson Park and driving down Broadway between 9:00 and 10:00 p.m. led by a band in a delivery truck hidden from view by white sheets. Thousands of local residents lined the street to see the torchlit spectacle. A banner read "100 per cent American." Klan members in the lead car handed a letter to Mattoon's police chief, Joseph Ellsworth "Elva" Portlock (1877-1932), which read, in part, "Your city has one of the worst reputations in the state for lawless characters, and we want it stopped at once, or we will take a hand in it, and see that it is stopped, or there will be trouble. We stand for law and order, first, last and always. Take notice and govern yourself accordingly." It was signed by the Ku Klux Klan committee from Champaign, Illinois. After the parade, the Klansmen reportedly conducted rituals and burned a 35-foot cross in Bell's Woods.

Mattoon Klansmen attended a rally at the Edgar County fairgrounds near Paris in July, also providing band members for the occasion. Thousands of attendees turned out to hear several Protestant pastors give speeches, including Rev. Armon Cheek of the Universalist Church and Rev. W.W. Sniff of Central Chrisitian Church of Terre Haute, Indiana. The Klan's popularity led to a relaxed attitude regarding its secrecy. The *Daily Journal-Gazette* openly identified the exalted cyclops of the Paris Division Klan of the Realm of Illinois as James B. Dively (1896-1987), a World War

1 veteran and Edgar County elementary school teacher from southern Illinois.

Mattoon Klansmen also attended a statewide rally of approximately 10,000 in Shelbyville on August 7. Captain John Killian Skipwith, Sr. (1848-1933), a Confederate veteran (enlisted at the age of 13 and served with Nathan Bedford Forrest) and grand cyclops of the Louisiana Ku Klux Klan, was a featured speaker at that event. Skipwith was under investigation for his alleged involvement in the murder of two African American men in Lousiana in 1922. He told the assembled crowd that the state was manufacturing its case against him and the prosecution was being funded by "those Jews in Wall Street."

On Labor Day at Peterson Park in Mattoon, the All American Chautauqua Service invited Rev. J.F. McMahan to publicly debate Thomas Sunderland, a Catholic from Montana, on the issue of whether or not the Klan's principles were "American, patriotic, constitutional, just and Christian." The *Daily Journal-Gazette* did not disclose the winner, but did say the event was well-attended by visitors from surrounding communities. Chautauquas were a popular form of entertainment in the late nineteenth and early twentieth centuries, featuring musical performances, lectures, and debates.

Behind its public facade, the Klan was, at its heart, still a vigilante organization that used threats and intimidation to enforce its agenda. This side of the Klan reared its ugly head in Mattoon in the autumn of 1923 when Klan members chased a black barber named James P. Cranshaw from town. J. P. Cranshaw owned a barber shop at 1712 Broadway Avenue and lived with his wife in a house on Shelby Avenue. On Thursday, November 15, 1923, he was arrested and fined $200 for disorderly conduct and resisting arrest for running from two police officers. The officers attempted to stop him and a Chicago-based cabaret dancer named Mary Evans after they jumped from a car at 1:30 a.m. Chief Joseph Portlock told the *Daily Journal-Gazette* Cranshaw was arrested "due to the continuous reports he had been driving out with white women." The woman, Evans, was fined $52 and released.

That night, robed Klansmen lit a cross on Cranshaw's front lawn, fired several shots into the air, and left a note on his door that read, "Jim Cranshaw, your room is worth more than your company. Leave town at once." By Saturday, the newspaper reported Cranshaw had fled Mattoon. A policeman discovered another note, this one unsigned, pasted to the window of his barber shop early Saturday morning that threatened "Let this be your last day in this town, n---ers; leave at once."

Until 1900, Coles County had a small but growing African American population. Black entrepreneurs opened barber shops and restaurants, others worked for the railroad, and several black women taught at local schools. Austin Perry (1833-1908), a barber, was elected Second Ward alderman as a Republican in Mattoon in 1883. There were 299 African Americans living in Coles County in 1900, but that number fell to 179 by 1930. It's not clear what factors led to this population decline, but as illustrated by the case of J.P. Cranshaw, Klan intimidation should be counted among them. The African American population of Coles County would not surpass 300 until 1970.

The Mattoon Klan continued its activities into 1925, when Rev. J.F. McMahan unsuccessfully ran for school board president. He hosted a large Klan gathering at the First Christian Church on Sunday, April 26, 1925, involving members from Mattoon, Champaign, and neighboring towns. They were served a picnic supper by the church women's society, then headed to Peterson Park to listen to a sermon by McMahan. The *Daily Journal-Gazette* estimated 1,500 were in attendance. It's not clear how many of Coles County's 36,000 residents were active Klan members, but based on newspaper reports, it must have been several hundred.

When Cora Stallman's body was found in a cistern on her sister's farm southeast of Humboldt on August 1, 1925, one of the many threatening letters she received was signed "K.K.K." Thomas Seaman, her brother-in-law, told newspapers that local residents not deemed supportive enough of the Klan had also received threatening letters, but it was unclear whether Stallman's death was related. An unnamed spokesperson for the Klan denied all involvement and pointed the finger at "blackmailers." "The Ku Klux Klan, according to the neighbors, has been strong in the county..." one article said. Two years earlier, the Klan had held a large rally in a grove a half-mile west of Humboldt complete with a band and nighttime ceremonies.

By the time, however, conviction of David Curtiss Stephenson (grand dragon of the KKK in Indiana) for rape and murder, criminal indictments, anti-mask laws, factionalism, and public backlash had taken their toll, and by 1930 the "Invisible Empire" had crumbled across the United States. Membership plummeted from several million to tens of thousands. The Illinois Theatre in Champaign, which housed the headquarters for local branches of the KKK in east central Illinois, burned down in 1927. Rev. Jesse F.

McMahan died on April 9, 1957 at the age of 76. His obituary made no mention of his Klan activities.

SHAGGY ROW AND MAYOR "DAYLIGHT" WELCH

Today, Commercial Avenue is a quiet street of mixed residential and commercial development on Mattoon's west side. It is anchored at one end by the Lorenz Supply Company and by Lytle Park at the other. At the turn of the last century, however, this street was notoriously known as "Shaggy Row," a collection of shacks, factories, and boarding houses where assaults, thefts, and shootings were common. Some called it Mattoon's red-light district. But it was also an integrated neighborhood where black and white residents freely mingled, even married and settled down. Shaggy Row met its demise in the election of 1911, when reform candidates swept away politically influential saloon keepers and cracked down on illicit gambling, liquor, and prostitution in the city.

Platted in 1855 and chartered as a city in 1861, Mattoon grew up around the juncture of the Terre Haute & Alton Railroad and Illinois Central Railroad. The Peoria, Decatur & Evansville Railroad soon followed. Hotels, theaters, barbershops, restaurants, and stores opened downtown to serve the growing population. Young men who worked for the railroads and in other local industries often sought unwholesome diversions like pool halls, gambling parlors, saloons, cigar shops, and "houses of ill-fame". At the same time, churches and organizations like the Anti-Saloon League, Woman's Christian Temperance Union, and Citizens' League worked to eliminate vice from the city.

One way Mattoon controlled liquor sales was by issuing saloon licenses. A proprietor could be fined and his business shuttered if he operated without a license, but city officials had to be willing to enforce those rules. Years before the Eighteenth Amendment to the U.S. Constitution banned the production, transport, and sale of intoxicating liquors, temperance organizations tried other ways to prohibit alcohol. In Mattoon's 1905 municipal election, a slim majority voted against the city issuing saloon licenses. Although the vote was nonbinding, by placing the license question on the ballot, reformers sought to show popular sentiment was against the sale of liquor.

Saloon keepers fought back by bankrolling candidates who would look the other way while they continued to operate, sometimes without a license. If newspaper reports and court records are to be believed, many of these proprietors engaged in illicit gambling and prostitution on the side. William Henry "Colonel Bill" Knight (1866-1913) and George Andrew Kizer (1871-1935) were two of Mattoon's most prominent saloon keepers. Bill Knight's place of business was at 2001 Western Avenue. George Kizer owned a saloon and later a cigar store at 1406 Broadway. He was a Democratic kingmaker and a member of the local Democratic central committee from 1904 to 1906.

"George Kizer, the gambler, is the recognized leader of the democratic hosts in Mattoon to-day," the *Mattoon Gazette*, quoting the *Mattoon Commercial*, wrote in 1899. "Nothing of importance is done without his sanction and consent, and his every wish is without hesitation complied with... He makes and unmakes candidates with a simple wave of his hand... Kizer, the gambler, with his satellites which swarm around him in countless numbers, is a power in Mattoon."

In the spring of 1905, Kizer backed Charles T. "Daylight" Welch (1868-1924) for first ward alderman, which encompassed an area on either side of Broadway Avenue. Welch was a Catholic pawn broker and money lender who did business out of a storefront at 1712 Broadway. In January 1905, George Kizer struck a man named Robert "Boxy" Boyle in the head with a hammer at the Peerless Saloon on Broadway in retaliation for Boyle giving Welch a black eye a few days earlier. According to Boyle, Kizer accused him of punching "his best friend." That same year, both Kizer and Welch were under indictment. Kizer was taken to court for keeping a gaming house and Welch with charging unlawful interest. Welch failed to win his party's nomination that year, but succeeded in 1906. In those days, aldermen served one-year terms and mayors served two years.

An anonymous Democratic "Voter", writing in the *Mattoon Journal-Gazette*, the city's Republican organ, implored voters not to choose Welch. "His position on gambling and kindred evils is too well known..." he wrote. "Not that one alderman can bring back into power the gambling element, but one alderman can in a great measure hamper the authorities, and by aiding and abetting those who follow the destinies of the green cloth to that extent help evil doers." Welch defeated Republican Dr. W.W. Williams 148 to 134.

Mattoon, however, was a predominantly Republican city. In the 1907 municipal election, ten Republican aldermen were elected to the Democrats' four. Republican L.L. Lehman defeated Democrat Henry Shaw in the mayoral race 1,453 to 958. As one of four Democratic aldermen, Welch gained in prominence despite his critics. That this purportedly immoral businessman could one day become mayor of Mattoon was unthinkable to the Republican majority, but Bill Knight and George Kizer conspired to make that a reality.

Bill Knight's saloon was located on Western Avenue within walking distance of the intersection of Western and N. Railroad Avenue, otherwise known as "Shaggy Row." The first mention of Shaggy Row in a local newspaper was an 1892 blurb in *The Mattoon Gazette* about the Mattoon Buggy Pole Company building an addition to their factory in the neighborhood. Stories of arson, shoot-outs, brawls, attempted suicide, and murder followed. While reporting on the murder of Howard Jackson by Sid Hall, the *Gazette* lamented that Shaggy Row had "come to stand for all that is bad and debauched." Bill Knight owned several houses on that street, which fell within the boundaries of Mattoon's fifth ward. N. Railroad Avenue was renamed Cottage Avenue in September 1903.

In February 1904, Thomas C. Rowe (1855-1928), Democratic alderman of the fifth ward and chairman of the police committee, read a salacious report at the city council publicly accusing Bill Knight and his younger brother Charles Walter Knight (1876-1938) of running gambling and prostitution out of the Annex Hotel and Bar, 1812-14 Western Avenue. The Knight family had moved to Mattoon from Nashville, Brown County, Indiana in 1878 or '79 and quickly established themselves as local saloon keepers.

"I know that there are four or five prostitutes harbored at the Annex," Policeman Dan Graham alleged in his affidavit. "I am satisfied that liquor is being sold there Sunday after hours. Alarm bells are connected so that it is impossible to catch them selling liquor in violation of the ordinance. I know that William Knight harbors two known prostitutes above his saloon."

Policeman Mat Donahue concurred, alleging, "I have seen prostitutes go into and out of the Annex. I am informed that there are three or four at that place... I think more liquor is sold on Sunday at this place than during any other day of the week. I have seen parties go in and out of William Knight's place of business on Sunday. I am informed that prostitutes are harbored up stairs. I am told that there have been from two to seven up stairs at one time." Three more policemen echoed their statements, and City Marshal Dennis Lyons endorsed them. Both Bill and Charles Knight allegedly kept guards near the stairs who pushed buttons connected to alarms above their saloons to warn patrons of any raid, making it difficult if not impossible to collect evidence. Alderman Rowe pleaded with his colleagues to revoke Charles Knight's saloon license.

A majority on the city council balked at the accusations. The Annex was a hotel, one alderman argued. If patrons of the illustrious Dole House Hotel were allowed to come and go and eat their dinner on Sunday, why not patrons of the Annex? Besides, these critics said, if evidence against the Knight brothers was so strong, why haven't they been arrested? "If any saloonkeeper violates the law it is the duty of the police force to discover the fact and get the evidence and prosecute him," fourth ward Alderman R.J. Coy, a Republican, reportedly said.

The motion to revoke Charles Knight's saloon license failed eight to six.

The reformers called their bluff, and over the next three months, Charles was charged multiple times with selling liquor on Sundays, "keeping a public nuisance," selling liquor to a minor, keeping a "house of ill fame", keeping a tippling house (later known as a "speakeasy"), and gaming, among other misdemeanors. He pleaded guilty and paid over $280 in fines. Bill Knight pleaded guilty to similar charges and paid over $155 in fines. $280 in 1904 is roughly equivalent to $8,066 in 2020.

While alderman argued over the presence of prostitution on Western Avenue, no one argued about its presence on Shabby Row. Among the dozens of newspaper articles attesting to illicit boarding houses on that street, one name stands out: Isabelle Scott (1877-1907), who operated out of a house owned by Bill Knight at 2217 Cottage Avenue. Madame Isabelle Scott first appeared in *The Mattoon Daily Journal* in September 1902 when she was indicted alongside several other women, including Lillian Webster and Lulu Holloway, for "keeping a house of ill fame." She was 25 years old and possibly suffering from the tuberculosis that would kill her less than five years later. In March 1903, she pleaded guilty to the charges and paid a fine of over $50. Almost exactly one year later, Isabelle was swept up in the same round of prosecutions as Bill and Charles Knight. Charles "Daylight" Welch was indicted as well, this time for failing to report as a pawnbroker to the sheriff as required by law.

Isabelle's multiple run-ins with the law on Shabby Row included being the accuser as well as the accused. On Thursday, October 1, 1903, two young broomcorn farmhands, J.L. Hall and George Rubins (using the alias James Denning), called on Isabelle Scott's establishment. Isabelle was laying low, so she told them she wasn't home and asked them to leave. Undeterred, the young men kicked in her door and began ransacking the house. They stole a gold watch and some cash from Anna Cobble, one of Isabelle's girls, and departed. Isabelle reported Hall and Rubins to the police, who caught the men and "sweated" a confession out of them along with the location of their stolen loot.

On a cold, rainy Wednesday afternoon over a year later, January 11, 1905, two young men, Frank Cannon and Peter Robinson, came calling. "I told them I was not receiving guests that day," she later told the Coles County magistrate. "I have been ill for some time and did not desire any company." Robinson, however, was not dissuaded and began kicking the door. Isabelle was having none of it. Perhaps because of the previous incident, she called for one of her girls to bring a revolver. She swung open the door and began shooting at the young men. Robinson later said she fired as many as eight shots, stopping only to grab a new pistol from her assistant, but Isabelle said it was only three.

"She fired straight at me, and I was afraid to turn for fear she'd get me," Robinson said. "I backed away as fast as possible and was not hit." Robinson and his friend fled. Isabelle took a cab alone to the police station and asked the magistrate to issue warrants for the two men, which he did. Robinson pleaded guilty to disorderly conduct the next morning and paid a fine of $5 plus court costs.

Madame Isabelle had connections with both Bill Knight and Alderman Charles Welch, and her connection to Bill Knight went beyond simply that of tenant and landlord. When she was indicted in October 1905, Knight acted as surety on her bond. In January of that same year, when Police Chief Lyons visited the houses of ill repute on Cottage Avenue and told their occupants to leave town, Knight entered a private contract with Isabelle to sell her the property because as homeowner, Chief Lyons had no right to evict her. When Isabelle needed money to travel to Hot Springs, Arkansas to seek relief from her tuberculosis, she mortgaged her household goods to Charles Welch. Welch then served as administrator of her estate when she died.

Two back-to-back Republican administrations, that of Mayor William Byers, 1905-1907, and Mayor L.L. Lehman, 1907-1909, turned up the heat on Bill Knight, George Kizer, and their liquor and gambling interests. In December 1905, Mayor Byers revoked Bill Knight's liquor license only a few months after it was issued because "upon thorough investigation, I find that you have been running a gambling house in connection with your place of business..." Chief Lyons arrested Knight and after a short trial, he was convicted of four counts of running his saloon without a license and fined over $200. Knight threatened to publicly expose his enemies before opening a new operation in the boom town of Casey, Illinois.

On the evening of Thursday, October 25, 1906, Chief Lyons and his men raided George Kizer's cigar store, the Smoke House on Broadway, and arrested 18 men. "A busy scene was presented to the officers as they entered the lair of the tiger," described a *Journal-Gazette* reporter. "Eighteen men—besides George Kizer, the alleged proprietor, and his brother, John Kizer—were assiduously courting the goddess of chance, either playing cards or 'rolling the bones'." The Kizer brothers initially marched the men down to the magistrate and entered pleas of guilty, but then changed their minds and demanded a jury trial. In March 1907, the city council granted George Kizer a liquor license for his former cigar store. The vote was a tie, with Alderman Charles Welch casting a vote in favor and Mayor S.D. Geary, who had been chosen to fill the remainder of Mayor Byers' term after Byers moved to Iowa, casting the tie breaking vote.

In the spring of 1907, the Anti-Saloon League of Illinois successfully lobbied the state to pass a Local Option Law allowing townships and precincts to vote on becoming "anti-saloon territory". Mattoon became a dry town, so the saloon men turned to politicians who would look the other way while they did business. When Alderman Charles Welch announced he was running for mayor in the 1909 municipal election, the reformers were indignant. In one temperance sermon, Reverend E.M. Martin of the First Presbyterian Church thundered, "We want more men with backbone to drive out such citizens as Daylight Welch, Redlight Knight and Midnight Kizer."

Welch defeated Republican Amos H. Messer by 239 votes, but his moment of victory also proved to be his ultimate undoing.

"Colonel Bill" Knight celebrated his friend's victory from jail. On March 24, 1909, a Coles County court found him guilty on 63 counts of selling liquor from his establishment at 2001 Western Avenue. He was sentenced to 1,660 days in Coles County Jail and given a $5,800 fine (equivalent to $163,415 in 2020).

More indictments followed. Mayor Welch wasn't even in office a year when, in September 1909, eight aldermen called on him to resign after he was seen flaunting the law by drinking in saloons. On September 25, he was formally indicted by a grand jury for Misfeasance and Malfeasance in Office. Seventh ward Alderman Michael J. Lynch was also indicted for illegal liquor selling, and later, for perjury. Since Welch's election, the saloons had been operating openly, and the reformers were spurred to action. At a religious revival in March 1910, hundreds called on Welch to enforce the drinking laws or resign.

Charles "Daylight" Welch served out the remainder of his term and ran for reelection as an Independent. On April 18, 1911, Republican Edward T. Guthrie defeated Welch by the largest margin in Mattoon's political history thus far: 2,050 to 746.

DAILY JOURNAL-GAZETTE APRIL 19, 1911

As for Shaggy Row, that spring it was also on the chopping block. On February 8, Ella Brown Turner and several of her "girls" vacated Madame Isabelle's old residence at 2217 Cottage Avenue and fled to Terre Haute after pleading guilty to "keeping a disorderly house." In March, a grand jury investigated Cottage Avenue and intended to prosecute property owners who allowed "houses of ill fame" to operate under their roofs, but in the early morning hours of March 20, a fire of unknown origin spread through that section. The notorious house at 2217 Cottage Avenue went up in flames, along with several adjacent residences.

On Thursday, May 4, 1911, police raided the second floor of a building at 2009 Western Avenue owned by Bill Knight and ran by Madame Rae Berry, who had previously been convicted of running a house of prostitution on Cottage Avenue. Madame Berry absconded to Terre Haute, Indiana. Bill Knight was convicted and paid his last fine for that particular offense. He died in September 1913 at the age of 48.

Mattoon's reformers had won. The "triple iniquity" of "Daylight Welch, Redlight Knight and Midnight Kizer" had been defeated. This era of open gambling, saloons, and vice was over.

REFERENCES

PROLOGUE

"'World's Fastest' machine puts little Lerna on the pop culture map." *Journal Gazette* (Mattoon) 30 May 2010.

"'Tales of Coles County' features spooky stories." *Daily Eastern News* (Charleston) 28 October 2010.

"Twisted Tales." *Times-Courier* (Charleston) 23 October 2007.

"Local paranormal group attracted to the spookier things in life." *JG-TC* (Mattoon) 17 October 2011.

TALES OF COLES COUNTY

Beltt, Bill. "John O'Hair Rides Riot into History." *Heartland* (December 1986).

Coleman, Charles H. and Paul H. Spence. "The Charleston Riot, March 28, 1864." *Journal of the Illinois State Historical Society* 33 (March 1940).

Easter-Shick, Nancy. *'Round the square: Life in downtown Charleston, Illinois, 1830-1998.* Charleston: Easter-Chick Publishing, 1999.

Neely, Mark E., Jr., *The Union Divided: Party Conflict in the Civil War North.* Cambridge: Harvard University Press, 2002.

Parkinson, John Scott. "Bloody Spring: The Charleston, Illinois Riot and Copperhead Violence During the American Civil War" (Ph.D. diss., Miami University, 1998).

Perrin, William Henry. *The History of Coles County, Illinois.* Chicago: W. Le Baron, 1879.

Sampson, Robert D. "'Pretty Damned Warm Times': The 1864 Charleston Riot and 'the Inalienable Right of Revolution'." *Illinois Historical Journal* 89 (Summer 1996).

Tibbals, Richard K. "'There has been a serious disturbance at Charleston...': The 54th Illinois vs. the Copperheads." *Military Images* 21 (July-August 1999).

Wilson, Charles Edward. *Historical Encyclopedia of Illinois and History of Coles County*. Chicago: Munsell Publishing Company, 1906.

Independent Gazette (Mattoon) 7 February 1864.

Plain Dealer (Charleston) 29 March 1864.

GHOST LORE

Stevenson, L.W. *A Family Possessed: A Ghost Story*. Mahomet: Mayhaven Publishing, 2000.

"Ghost Appears on the West Side." *Journal Gazette* (Mattoon) 13 January 1908.

"Spook Hunt Ceases." *Journal Gazette* (Mattoon) 15 January 1908.

"That Ghost Again Walks." *Journal Gazette* (Mattoon) 04 February 1908.

"Another Ghost in North Part of Town." *Journal Gazette* (Mattoon) 16 February 1908.

"Do Ghosts Inhabit the Residence at 2701 Western?" *Journal Gazette* (Mattoon) 26 July 1912.

"Charles Moore is Found Dead in Automobile." *Commercial-Star* (Mattoon) 15 November 1914.

"Death of Tracy Kingman Tuesday." *Journal Gazette* (Mattoon) 1 January 1920.

"Mrs. Kingman dies in Winnetka Sunday." *Journal Gazette* (Mattoon) 7 March 1932.

"Opening of theater in Charleston this week," *The Decatur Daily Review* (Decatur) 6 February 1938.

"Wedding Dress 75 Years Old on Display." *Journal Gazette* (Mattoon) 24 June 1947.

"Keepsakes on Loan to Tycer House." *Journal Gazette* (Mattoon) 11 September 1967.

"Haunted House in Charleston?" *Eastern News* (Charleston) 17 July 1968.

"At Night Come Ghostly Sounds." *Herald and Review* (Decatur) 05 February 1970.

"Marie Tycer, EIU professor, found dead." *Journal Gazette* (Mattoon) 11 March 1970.

"Ghosts roam local haunts..." *Eastern News* (Charleston) 28 October 1977.

"Tragedy results in lonely ghost." *Daily Eastern News* (Charleston) 29 October 1982.

"Haunted House." *Daily Eastern News* (Charleston) 25 October 1985.

Herald and Review (Decatur) 25 February 1989.

"Boo! Unexplained happenings still a mystery to couple." *Journal Gazette* (Mattoon) 26 October 1989.

"Odds and Ends." *Journal Gazette* (Mattoon) 3 November 1989.

"Odds and Ends." *Journal Gazette* (Mattoon) 9 February 1990.

"Phantom of the Theater: Will Rogers employee insists it's haunted," *The Charleston Chew* (Charleston) 19 July 2007.

"Charleston is Haunted." *Daily Eastern News* (Charleston) 30 October 2009.

"Spirits linger in Coles County." *JG-TC* (Mattoon) 30 October 2012.

"Will Rogers Theatre restoration remains a work in progress." *JG-TC* (Mattoon) 10 August 2017.

"Will Rogers partnership unlikely; no noticeable changes in years." *JG-TC* (Mattoon) 18 May 2018.

Ashmore Estates

Charleston and Mattoon Bicentennial Commissions. *History of Coles County, 1876-1976*. Dallas: Taylor Publishing Company, 1976.

Kleen, Michael. *Paranormal Illinois*. Atglen: Schiffer Publishing, 2010.

"Deplorable Condition of Affairs at Coles County Poor House." *Daily Courier* (Charleston) 12 August 1911.

"Ashmore Estates Told to Close." *Times-Courier* (Charleston) 10 May 1979.

"Ashmore Home Reprieve." *Times-Courier* (Charleston) 24 May 1979.

"Poor Farm Makes Money for Coles County." *Times-Courier* (Charleston) 2 January 1980.

"Ashmore Estates Situation Unclear." *Times-Courier* (Charleston) 17 April 1987.

"Ashmore Denies Juvenile Facility Zoning Permit." *Times-Courier* (Charleston) 19 December 1990.

"Ashmore estates Awaits a Little Cleanup, a Lot of Use." *Times-Courier* (Charleston) 8 June 1991.

"Be afraid, very afraid..." *Daily Eastern News* (Charleston) 31 October 1997.

"Coles County to Sell Ashmore Estates." *Times-Courier* (Charleston) 17 January 1998.

"County Still Responsible for 'Poor Farm' Cemetery." *Times-Courier* (Charleston), 20 July 2001.

"Spring Break, Townie Style." *Daily Eastern News* (Charleston) 12 March 2004.

"Ashmore's haunting rumors are false." *Daily Eastern News* (Charleston) 29 October 2004.

"Keep Out... until Halloween." *Times-Courier* (Charleston) 31 August 2006.

"Investigators Say Ashmore Estates is Haunted." *Coles County Leader* (Tuscola), 27 October 2006.

"TV team uses technology to root out spirits at Ashmore Estates." *Times-Courier* (Charleston) 20 July 2008.

"Coles County Poor Farm: Local resident recalls memories of living there during her childhood." *Times-Courier* (Charleston) 19 October 2009.

"Documentary producers make return visit to Ashmore Estates." *Times-Courier* (Charleston) 30 October 2009.

"'Ghost Adventures' looks to scare up good story at Ashmore Estates." *JG-TC* (Mattoon) 4 May 2011.

"Ashmore Estates on TV Friday." *JG-TC* (Mattoon) 20 September 2011.

"Owner: Ashmore Estates to see repairs." *JG-TC* (Mattoon) 1 February 2013.

"Ashmore Estates repairs planned." *JG-TC* (Mattoon) 18 February 2013.

"More than 100 turn out to support damaged historic site Ashmore Estates." *JG-TC* (Mattoon) 3 March 2013.

"Ashmore Estates building sold at auction for $12,700." *JG-TC* (Mattoon) 29 April 2013.

"Ashmore Estates repurposed under new ownership." *Daily Eastern News* (Charleston) 8 October 2014.

"Ashmore Estates has new owner, new plans." *JG-TC* (Mattoon) 15 October 2014.

EASTERN ILLINOIS UNIVERSITY

BURL IVES

Ives, Burl. *Wayfaring Stranger*. New York: Whittlesey House, 1948.

Scott, Beth and Michael Norman. *Haunted America, Volume 1*. New York: Tom Doherty Associates, LLC, 1994.

"President Lord enforces high standard of living." Eastern Illinois University. *The Warbler*. Charleston: 1974.

"Ives returns to college, earns honorary degree." Eastern Illinois University. *The Warbler*. Charleston: 1986.

"Latest claim to fame has EIU divided." *Chicago Tribune* (Chicago) 2 January 1992.

NAPOLEON

"His Majesty Napoleon." Eastern Illinois University. *The Warbler*. Charleston: 1959.

"Traditionalists Resurrect Past with Napoleon II." Eastern Illinois University. *The Warbler*. Charleston: 1966.

Kozy, Amy. "Napoleon: The dog, not the emperor." Eastern Illinois University. *The Warbler*. Charleston: 1995.

"Campus mascot... suffers wound—needs cash." *Eastern State News* (Charleston) 23 September1953.

"Napoleon missing; campus panics." *Eastern State News* (Charleston) 28 October 1953.

"'Nickels for Napoleon'... will save his life." *Eastern State News* (Charleston) 14 April 1954.

"Doctor calls dog 'difficult patient'." *Eastern State News* (Charleston) 26 May 1954.

"Lincoln Hall Notes." *Eastern State News* (Charleston) 13 October 1954.

"Canine confusion... English class moves out; dogs move in." *Eastern State News* (Charleston) 24 November 1954.

"Nap narrates assembly." *Eastern State News* (Charleston) 18 May 1955.

"Napoleon Showing Signs of Losing His Once-Mighty Grip!" *Eastern State News* (Charleston) 2 May 1956.

"The Sounding Board." *Eastern State News* (Charleston) 9 May 1956.

"'Nap' to Greet Alums." *Eastern State News* (Charleston) 17 October 1956.

"Nap Found Dead, Laid to Rest On Campus." *Eastern State News* (Charleston) 11 May 1960.

"Memorial for Campus Mascot to be Placed in Union Lounge." *Eastern State News* (Charleston) 7 February 1964.

"Napoleon II Killed in Hit-And-Run." *Eastern News* (Charleston) 16 March 1966.

THE PHANTOM

"Where The Action Is." *Eastern News* (Charleston) 13 July 1966.

"'Phantom' Strikes Again." *Eastern News* (Charleston) 23 April 1968.

"Phantom Starts with Watermelon; Continues Capers." *Eastern News* (Charleston) 9 May 1969.

"Phantom respects cops." *Eastern News* (Charleston) 3 October 1969.

"Phantom for senator." *Eastern News* (Charleston) 24 October 1969.

"Mickey Mouse McAfee." *Eastern News* (Charleston) 31 October 1969.

"Phantom protests recent pretenders." *Eastern News* (Charleston) 7 November 1969.

"Eastern has 31-year-old 'Big Ben'." *Eastern News* (Charleston) 14 November 1969.

"Where is Phantom?" *Eastern News* (Charleston) 22 September 1970.

"Phantom lives!" *Eastern News* (Charleston) 9 October 1970.

"Phantom sign not up to par." *Eastern News* (Charleston) 23 October 1970.

"Phantom strikes." *Eastern News* (Charleston) 18 April 1973.

"Tune in tonight." *Eastern News* (Charleston) 11 May 1973.

"Request Phantom's return." *Eastern News* (Charleston) 14 May 1973.

"Phantom strikes." *Eastern News* (Charleston) 30 October 1973.

"Old radio 'do-gooder' lurks here at Eastern." *Eastern News* (Charleston) 22 January 1974.

"'The Shadow' leaves trail of broken locks." *Eastern News* (Charleston) 28 January 1974.

"Where's 'Shadow' Now?" *Eastern News* (Charleston) 17 April 1974.

"Identity of Phantom still remains a mystery." *Eastern News* (Charleston) 21 October 1988.

PEMBERTON HALL

Allen-Kline, Margaret. "'She Protects Her Girls': The Legend of Mary Hawkins at Pemberton Hall." M.A. thesis, Eastern Illinois University, 1998.

Christensen, Jo-Anne. *Ghost Stories of Illinois*. Edmonton: Lone Pine, 2000.

Huchel, Brian. "A Ghost in the Hall." Eastern Illinois University. *The Warbler*. Charleston: 1995.

Kleen, Michael. *Paranormal Illinois*. Atglen: Schiffer Publishing, 2010.

_____. *The Legend of Pemberton Hall*. Charleston: Black Oak Press, Illinois, 2008.

Quinn, Kelli. "A Ghost's Story: Few Know the Truth of Pemberton's Mary." Eastern Illinois University. *The Warbler*. Charleston: 1998.

Scott, Beth and Michael Norman. *Haunted Heartland: True Ghost Stories from the American Midwest*. New York: Barnes & Noble Books, 1985, 1992.

Scott, Beth and Michael Norman. *Haunted America, Volume 1*. New York: Tom Doherty Associates, LLC, 1994.

Taylor, Troy. Haunted Illinois: Travel Guide to the History and Hauntings of the Prairie State. Alton: Whitechapel Productions Press, 2004.

"Miss Mary E. Hawkins Died This Morning." *Daily Courier* (Charleston) 30 October 1918.

"Mary E. Hawkins: A Most Worthy Woman." *Daily Courier* (Charleston) 31 October 1918.

"Pemberton Hall Most Historical Building On Campus." *Eastern News* (Charleston) 22 October 1965.

"Ghosts in Pem? True or not, myths persist." *Eastern News* (Charleston) 15 October 1976.

"Myth of Pem ghost based on live coed." *Eastern News* (Charleston) 5 November 1976.

"Halloween brings out Pem's 'spirit.'" *Eastern News* (Charleston) 27 October 1978.

"Was 'Mary' dorm's late-night visitor?" *Herald and Review* (Decatur) 31 October 1984.

"Pemberton students share eerie stories of fourth-floor murder tale." *Daily Eastern News* (Charleston) 25 October 1985.

"Pemberton prowler tales persist." *Daily Eastern News* (Charleston) 2 November 1989.

"A legend exhumed." *Daily Eastern News* (Charleston) 29 October 1993.

"Remember Mary? Here's the story behind EIU's Pem Hall ghosts." *Times-Courier* (Charleston) 26 October 1994.

"Students scare up ghosts." *Daily Eastern News* (Charleston) 31 October 1997.

"Pemberton's legend, Mary." *Daily Eastern News* (Charleston) 31 October 2008.

"Ghost of Pemberton just a story." *Daily Eastern News* (Charleston) 30 October 2009.

"Expanding a legacy: Hawkins descendant comes to EIU." *JG-TC* (Mattoon) 27 September 2014.

CEMETERY LORE

Lewis, Chad and Terry Fisk. *The Illinois Road Guide to Haunted Locations.* Eau Claire: Unexplained Research Publishing, 2007.

Peck, Marsha. "Old Dry Grove Cemetery." *Heartland* (May 1986).

"Digging up the past." *Daily Eastern News* (Charleston) 30 October 1989.

"Cemetery in Ashmore desecrated by vandals." *Herald and Review* (Decatur) 07 August 1990.

"Witch's Grave in Coles County?" *Coles County Leader* (Tuscola) 31 October 2003.

"Mattoon, Ashmore cemeteries part of book of haunted places in Illinois." *Journal Gazette* (Mattoon) 09 January 2008.

"Charleston is Haunted." *Daily Eastern News* (Charleston) 30 October 2009.

"Mattoon-based thriller gets a name." *Journal Gazette* (Mattoon) 14 May 2010.

"Emergency crews to make some noise for film crew." *Journal Gazette* (Mattoon) 3 September 2010.

"Murder mystery filmed in Pemberton." *Daily Eastern News* (Charleston) 7 September 2010.

MAD GASSER OF MATTOON

Bartholomew, Robert E. and Jeffrey S. Victor. "A Social-Psychological Theory of Collective Anxiety Attacks: The 'Mad Gasser' Reexamined." *The Sociological Quarterly* 45 (Spring 2004).

Maruna, Scott. *The Mad Gasser of Mattoon: Dispelling the Hysteria*. Jacksonville, IL: Swamp Gas Book Co., 2003.

"'Anesthetic Prowler' on Loose." *Daily Journal-Gazette* (Mattoon) 2 September 1944.

"Anesthetic Prowler Adds Victim." *Daily Journal-Gazette* (Mattoon) 6 September 1944.

"Victims of Gas Prowler Now 25." *Daily Courier* (Charleston) 9 September 1944.

"Many Prowler Reports; Few Real." *Daily Journal-Gazette* (Mattoon) 11 September 1944.

"'Gas Calls' at Vanishing Point." *Daily Journal-Gazette* (Mattoon) 13 September 1944.

"Mad Gasser legend is 50." *Journal Gazette* (Mattoon) 1 September 1994.

"Two authors say Mad Gasser was real." *Journal Gazette* (Mattoon) 26 February 2003.

"'Mad Gasser' author points finger at 'brilliant' chemistry student." *Journal Gazette* (Mattoon) 30 June 2003.

"One former Mattoon resident chalks Mad Gasser case up to mass hysteria." *Journal Gazette* (Mattoon) 11 March 2005.

"Debating the Mad Gasser" in Mattoon Sesquicentennial. *Journal Gazette* (Mattoon) 17 August 2005.

"Public quotes regarding Mad Gasser fear." *Journal Gazette* (Mattoon) 18 August 2005.

"'Mad Gasser' attacks drew attention to Mattoon." *JG-TC* (Mattoon) 23 September 2014.

"Former Mattoon resident writes book about 'Mad Gasser' incident." *JG-TC* (Mattoon) 26 October 2014.

"75 years ago, Mattoon fearful of 'Mad Gasser'." *JG-TC* (Mattoon) 31 August 2019.

ROADS LESS TRAVELED

Peck, John Mason. *A Gazetteer of Illinois, in Three Parts.* Philadelphia: Grigg & Elliott, 1837.

"Cars in Collision at Dead Man's Grove Corner." *The Daily Journal-Gazette and Commercial Star* (Mattoon) 2 May 1931.

"Sullivan Young Man Killed." *The Daily Journal-Gazette and Commercial Star* (Mattoon) 1 February 1935.

"Kerans Exonerated in Death of Harold Conard." *The Daily Journal-Gazette and Commercial Star* (Mattoon) 5 February 1935.

"3 Autos Collide at Dead Man's Grove." *The Daily Journal-Gazette and Commercial Star* (Mattoon) 17 January 1939.

"Youth Escapes Burning Auto." *The Daily Journal-Gazette and Commercial Star* (Mattoon) 2 March 1951.

"Dead Man's Grove Curve or Just Dead Man's Curve?" *The Daily Journal-Gazette and Commercial Star* (Mattoon) 29 May 1953.

"Curve not deadly: officials." *Herald and Review* (Decatur) 1 June 1984.

Journal-Gazette (Mattoon) 23 June 1987.

"Sentence includes jail time for DUI." *Herald and Review* (Decatur) 6 August 1987.

"Woman hurt, ticketed in accident on Illinois 316." *The Daily Journal-Gazette* (Mattoon) 9 June 1995.

"Truck overturns on Dead Man's Curve drive; driver OK." *Journal-Gazette* (Mattoon) 3 May 1999.

"Real tragedy at rumored haunted bridge." *Daily Eastern News* (Charleston) 27 October 2005.

"Airtight Bridge to go retro with wood deck." *Journal Gazette* (Mattoon) 20 February 2010.

"Woman hurt in accident." *JG-TC* (Mattoon) 27 June 2012.

CRIME

FRONTIER CRIME

Perrin, William Henry. *The History of Coles County, Illinois*. Chicago: W. Le Baron, 1879.

Wilson, Charles Edward. *Historical Encyclopedia of Illinois and History of Coles County*. Chicago: Munsell Publishing Company, 1906.

LYNCHINGS

Easter-Shick, Nancy. *'Round the square: Life in downtown Charleston, Illinois, 1830-1998*. Charleston: Easter-Chick Publishing, 1999.

Lupton, John A. "'In View of the Uncertainty of Life': A Coles County Lynching." *Illinois Historical Journal* 89 (Autumn 1996).

Wilson, Charles Edward. *Historical Encyclopedia of Illinois and History of Coles County*. Chicago: Munsell Publishing Company, 1906.

"Shocking Tragedy—Man Shot by his Son in Law." *Mount Carmel Register* (Mount Carmel, IL) 31 October 1855.

"Strangled by a Mob." *The Daily Inter Ocean* (Chicago) 27 June 1888.

"Speedy Justice." *The Herald* (Decatur) 27 June 1888.

"A Terrible Affair!" *The Mattoon Gazette* (Mattoon) 29 June 1888.

"That Lynching Bee." *Daily Republican* (Decatur) 14 July 1888.

Decatur Weekly Republican (Decatur) 19 July 1888.

"Indicted for the Hanging of William Moore." *Chicago Tribune* (Chicago) 8 October 1888.

"First Coles County Clerk Murdered; Killer Lynched." *Daily Journal Gazette* (Mattoon) 1 September 1955.

"Coles County Gets Weapon: Convicted Slayer Denounced Lynching Mob in his Will." Herald and Review (Decatur) 11 March 1962.

"Family feud leads to mob lynching." *Herald and Review* (Decatur) 2 June 1985.

"Murder, lynching a 'blot on Charleston's character'." *Journal Gazette* (Mattoon) 29 June 2010.

"19th-century mob rule in Charleston." *Herald and Review* (Decatur) 15 August 2011.

John Mason

"Murder in Cold Blood! John Mason Shot and Killed." *The Mattoon Commercial* (Mattoon) 22 April 1880.

The Inter Ocean (Chicago) 22 April 1880.

Charleston Plain Dealer (Charleston) 22 April 1880.

Mattoon Gazette (Mattoon) 23 April 1880.

The Pantagraph (Bloomington) 16 November 1880.

The Rock Island Argus (Rock Island) 18 November 1880.

The Inter Ocean (Chicago) 29 November 1880.

"Acquitted." *The Decatur Daily Review* (Decatur) 30 November 1880.

"Mother of Mrs. R. L. Harvey Passes Away." *The Journal-Gazette* (Mattoon) 8 March 1918.

The Journal-Gazette (Mattoon) 9 March 1918.

The Strange Death of Cora Stallman

"Woman Ends Her Life in a Cistern." Daily Journal-Gazette and Commercial-Star (Mattoon) 1 August 1925.

"Veiled Threat Adds New Mystery to Death of Coles County Woman." Decatur Herald (Decatur) 2 August 1925.

"Autopsy Reveals Coles Cistern Victim Did Not Meet Death in Water." Decatur Herald (Decatur) 3 August 1925.

"Weird Chain of Incidents Baffles Police." Chicago Daily Tribune (Chicago) 3 August 1925.

"Mattoon, Ill. Murder is Mysterious." The Daily Independent (Murphysboro, IL) 3 August 1925.

"Turn to Threatening Letters for Key to Coles Cistern Death." Decatur Herald (Decatur) 4 August 1925.

"Hatred Seen as Sole Motive in Cistern Death." Chicago Daily Tribune (Chicago) 4 August 1925.

"Shirley Says Miss Stallman was a Suicide." Daily Journal-Gazette and Commercial-Star (Mattoon) 4 August 1925.

"Cistern Victim Took Own Life, Sister Insists." Chicago Daily Tribune (Chicago) 5 August 1925.

"'We Believe it is a Case of Suicide'." Daily Journal-Gazette and Commercial-Star (Mattoon) 5 August 1925.

"Position of Stallman Body When Found, Blow to Theory of Suicide." Decatur Herald (Decatur) 6 August 1925.

"Stallman Mystery Gets Deeper." Daily Journal-Gazette and Commercial-Star (Mattoon) 6 August 1925.

"Woman Thrown into Farm Well, Coroner Says." Chicago Daily Tribune (Chicago) 6 August 1925.

"Stallman Quiz at Standstill." Decatur Herald (Decatur) 8 August 1925.

"No Date Yet Set for Stallman Inquest." Daily Journal-Gazette and Commercial-Star (Mattoon) 21 August 1925.

"Inquiry into Death of Coles Woman Will Be Started This Afternoon." Decatur Herald (Decatur) 27 August 1925.

"No Solution is Reached in Stallman Case." Daily Journal-Gazette and Commercial-Star (Mattoon) 28 August 1925.

"Miss Stallman Did Not Drown." The Decatur Review (Decatur) 28 August 1925.

"Inquest in Stallman Case Resumed Today." Daily Journal-Gazette and Commercial-Star (Mattoon) 31 August 1925.

"Open Verdict is Reached in Stallman Case." Daily Journal-Gazette and Commercial-Star (Mattoon) 1 September 1925.

"Coroner's Jury Returns Open Verdict in Coles Cistern Death Mystery." Decatur Herald (Decatur) 1 September 1925.

"Stallman Case Evidence to go Before Grand Jury." Daily Journal-Gazette and Commercial-Star (Mattoon) 14 October 1925.

THE COX MURDERS

Sawyer, Diane. *The Mattoon Murders*. Jonesboro, Ark: Southern Publishing Co., 1982.

Cox, William. "A Tragic Saturday That Shattered My Family." *Awake!*, October 22, 1986.

"For Friends the Vigil Was Lonely." *Journal Gazette* (Mattoon) 29 April 1968.

"Slayings Trigger County's Biggest Manhunt." *Journal Gazette* (Mattoon) 29 April 1968.

"Youth Held—5 Children Killed." *Wausau Daily Herald* (Wausau, WI) 29 April 1968.

"Youth Charged in Mattoon Slayings." *Decatur Herald* (Decatur) 29 April 1968.

"Fuller Charged With 5 Slayings." *The Decatur Review* (Decatur) 29 April 1968.

"Girlfriend Says Accused Slayer Hated Family." *Journal Gazette* (Mattoon) 30 April 1968.

"Accused Youth Was Refused Permission to Marry Cox Girl." *Decatur Herald* (Decatur) 30 April 1968.

"Cox Family Looking for New Home." *Journal Gazette* (Mattoon) 3 May 1968.

"Fuller Pleads Innocent." *Journal Gazette* (Mattoon) 13 May 1968.

"Glenn Says He Will Ask Death Penalty." *Journal Gazette* (Mattoon) 14 October 1968.

"Cox Family May Testify in Murder Trial." *Journal Gazette* (Mattoon) 15 October 1968.

"Testimony Quotes Fuller: 'I Did It'." *Journal Gazette* (Mattoon) 24 October 1968.

"Fuller 'Didn't Want to Murder'." *Decatur Herald* (Decatur) 5 November 1968.

"Fuller Tells Why He Killed Children." *The Decatur Review* (Decatur) 7 November 1968.

"I was Real Hot, a Dry Hot...I Cried on Sunday." *Journal Gazette* (Mattoon) 7 November 1968.

"Three Cox children testify." *Journal Gazette* (Mattoon) 9 November 1968.

"Fuller 'Planned to Kill'." *The Decatur Review* (Decatur) 9 November 1968.

"Fuller Draws 70 to 99 Years." *Journal Gazette* (Mattoon) 10 December 1968.

"The innocence lost" in Mattoon Sesquicentennial. *Journal Gazette* (Mattoon) 17 August 2005.

"Man seeking parole in 1968 Mattoon murders." *Herald and Review* (Decatur) 13 June 2014.

"Fifty years later, they remain 'Taken Before Their Time'." *The News-Gazette* (Champaign) 2 May 2018.

THE TRAGIC '70s

"Police probe fatal stabbing." *Journal Gazette* (Mattoon) 28 August 1972.

"Report suspects located in stabbing probe." *Journal Gazette* (Mattoon) 29 August 1972.

"Police seek woman." *Journal Gazette* (Mattoon) 2 September 1972.

"FBI joins probe of slaying." *Journal Gazette* (Mattoon) 22 September 1972.

"Woman to Be Arraigned Today in Stabbing Case." *Decatur Herald* (Decatur) 6 November 1972.

"Manslaughter plea heard." *Journal Gazette* (Mattoon) 8 March 1973.

"Woman sentenced in fatal Mattoon stabbing." *Journal Gazette* (Mattoon) 9 March 1973.

"Police search for coed." *Journal Gazette* (Mattoon) 6 July 1973.

"Coed found dead." *Journal Gazette* (Mattoon) 9 July 1973.

"Violent death indicated." *Southern Illinoisan* (Carbondale) 9 July 1973.

"Woman Had Been Shot in Head: Sheriff." *Decatur Herald* (Decatur) 11 July 1973.

"Jury verdict murder." *Journal Gazette* (Mattoon) 18 July 1973.

"Reward offered by city." *Eastern News* (Charleston) 18 July 1973.

"Grisly Slayings Shock, Baffle Area Lawmen." *The Terre Haute Tribune* (Terre Haute) 22 July 1973.

"Young girl's body found near city." *Journal Gazette* (Mattoon) 18 July 1973.

"Coles authorities continue investigations into deaths." *Journal Gazette* (Mattoon) 13 August 1973.

"Cause of girl's death not found." *Journal Gazette* (Mattoon) 17 August 1973.

"'No news' latest report in Rardin murder case." *Eastern News* (Charleston) 29 August 1973.

"Foster bound over on slaying charge." *Journal Gazette* (Mattoon) 10 October 1973.

"Murder of EIU coed remains unsolved." *Herald and Review* (Decatur) 1 January 1974.

"Woman Found Dead Near Lake Paradise." *Times-Courier* (Charleston) 11 March 1974.

"Authorities Not Certain If Foul Play Involved." *Times-Courier* (Charleston) 12 March 1974.

"Official confirms woman strangled." *Journal Gazette* (Mattoon) 13 March 1974.

"Hideous crime must open eyes." *Journal Gazette* (Mattoon) 28 March 1974.

"No arrests made in Shriver case." *Journal Gazette* (Mattoon) 29 March 1974.

"Drop murder charge." *Journal Gazette* (Mattoon) 11 April 1974.

"Investigators without clues in two area murders." *Journal Gazette* (Mattoon) 16 April 1974.

"Sheriff considers reward offer to help solve slaying of girl." *Journal Gazette* (Mattoon) 4 February 1975.

"Lanman search is underway." *Journal Gazette* (Mattoon) 5 March 1977.

"Andy Lanman's Body Found South of City." *Times-Courier* (Charleston) 21 March 1977.

"Foul play not ruled out in EIU student's death." *Journal Gazette* (Mattoon) 21 March 1977.

"No Visible Wounds on Andy Lanman Body." *Times-Courier* (Charleston) 22 March 1977.

"Lanman test results secret." *Journal Gazette* (Mattoon) 5 April 1977.

"Lanman Died of Massive Overdose." *Times-Courier* (Charleston) 15 April 1977.

"Stuffle denies charges he tried to divert probe." *Journal Gazette* (Mattoon) 22 April 1977.

"Woman's Body Found in Creek Near Toledo." *Decatur Herald* (Decatur) 25 April 1977.

"Sheriff seeks suspects, motives in murder case." *Journal Gazette* (Mattoon) 25 April 1977.

"Death Ruled Homicide." *Decatur Herald* (Decatur) 19 May 1977.

"No suspects in murder." *Journal Gazette* (Mattoon) 26 April 1977.

"Jury to convene May 9 to probe Lanman case." *Journal Gazette* (Mattoon) 29 April 1977.

"Campaign initiated to solve murders." *Journal Gazette* (Mattoon) 9 July 1977.

"Reward Nets No Leads in Coles Deaths." *Decatur Herald* (Decatur) 19 July 1977.

"Why was no arrest made?" *Journal Gazette* (Mattoon) 4 February 1978.

"Lanman's death still unsolved after one year." *Eastern News* (Charleston) 1 March 1978.

"Convict indicted for murder." *Journal Gazette* (Mattoon) 7 April 1978.

"Jerry Ross murder trial rescheduled." *Journal Gazette* (Mattoon) 24 June 1978.

"Confession alleged." *Journal Gazette* (Mattoon) 29 September 1978.

"State rests its case in Ross trial." *Journal Gazette* (Mattoon) 30 September 1978.

"Ross found guilty." *Journal Gazette* (Mattoon) 4 October 1978.

"Trials result in convictions." *Journal Gazette* (Mattoon) 5 January 1979.

"Drug death suit asks $3 million." *Journal Gazette* (Mattoon) 27 February 1979.

"Charges link 3 men to Lanman overdose." *Eastern News* (Charleston) 28 February 1979.

"Trial Opens for Suspect In '74 Killing of Deputy." *St. Louis Post-Dispatch* (St. Louis) 7 January 1982.

"Wright acquitted of murder." *Decatur Herald* (Decatur) 3 February 1982.

"Rardin murder case alive." *Journal Gazette* (Mattoon) 25 February 1982.

"No foolin', urban myths abound in Coles County." *Times-Courier* (Charleston) 31 March 2006.

AIRTIGHT BRIDGE MURDER

Kleen, Michael. *Paranormal Illinois*. Atglen: Schiffer Publishing, 2010.

"Headless Body Found at Bridge." *Times-Courier* (Charleston) 20 October 1980.

"Identity of headless body sought." *Journal Gazette* (Mattoon) 20 October 1980.

"Bridge mystery unsolved." *Times-Courier* (Charleston) 21 October 1980.

"Lynch: Victim's blood type 'rare'." *Journal Gazette* (Mattoon) 21 October 1980.

"Doctor Deduces Clues in 'Airtight Case'." *Times-Courier* (Charleston) 22 October 1980.

"Sheriff seeking clues of woman's identity." *Daily Eastern News* (Charleston) 22 October 1980.

"Bizarre murder case isn't unique." *Journal Gazette* (Mattoon) 23 October 1980.

"Authorities still seek clues." *Journal Gazette* (Mattoon) 28 October 1980.

"Lucas suspected in area slaying." *Herald & Review* (Decatur) 18 August 1984.

"Few new details in Airtight Bridge inquiry." *Journal Gazette* (Mattoon) 24 November 1992.

"Progress slow in inquiry of Airtight Bridge murder." *Journal Gazette* (Mattoon) 10 December 1992.

"Real tragedy at rumored haunted bridge." *Daily Eastern News* (Charleston) 27 October 2005.

"Airtight Bridge murder victim honored by daughter who barely knew her." *Times-Courier* (Charleston) 5 December 2008.

"Arrest announced in 1980 Airtight Bridge murder." *JG-TC* (Mattoon) 4 March 2017.

"Cox long thought victim's husband was 'prime suspect'." *JG-TC* (Mattoon) 8 March 2017.

"Husband pleads guilty in Airtight Bridge case." *JG-TC* (Mattoon) 4 November 2017.

"A 37-year-old mystery solved." *JG-TC* (Mattoon) 16 December 2017.

"Reopening case led to confession in Airtight Bridge murder." *Southern Illinoisan* (Carbondale) 17 December 2017.

THE MILLENNIUM MURDERS

"Campus Feels Closure: Boulay found guilty of murder, sentenced 24 years." Eastern Illinois University. *The Warbler*. Charleston: 1999.

"Apartment blaze: Students belongings razed." Eastern Illinois University. *The Warbler*. Charleston: 2000/2001.

"Sharing life tales in honor of Miss Blumberg." Eastern Illinois University. *The Warbler*. Charleston: 2000/2001.

"Eastern student murdered: McNamara remembered for her academics and athletics." Eastern Illinois University. *The Warbler*. Charleston: 2002.

"EIU student held in murder." *Herald and Review* (Decatur) 4 February 1998.

"Freshman found murdered." *Daily Eastern News* (Charleston) 4 February 1998.

"Bond set for suspect in strangling." *Journal Gazette* (Mattoon) 5 February 1998.

"Campus mourns loss of student." *Daily Eastern News* (Charleston) 6 February 1998.

"Note reveals he 'lost it'." *Journal Gazette* (Mattoon) 3 March 1999.

"Boulay sentenced: One-time EIU student gets 24 years for murder." *Journal Gazette* (Mattoon) 19 May 1999.

"Woman found dead in Charleston." *Journal Gazette* (Mattoon) 30 June 1999.

"Body found on Seventh." *Daily Eastern News* (Charleston) 30 June 1999.

"Children were there to see mom die." *Journal Gazette* (Mattoon) 1 July 1999.

"Police: Child woke to find mom dead." *Journal Gazette* (Mattoon) 2 July 1999.

"Police interview neighbors, friends, family in Charleston murder case." *Journal Gazette* (Mattoon) 13 July 1999.

"Grief-stricken family hoping for break in case." *Journal Gazette* (Mattoon) 30 September 1999.

"Young woman is found shot to death at shop in O'Fallon, Ill." *St. Louis Post-Dispatch* (St. Louis) 2 January 2000.

"St. Louis police officers arrive at EIU to investigate New Year's Eve shooting death of student in O'Fallon." *Journal Gazette* (Mattoon) 3 January 2000.

"Sorority coping with another fallen 'sister'." *Journal Gazette* (Mattoon) 4 January 2000.

"O'Fallon police send details of woman's slaying to special FBI unit." *St. Louis Post-Dispatch* (St. Louis) 9 January 2000.

"Students mourn loss of Eastern junior." *Daily Eastern News* (Charleston) 10 January 2000.

"Memorial service to honor Eastern student." *Daily Eastern News* (Charleston) 11 January 2000.

"Composites of possible attacker, witness posted." *Daily Eastern News* (Charleston) 18 January 2000.

"Apparent lack of motive makes woman's slaying harder to solve." *St. Louis Post-Dispatch* (St. Louis) 10 April 2000.

"Police still need leads in slaying of woman a year ago." *St. Louis Post-Dispatch* (St. Louis) 31 December 2000.

"Eastern student murdered." *Journal Gazette* (Mattoon) 13 June 2001.

"Student's death being investigated." *Daily Eastern News* (Charleston) 13 June 2001.

"Police probe EIU student's death." *Herald and Review* (Decatur) 13 June 2001.

"Rolling Meadows woman slain at EIU." *Chicago Tribune* (Chicago) 13 June 2001.

"EIU student's death a homicide." *Chicago Tribune* (Chicago) 14 June 2001.

"Autopsy results point to strangulation." *Journal Gazette* (Mattoon) 14 June 2001.

"EIU student charged in murder case." *Journal Gazette* (Mattoon) 15 June 2001.

"Authorities wait for lab tests before filing formal charges." *Journal Gazette* (Mattoon) 16 June 2001.

"Eastern student charged with first degree murder." *Daily Eastern News* (Charleston) 18 June 2001.

"Mertz charged with 6 counts of first-degree murder." *Journal Gazette* (Mattoon) 28 June 2001.

"McNamara murder heightens frustration for Warner's family." *Journal Gazette* (Mattoon) 29 June 2001.

"Trial date set for EIU student accused in coed's killing." *Herald and Review* (Decatur) 24 July 2001.

"State to seek death penalty." *Journal Gazette* (Mattoon) 6 September 2001.

"Candlelit memorial draws 1,500 to honor McNamara." *Daily Eastern News* (Charleston) 17 September 2001.

"Police are seeking to question murder suspect in 3rd slaying." *St. Louis Post-Dispatch* (St. Louis) 14 February 2002.

"Parents of slain student say report of possible suspect is no big surprise." *St. Louis Post-Dispatch* (St. Louis) 25 February 2002.

"Judge grants defense request to delay Mertz trial." *Journal Gazette* (Mattoon) 11 September 2002.

"Ferguson: Physical evidence, DNA led to Mertz." *Journal Gazette* (Mattoon) 4 February 2003.

"Officer: McNamara died in bathroom." *Journal Gazette* (Mattoon) 5 February 2003.

"Mertz jury to hear testimony on other break-ins." *Journal Gazette* (Mattoon) 6 February 2003.

"McNamara's arm wound, Martz's watch 'correlate'." *Journal Gazette* (Mattoon) 7 February 2003.

"Cellmate testifies that Mertz bragged of killing McNamara." *Journal Gazette* (Mattoon) 8 February 2003.

"Jury quickly finds Mertz guilty." *Journal Gazette* (Mattoon) 13 February 2003.

"Trial evidence was gathered by an 'All-American girl'." *Journal Gazette* (Mattoon) 14 February 2003.

"Mertz lnked to Warner murder." *Journal Gazette* (Mattoon) 19 February 2003.

"Defense tries to clear Mertz in other cases." *Herald and Review* (Decatur) 22 February 2003.

"Mertz going to death row." *Journal Gazette* (Mattoon) 27 February 2003.

"Warner's family sure Mertz was killer." *Journal Gazette* (Mattoon) 7 March 2003.

"State will seek life term in slaying of student." *St. Louis Post-Dispatch* (St. Louis) 3 September 2004.

"In court, father tells of grisly scene." *St. Louis Post-Dispatch* (St. Louis) 3 April 2007.

"Guilty verdict in killing of Illinois student." *St. Louis Post-Dispatch* (St. Louis) 14 April 2007.

"Phillips gets 55-year term for killing Amy Blumberg." *St. Louis Post-Dispatch* (St. Louis) 30 May 2007.

"Convicted murderer of EIU student scheduled to get out on parole." *Journal Gazette* (Mattoon) 12 November 2010.

"EIU vigil remembers Andrea Will on day her murderer is released from prison." *Herald and Review* (Decatur) 17 November 2010.

"Bill to keep tabs on freed killers goes to Quinn." *Chicago Tribune* (Chicago) 30 June 2011.

"State's attorney finishes 20 years." *JG-TC* (Mattoon) 1 December 2012.

Disasters

Carey, J.P. "The Central Illinois Tornado of May 26, 1917." *Geographical Review* 4 (August 1917).

Perrin, William Henry. *The History of Coles County, Illinois*. Chicago: W. Le Baron, 1879.

Power, John C. *History of the Early Settlers of Sangamon County, Illinois*. Springfield, IL: Edwin A. Wilson & Company, 1876.

Williams, Jack Moore. *History of Vermilion County, Illinois*, Vol. 1. Topeka: Historical Publishing Company, 1930.

Wilson, Charles Edward. *Historical Encyclopedia of Illinois and History of Coles County*. Chicago: Munsell Publishing Company, 1906.

"Twelve Dead, Score Hurt on Interurban." *The Daily Review* (Decatur) 30 August 1907.

"12 Are Killed Outright." *Journal Gazette* (Mattoon) 30 August 1907.

"27 Killed, 50 Hurt in Trolley Crash." *The New York Times* (New York City) 31 August 1907.

"Fifteen killed in trolley wreck." *Paxton Daily Record* (Paxton) 31 August 1907.

"20 Killed on Interurban." *The Daily Free Press* (Carbondale) 31 August 1907.

"Both motormen are held for criminal negligence." *Journal Gazette* (Mattoon) 2 September 1907.

"Victims now seventeen." *Journal Gazette* (Mattoon) 3 September 1907.

"Illinois Wind Killed 150." *The Chicago Sunday Tribune* (Chicago) 27 May 1917.

"200 Killed in Illinois Tornado." *Sunday Review* (Decatur) 27 May 1917.

"54 Dead in Mattoon; 38 in Charleston." *The Decatur Herald* (Decatur) 28 May 1917.

"Relief sent stricken at Mattoon, Ill." *The Rock Island Argus* (Rock Island) 28 May 1917.

"Thrilling experiences of Saturday's big storm." *Journal Gazette* (Mattoon) 28 May 1917.

"Mattoon lays plans for rise out of wreck." *The Chicago Daily Tribune* (Chicago) 29 May 1917.

"Tornado-devastated cities require help." *The Decatur Herald* (Decatur) 29 May 1917.

"Fairgrounds are wrecked." *Journal Gazette* (Mattoon) 31 May 1917.

"8 States Storm-Swept." *The Nashville Journal* (Nashville, IL) 31 May 1917.

"CIPS in Mattoon: The early years." *Journal Gazette* (Mattoon) 24 March 1979.

"Blair Burns." *Daily Eastern News* (Charleston) 29 April 2004.

"Blair Hall Burns: Historic EIU building severely damaged." *Journal Gazette* (Mattoon) 29 April 2004.

"Burned, but not beaten." *Daily Eastern News* (Charleston) 30 April 2004.

"Cooley said workers not at fault for Blair fire." *Daily Eastern News* (Charleston) 23 August 2004.

"Tornado devastates area" in Mattoon Sesquicentennial. *Journal Gazette* (Mattoon) 17 August 2005.

"18 killed in Interurban collision" in Mattoon Sesquicentennial. *Journal Gazette* (Mattoon) 17 August 2005.

"Blair Hall is a part of history." *Daily Eastern News* (Charleston) 25 April 2006.

"December 1836 'Sudden Change' a dangerous event for early settlers." *The Pantagraph* (Bloomington) 14 December 2008.

GHOST TOWNS

Charleston and Mattoon Bicentennial Commissions. *History of Coles County, 1876-1976*. Dallas: Taylor Publishing Company, 1976.

Coles County, Illinois Cemeteries Map. Coles County Genealogical Society, 2001.

Coles County Map & Tour Guide. Phelps Map Service, 2011.

"Church Nears Centennial: St. Omer's, Near Ashmore, Plans Special Service." *The Decatur Daily Review* (Decatur) 19 September 1940.

"Discovering Coles County Driving Tours." *Journal Gazette* (Mattoon) 22 June 1979.

"Diona, Johnstown, Farmington Rich in History." *Daily Journal-Gazette and Commercial-Star* (Mattoon) 7 January 1935.

Perrin, William Henry. *The History of Coles County, Illinois*. Chicago: W. Le Baron, 1879.

Ku Klux Klan

Kacich, Tom, et al. *Hot Type: 150 Years of the Best Local Stories from the News-Gazette*. Champaign: Sports Publishing L.L.C., 2002.

Ogbomo, Onaiwu. Photographic Images and the History of African Americans in Coles County, Illinois. Office of African American Studies and the Tarble Arts Center, Eastern Illinois University, 2002. https://www.eiu.edu/africana/pages/colescounty/index.htm

"Paris Boasts of a Ku Klux Klan." *Daily Journal-Gazette and Commercial-Star* (Mattoon) 26 May 1922.

"K.K.K. Makes Gift to Pastor." *Daily Journal-Gazette and Commercial-Star* (Mattoon) 29 July 1922.

"Klansmen to Hold Public Meeting Here." *Daily Journal-Gazette and Commercial-Star* (Mattoon) 8 August 1922.

"Ku Klux Klan Lecture Draws Large Audience." *Daily Journal-Gazette and Commercial-Star* (Mattoon) 14 August 1922.

"Mayor of Decatur in Ku Klux Klan Warning." *Daily Journal-Gazette and Commercial-Star* (Mattoon) 16 August 1922.

"Rev. M'Mahan Admits He Belongs to Klan." *Daily Journal-Gazette and Commercial-Star* (Mattoon) 17 October 1922.

"Mattoon Klan at Shelbyville." *Daily Journal-Gazette and Commercial-Star* (Mattoon) 31 October 1922.

"Bitter Scenes at Meeting of 1st Christian." *Daily Journal-Gazette and Commercial-Star* (Mattoon) 5 December 1922.

"Mattoon Minister to Speak on Klan in Paris." *Daily Journal-Gazette and Commercial-Star* (Mattoon) 24 January 1923.

"Big Parade of Klansmen Sat. Night." *Daily Journal-Gazette and Commercial-Star* (Mattoon) 28 May 1923.

"Thousands Attend Klan Celebration." *Daily Journal-Gazette and Commercial-Star* (Mattoon) 30 July 1923.

"Klan Day at Chautauqua Draws 10,000." *Daily Journal-Gazette and Commercial-Star* (Mattoon) 8 August 1923.

"Labor Day Program Held in this City." *Daily Journal-Gazette and Commercial-Star* (Mattoon) 4 September 1923.

"Klan Celebration Held Near Humboldt." *Daily Journal-Gazette and Commercial-Star* (Mattoon) 5 October 1923.

"Heavily Fined on Disorderly Charge." *Daily Journal-Gazette and Commercial-Star* (Mattoon) 15 November 1923.

"Ku Klux Card on Cranshaw's Door." *Daily Journal-Gazette and Commercial-Star* (Mattoon) 16 November 1923.

"Cranshaw Reported to Have Left City." *Daily Journal-Gazette and Commercial-Star* (Mattoon) 17 November 1923.

"Mattoon School Election Will be Hard Fought." *Daily Journal-Gazette and Commercial-Star* (Mattoon) 11 April 1925.

"Christian Church Services Held in Park." *Daily Journal-Gazette and Commercial-Star* (Mattoon) 27 April 1925.

"Weird Chain of Incidents Baffles Police." *Chicago Daily Tribune* (Chicago) 3 August 1925.

"Mattoon, Ill. Murder is Mysterious." *The Daily Independent* (Murphysboro, IL) 3 August 1925.

"Rev. McMahan Dies After Long Illness." *Daily Journal-Gazette* (Mattoon) 10 April 1957.

SHAGGY ROW AND MAYOR "DAYLIGHT" WELCH

The Mattoon Gazette (Mattoon) 25 March 1892.

"Used Their Guns: And the Swing Went a Little Bit Higher." *Mattoon Gazette* (Mattoon) 4 June 1897.

"An Expression From the Democratic Candidate for City Attorney." *Mattoon Gazette* (Mattoon) 31 March 1899.

"It is Murder: Notorious Shaggy Row the Scene of Another Tragedy." *Mattoon Gazette* (Mattoon) 11 May 1900.

"Trouble On Shaggy Row in Which Colored Gentry Mix." *Mattoon Daily Journal* (Mattoon) 27 January 1902.

"Shot at Him: Lil Webster, Keeper of a Shaggy Row Resort, Makes it Warm." *Mattoon Daily Journal* (Mattoon) 15 May 1902.

"Bill Is Wrathy Because He Finds He Has No Insurance on Burned Property." *Mattoon Daily Journal* (Mattoon) 18 June 1902.

"The Saloon Situation." *Mattoon Daily Journal* (Mattoon) 17 July 1902.

"Excitement On Shaggy Row Late Sunday Afternoon." *Mattoon Daily Journal* (Mattoon) 28 July 1902.

"Robbed Him: Fred Langley Badly Beaten on Strenuous 'Shaggy Row.'" *Mattoon Daily Journal* (Mattoon) 19 January 1903.

Mattoon Daily Journal (Mattoon) 31 March 1903.

"Canaries Visit Shaggy Row and Get Into Trouble." *Mattoon Daily Journal* (Mattoon) 2 October 1903.

"Rubins is Correct Name of Young Man Accused of Robbing Anna Cobble." *Mattoon Daily Journal* (Mattoon) 7 October 1903.

"'Kippy' Burns Indicted." *Mattoon Daily Journal* (Mattoon) 26 October 1903.

"Low Comedy: Denizen on Cottage Avenue Does His Little Stunt." *Mattoon Daily Journal* (Mattoon) 14 December 1903.

"Dodge, Brothers, All of You, Dodge." *The Mattoon Daily Journal* (Mattoon) 24 February 1904.

"Warrant Issued for Arrest of Charles Knight, Charge with Sunday Selling." *Mattoon Daily Journal* (Mattoon) 26 February 1904.

"Knight Fined." *The Mattoon Commercial* (Mattoon) 10 March 1904.

"Knight Trial is On." *Mattoon Daily Journal* (Mattoon) 2 May 1904.

Mattoon Daily Journal (Mattoon) 6 May 1904.

"Bold Robbers Raid Alleged Gambling Den: George Kizer is Relieved of About One Thousand Dollars in Coin and His Jewelry Early Tuesday Morning." *Mattoon Daily Journal* (Mattoon) 1 November 1904.

"Witness Disappears: State is Forced to Dismiss Alleged Holdup Case this Afternoon." *Mattoon Daily Journal* (Mattoon) 13 December 1904.

"Disorderly Charge Against Two Boys Preferred by Isabel Scott." *Mattoon Morning Star* (Mattoon) 12 January 1905.

"Repulsed Invaders: Madame Isabel Scott Opens Fire on Belligerent Men--Has Them Arrested." *Mattoon Journal-Gazette* (Mattoon) 12 January 1905.

"An Echo of the Election." *Mattoon Journal-Gazette* (Mattoon) 13 January 1905.

"Authorities Commence War on Tenderloin District." *Mattoon Journal-Gazette* (Mattoon) 25 January 1905.

"Mrs. Garner as Reformer." *Mattoon Journal-Gazette* (Mattoon) 11 February 1905.

"Inquisitors in Session." *Mattoon Journal-Gazette* (Mattoon) 6 March 1905.

"'Evils of the City'." *Mattoon Journal-Gazette* (Mattoon) 15 April 1905.

"Where the Fault Lies." *Mattoon Journal-Gazette* (Mattoon) 17 April 1905.

"William Byers Chosen to Govern the City." *Mattoon Journal-Gazette* (Mattoon) 19 April 1905.

"Knight's in Limelight: Keeper of West Side Restaurant on Trial for Keeping Disorderly House." *Mattoon Journal-Gazette* (Mattoon) 18 May 1905.

"'They Have to Leave Shaggy,' Says Chief Lyons." *Mattoon Journal-Gazette* (Mattoon) 6 June 1905.

"Col. Bill Knight in the Toils." *Mattoon Journal-Gazette* (Mattoon) 9 June 1905.

"Case Against Bill Knight Dismissed." *Mattoon Journal-Gazette* (Mattoon) 10 June 1905.

"Isabel Pays Penalty." *Mattoon Journal-Gazette* (Mattoon) 14 August 1905.

"Will 'Bill' Knight Get His License Tonight?" *Mattoon Journal-Gazette* (Mattoon) 3 October 1905.

"Nary Sexson is Again Arrested." *Mattoon Journal-Gazette* (Mattoon) 16 October 1905.

"Liquidate Their Fines." *Mattoon Journal-Gazette* (Mattoon) 20 October 1905.

"Isabelle Indicted." *Mattoon Journal-Gazette* (Mattoon) 26 October 1905.

"'Bill' Knight's License Revoked by the Mayor." *Mattoon Journal-Gazette* (Mattoon) 13 December 1905.

"Bill Knight Again Placed Under Arrest." *Mattoon Journal-Gazette* (Mattoon) 16 December 1905.

"Public Should Support the Mayor." *Mattoon Journal-Gazette* (Mattoon) 16 December 1905.

"Bill Knight is Guilty: Saloonkeeper Convicted of Running Saloon Without a License." *Mattoon Journal-Gazette* (Mattoon) 19 December 1905."

"Col. Bill Knight Issues a Defi to His Enemies." *Mattoon Journal-Gazette* (Mattoon) 30 December 1905."

"Gets Permit for Saloon." *Mattoon Journal-Gazette* (Mattoon) 22 February 1906."

"Welch Should be Defeated." *Mattoon Journal-Gazette* (Mattoon) 13 April 1906.

"Williams is Defeated by Welch in Ward One." *Mattoon Journal-Gazette* (Mattoon) 17 April 1906.

"Police Make Raid on the George Kizer 'Cigar Store'." *Mattoon Journal-Gazette* (Mattoon) 26 October 1906.

"Far-Reaching Law on Statute Books: One of the Most Remarkable Temperance Acts Ever Passed Enacted in Illinois." *Mattoon Journal-Gazette* (Mattoon) 13 June 1907.

"Isabelle Scott Dies at Hot Springs." *Mattoon Journal-Gazette* (Mattoon) 26 July 1907."

"Make Raid on Domicile." *Mattoon Journal-Gazette* (Mattoon) 29 July 1907."

"Residents of 'Row' Fined for Disorderly." *Mattoon Journal-Gazette* (Mattoon) 8 August 1907."

"City's Treasury is Replenished: Dean Burchill and Two 'Girls' Caught in Shaggy Row Raid Wednesday Night." *Mattoon Journal-Gazette* (Mattoon) 2 July 1908.

"White Woman and Colored Husband Arrested." *Mattoon Morning Star* (Mattoon) 15 August 1908.

"Twenty One Indictments Are Returned by the Grand Jury." *Mattoon Journal-Gazette* (Mattoon) 17 September 1908.

"Severe Blow to the 'Row'." *Mattoon Journal-Gazette* (Mattoon) 24 September 1908.

"Police Make Raid on Shaggy Row." *Mattoon Journal-Gazette* (Mattoon) 15 October 1908.

"Shaggy Row to be Cleaned Out." *Mattoon Journal-Gazette* (Mattoon) 19 October 1908.

"Daylight Welch, Redlight Knight, and Midnight Kizer." *Mattoon Journal-Gazette* (Mattoon) 22 February 1909.

"Just Playin' Politics." *Mattoon Journal-Gazette* (Mattoon) 23 February 1909.

"Shaggy Row Resort Raided by Police." *Mattoon Journal-Gazette* (Mattoon) 27 February 1909.

"Both Kizer and Knight." *Mattoon Journal-Gazette* (Mattoon) 16 March 1909.

"Indicted Mattoon Men Denied Change of Venue." *Mattoon Journal-Gazette* (Mattoon) 18 March 1909.

"'Bill' Kight Found Guilty on Every Count in Indictment; is Given the Maximum Sentence." *Mattoon Journal-Gazette* (Mattoon) 24 March 1909.

"City Placed in Control of Welch-Kizer-Knight Gang." *Mattoon Journal-Gazette* (Mattoon) 21 April 1909.

"Mayor Welch is Indicted." *Mattoon Journal-Gazette* (Mattoon) 25 September 1909.

"1,000 Demand Enforcement of the Law or Resignation." *Mattoon Journal-Gazette* (Mattoon) 28 March 1910.

"M.J. Lynch for Perjury." *Mattoon Journal-Gazette* (Mattoon) 7 May 1910.

"Joints Run Wide Open: Numerous Places on Broadway and Western Avenue Where Booze can be Had." *Mattoon Journal-Gazette* (Mattoon) 11 June 1910.

"Soiled Ones Given Fines." *Daily Journal-Gazette* (Mattoon) 8 February 1911.

"To Clean Up Shaggy Row." *Daily Journal-Gazette* (Mattoon) 1 March 1911.

"Grand Jury After Shaggy." *Daily Journal-Gazette* (Mattoon) 9 March 1911.

"No. 2217 Cottage is a Thing of the Past." *Daily Journal-Gazette* (Mattoon) 20 March 1911.

"REPUDIATE WELCHISM: Welch Sent to Political Grave." *Daily Journal-Gazette* (Mattoon) 19 April 1911.

"Majority is Increasing: Guthrie Defeats Welch at Tuesday's Election by Margin of 1304." *Daily Journal-Gazette* (Mattoon) 21 April 1911.

"Complaint Lodged Against Bill Knight." *Daily Journal-Gazette* (Mattoon) 5 May 1911.

"Madame Berry is Called as Witness." *Daily Journal-Gazette* (Mattoon) 12 May 1911.

"Colonel Bill Found Guilty." *Daily Journal-Gazette* (Mattoon) 13 May 1911.

"William H. Knight Dies in the Hospital." *Daily Journal-Gazette* (Mattoon) 12
    September 1913.

Index

MORE PRAISE FOR THE AUTHOR

"A long-time researcher... regional historian, author and raconteur – Kleen is a man of many talents."

- McDonough County Choice
March 9, 2010

"It doesn't take long... to come to the understanding that the future of Illinois folklore is in very capable hands as long as Kleen is at the helm. He artfully and passionately scours the entire state of Illinois, finding interesting and horrifying tales that somehow, until now, were confined to their local boundaries."

- Scott Markus, author of *Voices from the Chicago Grave*

"Thankfully roughly eight or so years ago I stumbled across this amazing set of stories and articles related to our own history here in Coles County. The author amazed me something fierce, his stories were very well written and kept my interest even after many years of shoving my face into numerous books."

- Katherine McGee-Overstreet
JG-TC, July 7, 2013

"Michael Kleen has a great fondness for the Midwest, a Master's degree in History, and an insatiable thirst for ghost stories. Lucky for us, he has been able to skillfully combine all of his passions in his new book, Paranormal Illinois. Painstakingly and lovingly compiled, Kleen's books will be sure to become indispensable primers for both Midwestern ghost hunters and local folklore buffs alike."

- Smile Politely.com
June 11, 2010

"Michael Kleen gets a kick out of ghost stories and he's willing to travel to see if there's any truth to these legends."

- *The Times* (Streator)
June 24, 2010

About the Author

Michael Kleen has a M.A. in History from Eastern Illinois University and a M.S. in Education from Western Illinois University. He is the author of *Witchcraft in Illinois: A Cultural History*, *Haunting Illinois*, *Paranormal Illinois*, *Six Tales of Terror*, and *Tales of Coles County*, among other works. He also edited and published the anthology *Secret Rockford*. He currently lives in Virginia with his wife, Kayla, and a corgi named Leo.

© GREG INDA

His nonfiction articles have appeared in publications like *Historic Illinois* and the *Journal of the Illinois State Historical Society*, and his short stories have appeared in anthologies like *Hunting Ghosts: Thrilling Tales of the Paranormal* and *Mythos: Myths & Tales of H.P. Lovecraft and Robert E. Howard*. In 2011, his short story "Coed Terror in the Ivory Tower of Doom" was adapted into a short film called *Headline News*, which won Best Actor for Michael Wexler as Dr. Ethan Campbell at the 2011 Chicago Horror Film Festival.

Michael has spoken about local history and folklore at conventions, libraries, cafes, museums, schools, and colleges; and he has presented research papers at the 2007, 2010, and 2011 Conference on Illinois History in Springfield. He has also been a guest on radio shows like The Mothership Connection on AM-1050 WLIP, Thresholds Radio, the Michael Koolidge Show, the Kevin Smith Show, and the Bobbie Ashley Morning Show, among others. He has also appeared on *30 Odd Minutes*, WGN Channel 9 News, WTVO Channel 17/FOX 39 News, WREX Channel 13 News, WICD Channel 15 News, and *Ghost Adventures*.

Follow his travels at:
www.michaelkleen.com